ZERO SUM

ZERO SUM

THE DREAD NOUGHT™ BOOK FOUR

MARC STIEGLER

DISRUPTIVE IMAGINATION

This Book is a work of fiction. All of the characters, organizations, and events portrayed in this novel are either products of the author's imagination or are used fictitiously. Sometimes both.

Copyright © 2023 Marc Stiegler
Cover Art by Bandrei at 99designs
https://99designs.com/profiles/bandrei
Cover copyright © LMBPN Publishing

LMBPN Publishing supports the right to free expression and the value of copyright. The purpose of copyright is to encourage writers and artists to produce the creative works that enrich our culture.

The distribution of this book without permission is a theft of the author's intellectual property. If you would like permission to use material from the book (other than for review purposes), please contact info@kurtherianbooks.com. Thank you for your support of the author's rights.

LMBPN Publishing
PMB 196, 2540 South Maryland Pkwy
Las Vegas, NV 89109

Version 1.00, September 2023
eBook ISBN: 979-8-88878-122-7
Paperback ISBN: 979-8-88878-123-4

THE ZERO SUM TEAM

Special thanks to the LMBPN Betas and the JIT team. You make everything better!

Beta Readers:
Rachel Beckford, John Ashmore, Kelly O'Donnell, Jim Caplan, Nat Roberts, Mary Morris

JIT Readers:
Daryl McDaniel
Zacc Pelter
Diane L. Smith
Jan Hunnicutt
Paul Westman

If I've missed anyone, please let me know!

Editor
Skyhunter Editing Team

DEDICATION

This book is dedicated to Diab Hammad, born in Palestine but the kind of person who truly Makes America Great

1

THE EMERALD REVEALED

The angry young man pressed his abdomen to feel the bomb implanted therein. Its comforting presence softened his indignation as he stared at his hand, once pale white, now a rich chocolate brown.

He flared his nostrils, which caused him to jerk. The surgery to widen his nose had never fully healed, and flexing his facial muscles sent an electric jolt of pain between his eyes. He blinked away the tears and looked at his hand again, willing himself to accept it.

Next, he reluctantly turned to the mirror and poked his contact lenses into place. His normally blue-gray eyes now matched his skin. It presented a more coherent look, at any rate.

But his face… He stared at a stranger's face.

For these last few days of his life, he had truly lost himself. He had long ago accepted that he lacked the rugged good looks of a ladies' man, but he had been comfortable with who he was.

His stomach twisted, and he retched into the toilet. The vomiting came as a side effect of the drugs that had left him with a black man's skin, a cocktail of amiodarone, cytotoxins, tetracyclines, and heavy metals. He had finished the course of treatment, but the side effects still scraped at his insides like leeches from the Black Lagoon.

He forced himself to look on the bright side. The deception was working perfectly. He looked like an African, and he had polished his British accent well enough to hide his Russian accent.

Time to go. He went to the janitors' closet in the basement of the Palais du Peuple and collected his mop and bucket. Fifteen minutes later, he started washing a corridor on the first floor.

The leader of the Judicial Council, which controlled the Congo's Supreme Court, swept close with his entourage. The Supreme Court had acted as the bulwark against fraud for the Congolese democracy, dismissing all suits by the loser of the last election to overturn the results. The death of this man would remove that obstacle, and the would-be dictator, who had pledged allegiance to Evgeni Sokolov, the director of the Gamma division of Alfa Group, would ascend to the presidency.

The Ruby Rager heaved a sigh of relief. He would no longer have to wear his disgraceful new appearance. He touched the place beside his liver where the large block of C-4 lay.

A wave of anger coursed through his veins as he thought about the current Congolese president. The fool had refused to cut his ties with the Western world and accept his proper place as a vassal of the Russian empire.

The rage felt good. He loved the uncomplicated purity of hatred and could ride it all day, though, once in a while, it felt as if the rage rode him. That felt even better.

He exploded.

Morte Noir's trip home with Remy passed quietly. Remy might normally talk like a perpetual motion machine, but the only thing she wanted at this moment was answers about her mother.

The Dark Mistress refused to answer any questions beyond assuring Remy that her mother was healthy and more or less happy in her loosely controlled captivity.

More than once, Morte Noir saw Remy's frustration rise to the point of considering a physical assault to get answers. The world's greatest assassin did not fret about the risk. On the one hand, she'd recently seen Remy's superhuman martial arts skills on display, and despite her formidable combat abilities, a dispassionate analysis suggested that Remy could take her.

However, Morte Noir judged not only people's skills but also their personalities. Remy had the strength of too much discipline and the weakness of too much empathy. She would not attack a woman taking her to the place she yearned to be.

The trip ended. Morte Noir opened the door to the second-floor sitting room and waved Remy in. "Laurie should be here in a few minutes. She's busy with the roses at the moment." She pointed at the window.

Remy followed Morte Noir's finger and hurried to look outside. In the vast garden, a figure in a shapeless burqa wielded a pair of pruning shears.

Though Remy couldn't see fine details, she recognized the woman. She pounded on the window and shouted, "Mom!"

Morte Noir coughed. "She can't hear you. That glass will stop a fifty-caliber bullet."

Remy whirled on her. "How do I get out there?"

The Mistress shook her head. "You don't."

Remy glared, but the Mistress stood unmoved. "Too dangerous." She pointed at the sky. "I don't think we're under surveillance, but we can never be sure."

Remy looked set to explode.

Morte Noir chuckled. "Patience." She turned and shouted through the door, "Little one?"

A petite young woman hurried up. "Yes, Mistress?"

Morte Noir nodded at the garden. "Please let Laurie know I have a gift for her. She needs to come claim it immediately."

The young woman bowed, spun, and rushed away.

The fluid grace of the girl's spin tickled Remy's memory. "She's quite good with a shuriken, isn't she?"

Morte Noir gave her a quizzical look.

Remy smiled triumphantly. "The Auction. She wore the burqa in the knife fight and spun to make the throw."

Morte Noir's eyes widened, and delight quirked her lips. "So, you've never seen her, but you recognize her. You *are* very good."

Remy watched through the window as Esin, clad in a burqa once more, accosted her mother.

Laurie looked up. Remy waved futilely. Her mother followed the girl.

By the time her mother arrived at the sitting room, she had stripped off the heavy black burqa, leaving her clad in shorts, sneakers, and a tank top. She saw her daughter and froze in shock and joy. "*Remy!*"

"*Mom!*"

Laurie ran across the room and met the running Remy halfway. They hugged for a never-ending moment, unbound by concepts of space or time.

Morte Noir said loudly, "Esin, come with me into the bedroom. Dave and Lisa are waiting for us. Time for your next training session."

Eventually, Remy and her mom separated. Laurie broke the spell. "Tea and cookies?" She moved to a corner of the room with cups and saucers.

Remy rushed past her. "Let me get that." She studied the boxes of tea. "Russian black tea. Most excellent!"

Laurie reached into a cupboard. "Lemon cookies."

For a few minutes, they performed the ritual they had practiced since Remy could heat water. The familiar operations kept Remy from sobbing in joy.

They sank onto the sofa together.

Laurie took a sip of her tea. "Morte Noir has been telling me about your exploits."

Remy stiffened. "Like what?"

Her mother raised an eyebrow. "Like breaking into the Kremlin for reasons even Morte Noir doesn't know, even though she lives up to her reputation of being the world's most knowledgeable purveyor of other people's secrets."

Remy smiled. "Nice to know we can keep her guessing."

Laurie continued. "And then you created a whole new country. Who does something like that?"

Remy's face turned wistful. "It's a lovely place. I hope to take you there."

Her mom stiffened. "I understand you have a fortress there." Her hand trembled as she took a sip of tea. "Is that where your father is?"

Remy nodded. "We built a hospital wing specifically for him. All the latest gear." She slumped. "None of it's any use. His brain function remains chaotic. Every once in a while, I think he's still in there somewhere." She looked away. "Then I think I'm just imagining it."

Remy gave Laurie a clinical description of her father's condition, punctuated with periodic pauses for despair. Her mother stroked her hair.

Remy took a breath. "At least the man who did this to him is dead."

Laurie pulled back. "You killed him?"

Remy shook her head. "I was going to." She got angry, then laughed at herself. "Morte Noir beat me to it."

Laurie stroked Remy's hair again. "Good woman, in her own wholly immoral and utterly unethical way."

Remy gave her a probing look. "Before the man who took Dad died, he claimed Dad did it to himself." She looked seriously into her mother's eyes, asking if there was any truth to that.

Laurie sighed. "It's true enough." She twisted away and picked up her tea uncomfortably. "You remember when we first submitted our research paper on the Memwriter?"

Remy held up a finger in warning. "Are you sure we want to talk about this? Morte Noir surely has this room bugged." She continued in a low voice, "Though, to be honest, I sort of promised her I'd give her the scoop if she brought me here."

Laurie burst into laughter. "Of course she has the room bugged!" She looked at the ceiling. "Listen to this part carefully. You'll want to hear it." She turned back to Remy. "I made the same promise. It's okay." She sighed. "In a peculiar sense, for some twisted reason, I trust her."

"Cool."

Laurie went back to the main topic. "Anyway, when we told you that no one responded to our paper, we didn't tell you that men came to our lab and tried to muscle us into leaving with them. Fortunately, a building security guard stopped in to check on us, and they left."

Remy pursed her lips. "AID." She started to explain, but Laurie nodded.

"So I've concluded, based on the background Morte Noir has given me." She looked down at her tea. "Anyway, we became concerned. We wracked our brains for why someone would want to kidnap us and steal the Memwriter."

Remy answered. "While you designed it to quickly add new knowledge to your mind, you can also use it to write false memories that feel more real than your true memories. If you insert fake lessons learned that lead to false conclusions, they can, in effect, rewrite your personality."

Lauries stared at her as enlightenment suffused her. "Of course." She went back to the subject. "Anyway, on a similar track, we knew that whatever people like that wanted, we didn't want them to get." Her hand tensed. "The Memwriter is a teaching tool, dammit!" she shouted into the air. "You hear that, Morte Noir? No one gets to misuse our stuff!"

Laurie took another bite of her cookie. "So we figured out another horrific use for our invention."

Remy tilted her head, listening attentively.

Laurie looked down at her feet. "You know we were able to write memories that would be triggered under certain circumstances."

Remy nodded eagerly. "All our financial accounts and passwords appeared in my mind after you were taken."

Her mother nodded. "We set triggers in our own minds, so if we were tortured, our memories would be overwritten with gibberish." She hesitated, then corrected herself. "Or rather, we arranged to have our memories overwritten with what looked like gibberish." She chuckled. "It actually follows a pattern based on AES encryption. If you know the password, you can identify which threads of memory were memwritten and which were real."

Remy leaned forward, excited. "So you can tell which parts of Dad's mind are true?"

Laurie nodded.

"And you can fix it."

Her mother winced. "We don't know how to erase the overwriting, but it seems possible that we can strengthen the real memories enough to transcend the gibberish."

A gleam filled Remy's eyes. "It's the same thing I did with Neil. Cassie's boyfriend, whose mind was rewritten by AID. What they did was much cruder, and I didn't have an algorithm describing the damage, but still..." She described how she had repaired Neil enough to become a functional person again.

Her mother smiled approvingly. "If you're trying to prove that you should help me with your father, you win."

Cassie watched as two Orinoco APCs stopped at the gatehouse at Rivendell. She resisted the urge to scratch her nose. To get to the itch, she would have to remove her darkened motorcycle helmet, and that was a no-no until the proper moment in the upcoming meeting. Instead, she quietly sweated in her motorcycle leathers until the conspiracy theorists arrived.

Before they had undertaken their fateful attempt to assassinate Dallas Ferris, she and Remy had put out a call on the EStorme image board for job applicants to come to Orinoco and interview. The purpose, they had explained in their post, was to find the people with the right stuff to assist in taking the war to the next level as they fought to protect the world from domination by the network of satanic pedophiles—the drinkers of babies' blood who secretly controlled most of the governments.

Early in their journey together, Cassie and Remy had convinced a small cadre of EStormers that Cassie-or-Remy was the Emerald. So when they put up the post that included a picture of a woman wearing the motorcycle gear that had kept them anonymous in that earlier undertaking, they had lots of supportive people vouching for them and for the legitimacy of their request.

Andrey had had a terrible time keeping the Rivendell job application submissions website from crashing under the strain. Almost a million EStormers had offered themselves for the mission.

Now the first two hundred vetted applicants had arrived.

Cassie had directed the Orinoco soldiers to set up rows of seating next to the sign that welcomed arrivals to Rivendell. She yelled for the EStormers, "Everyone, grab a chair and let me tell you about the next step in the Plan."

Two hundred fingers pointed skyward to say, *Where We Go One, We Go All.*

A man and a woman separated from the crowd and came toward her. Cassie stiffened, half-expecting them to kneel.

Instead, they stopped a few feet away, and the woman, smiling with the generous warmth of someone from the hills of Tennessee, asked, "Do you remember us? Tina and Brett?"

Cassie goggled in surprise, glad the darkened faceplate covered her reaction. She did remember. "You came to us in Virginia when we had the dump truck full of secret documents we needed to..." she struggled to remember the right word for "decrypt" in EStorme jargon. "bake for the Plan."

The woman straightened and beamed. It looked to Cassie like she wanted a hug.

Suppressing a sigh, Cassie hugged her, then her man, even though he was so tall that she needed to stand on tiptoes to reach him. She spoke sincerely. "I'm glad you made it here." She hesitated. "You understand, this is only an interview. We're looking for a handful of people right now. Odds are we'll send you home to stand back and stand by for the moment, ready to help in the next phase as we turn the Dark to Light."

The woman bobbed her head. The man drawled, "We're just happy to have the opportunity to try."

As they took their chairs, Cassie shook her head. Remy had been right. These were such good people. Fortunately, Remy did indeed have a Plan. And if they could pull it off, there *would* be a Great Awakening.

It just wouldn't be exactly the awakening everyone was expecting.

Cassie stepped up to the microphone to face the attentive EStormers. "Welcome to Orinoco."

The crowd shivered with excitement.

"And welcome here to Rivendell, the fortress of EStorme, from which we will unleash the final Storm."

This got such a loud cheer that it hurt her ears inside the helmet.

"But first, Rivendell must be protected. The secret cabal that runs the world will try everything in their power to destroy us here."

A hush fell.

"We have a new technology that will help us in our

fight. It's called the Memwriter. It's a training and education tool that will allow us to radically upgrade everyone's skills in a short time."

Someone raised his hand. "Will it hurt?"

Cassie laughed. "Only if we teach you physics."

Everyone laughed along with her, a little uncertainly.

"That was the only time it hurt my head, and I don't think it was the Memwriter. I think it was the physics."

That got a more relaxed wave of laughter.

"We'll be introducing you all to our new tech, but for now, only a handful of you will be selected to stay here to defend Rivendell."

Someone yelled, "What happens to the rest of us?"

Cassie nodded. "The rest of you will take your newfound abilities and go home. You'll wait for us to Call upon you later, when the Storm truly begins."

More cheering and raised *WWGOWGA* fingers greeted her promise.

Another person raised a hand to ask a question. Cassie gestured at him. He breathlessly asked, "Are you the Emerald?"

Cassie took a deep breath. She'd given the matter a great deal of thought, and after much argument with herself, sans useful input from Remy, who was incommunicado with her mother, she had made a decision.

She had no desire to be worshiped, but she knew someone who was in such danger that she needed people who were willing to sacrifice themselves to protect her. Therefore, Cassie swept off her helmet and revealed her partner's blonde hair and innocent blue eyes. "I *am* the Emerald."

Everyone stood, and a wild ovation swept across the field.

Cassie shouted into the microphone, "You can call me 'Remy.'"

2

ORDERS

Max Balakin, the leader of the most elite brigade of Ruby Rage sturmers, leaned over the bed and held his hand over the mouth of Italy's deputy director of the International Trade Administration.

The deputy woke and struggled against his hand.

The half-healed bones in Max's rib cage screamed in pain as he struggled with the man. Dammit, getting blown up during the Orinoco Revolution had really messed him up, and he had never fully recovered from the assassination attempt that had almost killed him in Arizona.

He growled to his lieutenant, "Take over."

The lieutenant clasped the director's mouth with one hand and tapped the victim's throat sharply with the other, then reached around to grab the back of the deputy's head.

The deputy jerked and relapsed into silence.

Max whispered some advice. "Sssh. If you scream, your wife and children will die before you do."

The deputy jerked again as he tried to pull his arms from beneath the covers to attack.

Max sighed. Since his lieutenant was busy holding the deputy down, he turned to another of his sturmers. "Tap him, please."

The sturmer smacked the deputy's temple, and the stunned man wilted.

Max jammed a ball gag into the target's mouth. The effort left him so spent that he could not continue, so he allowed his troops to flip the man, handcuff his hands behind his back, and flip him back. Max brushed back the thin hair on his mostly bald head. "I have a video of your wife you really must see."

Max placed a laptop on the side table and brought up the video. When the deputy's wife started to scream, Max muted the sound. He pursed his lips. "Really, you and your entire family have trouble understanding when silence is in order."

The deputy stared at him, eyes wide.

Max nodded. "Now that you are receptive, let me tell you what you will do." He explained that Russia needed vast supplies of the most sophisticated computer chips developed by Western civilization to build the most sophisticated weapons for the army. Nothing else would do.

"So, the next time you go into the office, you will meet with a representative from our embassy who will explain in detail how you will arrange for those chips to find their way onto cargo ships bound for Russia. You will do this because it is good for the world, good for Italy, and, of course, good for your family."

The deputy closed his eyes and nodded.

Max continued. "When the first shipment arrives in

Novorossiysk, I will deposit half a million dollars in an account assigned to you, and your family will return home. You will continue to work for us as long as we need goods that Western governments refuse to ship to us. Do you understand?"

The deputy nodded again.

Max winced twice as he removed the broken man's handcuffs and gag. "I look forward to working with you for many years. Cheer up." Max smiled in encouragement, which failed in its goal since even when he smiled, Max looked dour and angry. "You will grow very rich. It's going to be great."

Bryce held the secret conviction that Fort Meade had been built by a time-traveling toddler who plucked buildings from different architectural eras and tumbled them together with the enthusiasm generally found in a child's finger painting.

He picked his way through the parking lots to a modern building covered with reflective black glass. This one at least presented a proper rendition of the agency to the public. People looked at it and saw a dark reflection of themselves.

Once inside, the cacophony of styles gave way to simple bureaucratic conformity until you reached the deepest level of the building. It was so deep that most NSA keycards could not activate its doors and elevators. That level belonged to AID, the Analytical Intelligence Division.

Bryce suspected AID had won control of this level

easily because an experiment in horror must have been undertaken on it early in the building's history. The designers had apparently canvassed the nation's babies for the most ghastly green vomit, and the winning color was the one that most often caused sympathetic vomiting in onlookers. They had splashed this hue ubiquitously across the walls.

Bryce studiously avoided looking up from the floor as he walked over to the receptionist outside the director's office. He leaned over and gave her his most wicked smile. "So, what's the new director like?"

The receptionist's smile barely flickered before she turned to ice. "See for yourself."

Bryce's gut wrenched. Everyone who had met the new man was tight-lipped about him. He found the mystery irritating. They seemed intimidated by whoever, or whatever, they'd found in the inner sanctum.

Bryce was AID's top assassin. As a worst case, he could arrange a fatal accident for the director and hope for a better boss in the next round.

The receptionist waved him into the office.

The first thing Bryce saw was the thinning hair on the back of the director's head. The new boss sat hunched over a keyboard, studying a bank of monitors.

Bryce suddenly missed Dallas Ferris. The former director had been marked for death again and again, but he had beaten every attacker. Alas, he had met his match when Remy, Cassie, Dread Nought, and Morte Noir had accidentally combined forces against him.

Dallas had occupied a small, bare office, spending most

of his time in the adjoining conference room. He had listened to briefings and given orders, very hands-on yet happy to delegate.

The way the new boss picked through the screenfuls of data made Bryce suspect he was a micromanager. And a geek. Bryce shuddered at the thought of that combination.

Apparently, it was true that you never really appreciated a good boss until you lost him.

The new director held up a finger. "Hang on a second." A moment later, he continued, "Grab a chair and come over here."

Bryce rolled a chair over to the display area while he struggled with a memory. He had heard the director's voice on the phone; he was sure of it. Unfortunately, he couldn't place the call or the context.

The man turned to him, and Bryce suppressed a shudder as he looked into eyes filled with piercing intelligence but devoid of humanity.

The boss offered Bryce a trace of a smile. "Nice to meet you. I understand you're the second-best assassin in the world. I look forward to working with you. Perhaps together, we can make you Number One."

Bryce controlled his irritation. Since he'd failed to save Dallas, everyone figured Morte Noir had him beat. He started to object that he was already Number One but stopped. Defending himself would sound whiny.

The boss blinked. His eyes focused, and he connected with the here and now. "I've forgotten my manners. Let me introduce myself. You may call me the Doc."

Finally, Bryce remembered where he had heard the

Doc's voice. The memory struck him dumb and blind. It had been the first discussion of the techniques to be used to tear Cassie's boyfriend's mind apart.

The new director was the scientist who had run the torture experiments at Gitmo.

Bryce realized he should be afraid. The last thing he wanted was to be selected for one of the Doc's research projects.

He could kill the director right now. Bryce was the best assassin in the world, no matter how much people loved Morte Noir's work.

Even if he was only Number Two, he was still good enough to finish this encounter without muss or fuss.

Then he saw a crazy light in the Doc's eyes that seemed to say, *"Go ahead. Try it."* Perhaps he should hold off on direct action and see how things played out.

Still, he couldn't help poking the bear to hide his fear. "The Doc, huh? I thought you were just a science geek with a dash of sadism."

The Doc pursed his lips, no doubt mulling his recent defeat by Remy and Cassie in the wilds of southern Cuba. "You let Remy get away yet again at Camp No, though she was in a godforsaken jungle with no way out."

Bryce had mulled over that missed opportunity, and he felt the criticism was unjust. "I searched for her with infrared satellites, drones, and even dogs. She was nowhere to be found." He leaned forward and leveled his own accusation. "Did she get out the same way you did?" Bryce had puzzled over the Doc's mysterious disappearance as well. He really wanted an answer to that question.

The Doc did not fall for it. He smirked, then reverted to irritation. "And you let Remy's partner blow up my lab."

Bryce sighed. "Fair."

Having won the point, the Doc replied to Bryce's earlier comment. "You're not far off when you call me a science geek. That *is* my preferred occupation. *But...*" He grabbed a letter opener off his desk and threw it into a block of wood hanging on the wall that was carved in the shape of a human head. The letter opener stuck deep between the eyes. "I have many skills."

He nodded for Bryce to retrieve the opener. The Doc leaned back in the chair behind the desk. "In some sense, any scientist with a large project has to learn project management." His face twisted in distaste. "Dallas Ferris's decision to get himself killed left me short a critical operator."

He sighed. "Eventually, I'll find a replacement, but until we take Remy, I've decided to take a more hands-on approach."

Bryce flipped the letter opener from hand to hand before placing it on the desk. "I can handle Remy on my own."

The Doc stared at him. "Where is she now?"

Bryce coughed. "She's at Morte Noir's hideout."

The Doc nodded thoughtfully. "And that is where exactly?"

Bryce glared. Doc knew as well as anyone that that location had remained unknown despite AID's best efforts.

The Doc threw a hand in the air, dismissing the conversation. "I must have that girl, and I'm tired of excuses."

Bryce interrupted with the good news he'd been trying to deliver. "Do you really need her? I've cut a deal with Cassie to use the Quantum Key for us."

The Doc offered him polite though skeptical interest. "Details. What's the fine print?"

Bryce looked sheepish. "At the moment, she'll only do a few decryptions, and only if the messages obviously help us fight Gamma." He took a breath and continued, "I think I can persuade Remy's grandmother to help us on an ongoing basis. For a fee."

The Doc surmised the caveat. "But only to help fight Gamma."

Bryce shrugged.

The Doc gave him a small smile. "Well, that's something, I suppose. Though it's obviously a wholly inadequate basis on which to call a truce. I repeat, I need Remy. I need her yesterday."

He blew out an exasperated breath and spun his chair back to the displays. "Unfortunately, the acquisition of Remy is not our most pressing problem." He brought up a map of the world.

Bryce stood next to him and pointed at the scattered red splashes. "It looks like the planet has come down with a case of measles."

The Doc growled. "More like smallpox. Those are all the places where Ruby Rage agents have shifted the balance of power. Gamma is winning." A most unscientific anger filled his voice. "Their Ragers are more effective than my EStormers, yet they are nothing but meat bombs and fanatics with guns. They embody the essence of graceless crudity without nuance or art. How can they work so well?"

As Bryce watched, the Doc's science geek façade disintegrated in the face of someone else's better, if graceless, tech. The Doc, he realized, was jealous. An unknown stranger had beaten him.

Or was it a stranger? Bryce wondered if the Doc knew who it was. That would explain why he took it so personally.

The Doc took a breath and regained control. "That brings me to your first mission. I want you to steal a Russian Kinzhal hypersonic cruise missile."

Bryce blinked, then allowed a slow smile to cross his face. "That should be fun." He pursed his lips as he thought about the difficulties. "Though, uh, much as I hate to admit it, that could be more than a one-man job."

The Doc chuckled. "It should be the right size for a one man, one woman job."

Bryce peered at him suspiciously. "A woman?"

The Doc replaced the display of the Ruby Rage world map with a photo of a breathtaking woman.

Bryce shook his head. He never got tired of gazing upon the person who would apparently be his partner. "Morte Noir."

The Doc's eyes gleamed. "I thought that if I sweetened the pot properly, you wouldn't mind working with a team." He caught Bryce's eyes. "But let's be clear about the most important advantage of working with her."

Bryce knew the answer. "Deniability."

The Doc nodded. "If things go wrong, just snuff her. We'll explain that we sent you to stop her as our way of doing a neighborly service for our colleagues."

Bryce allowed no hint of his thoughts to show. Sure, stealing the missile would be difficult and dangerous, but it would be much easier and far safer to steal the missile than to kill Morte Noir.

The Doc held out a black business card with a time and location in silver letters. "I've set you up with a meeting. Get this done."

Bryce took the card. "Might I ask why we need a Russian cruise missile?"

The Doc looked into the distance. "To persuade our enemies to fight each other, of course. Kill multiple birds with one stone." He turned stern. "Bryce. I know you don't like me. You've demonstrated a sadly misplaced repugnance for the research necessary to extend our domination."

Bryce sat stiffly. "I don't have to like you. I'm a professional."

The Doc smiled, and this time, the expression reached his eyes. "Exactly. I expect your best. I know you'll deliver."

The way he said it made Bryce want to salute. Perhaps this crazy man understood some of the characteristics of leadership after all.

Bryce kept his hand at his side but answered sincerely. "You can count on it."

As he moved toward the door, the Doc offered some parting words. "One last thing."

Bryce turned, raising an eyebrow.

"I might be a science geek, but never again mistake me for a sadist. When we finally get Remy, I'll terminate that current line of research and get on with more important work."

Bryce nodded.

The Doc raised a finger. "But if you cross me, I have an avenue of investigation for which you'd be a perfect experimental volunteer."

Bryce shuddered at the word "volunteer."

The Doc pressed the point home. "If you screw with me, we'll see whether you still have the courage and mental wherewithal to call me a sadist when I'm done with you. Are we clear?"

Cassie stood outside the Cafe Tatti and tried to visualize all the ways this hookup could go wrong. Could *anyone* count that high?

She shook her head, and her glossy black hair shimmered in the light from the neon signs surrounding the parking lot. Her time was up.

Jake and Timmy sat at a corner table, trying to glare at every patron and every waiter all at the same time. They stiffened when they saw her enter.

Cassie gave them a cheery wave. She figured that if they were this angry, they'd been given orders not to interfere for anything less than a nuclear bomb alert. She swaggered over to them and touched each one on the shoulder. "You're going to just love the food here. Try the beef bourguignon. It melts in your mouth." At least, that was what Bryce had said.

She spun to the table at which her mark awaited her. They sat deep in the restaurant, near the passage to the kitchen and the rear exit.

As she approached, she disregarded Dale, who offered her an encouraging smile. She kept her focus on his companion, whose expression varied between anger, bemusement, doubt, and hope. He rose to meet her.

She offered her hand. "Augustus Luther? Nice to meet you."

"Cassie Parker. It's a miracle," Augustus muttered in reply.

Dale peered at the scar on her cheek. Based on the Insta pics from the sword fight by the Reflecting Pool, Joyce had told him that Cassie now carried a scar like Remy's. However, this wasn't *like* Remy's scar; it *was* Remy's scar. "Remy?"

Cassie's laugh held an irritated edge. "Sorry, Dale. Augustus got it right the first time." She took his hand in hers and guided his finger along the curved deformation. "She does extraordinary surgical work in the middle of a fight to the death, doesn't she?"

Dale shook his head. "Whoa."

Augustus looked at the two of them. "What are we talking about?"

Dale sat back in his chair. "Long story, but Cassie and

Remy match again." He chortled. "Poor Joyce. It's once more impossible to tell them apart."

Augustus interrupted. "Hopefully, henceforth, if we want to know which is which, we can just ask them." He turned a hawkish gaze on Cassie. "Right?"

Cassie struggled to answer. Dale was not surprised when she moved directly to a new topic. "I'd like to take Dale back to Rivendell for some memwriting."

Dale smiled. He'd had a secret intro to the machine when he'd been a captive at Cassie and Remy's HQ. Now he wouldn't have to hide it anymore. And he'd learn even more. "I'd like that."

A mischievous glint entered Cassie's eyes. "If we hurry, Dale should be able to graduate with the first class of EStormers."

Dale's smile faltered. "EStormers?"

Augustus shook his head. "You're going to give extraordinary knowledge, including advanced combat skills, to a bunch of conspiracy believers? Wouldn't that be, uh," he tried to find a tactful way to complete the question, "crazy dangerous?"

Cassie confessed to herself that she was having a great time tweaking her new partners. "Don't worry about the EStormers. We have them under control."

Augustus looked stunned and drew the entirely wrong conclusion that happened to be factually correct. "So, the analysis we stole was right. You can use the MemWriter to rewrite people's personalities." His eyes sparkled as his thoughts tried to span the possibilities. "Oh, my God."

Another thought occurred to him, and he looked at the agent with alarm. "This means she can rewrite you as well. Are you sure you want to take the chance?"

Dale stared a question at her. *Are you really rewriting those people's personalities?*

Cassie gave him a gentle smile she had learned from Remy. *Do you really think we'd do that?*

Dale swallowed. "Despite the effort she's making to scare us, I trust her."

Augustus looked doubtful. Cassie wondered if she could pull him in the rest of the way with an even bigger offer and use his greed to overcome his cautious suspicion. "What if I sweeten the pot? Would it be okay if I took Jake as well? Gave him a few thousand hours of memwritten sniper training? Nothing fancy. No electrical engineering or cyberwar stuff, just shooting practice. Would you like that?"

Dale and Augustus looked at her in surprise. Augustus glanced at Dale and choked out, "Would *he* like that?"

Dale pondered the matter. "Would it make him a lot better? He's already really good."

Cassie grimaced. "It would probably make him better. I can't say for sure." She shrugged. "But I need a guinea pig for this experiment, one way or the other. Jake would be a great candidate."

Augustus turned cautious again. "And he'll come out intact, only better."

Cassie sighed. "I *can* promise it won't hurt him." She

shook her head. "You wouldn't believe the stuff I've had memwritten into me."

Augustus rubbed his hands together. "I wanted to kidnap you and Remy so we could get the Memwriter for ourselves, but if you'll upgrade our agents' skills, that would be pretty good."

Cassie turned cold. "Not all of them."

Augustus looked puzzled.

Cassie explained, "If I see Curtis within a mile of a Memwriter, I'll cut him where it counts, and no technology will help him."

Augustus replied unsteadily, "Of course. I understand."

Cassie continued with the terms and conditions. "We'll start this deal slow, and the only people we'll augment will be the ones Dale vets."

Augustus turned a sly smile on Dale.

Cassie added, "And let's be clear. I'll vet your candidates with other sources as well." She didn't want Augustus trying to guess what sources, and she sure didn't want him investigating deep enough to figure out she had her hand on the pulse of the Utah Data Center, so she misdirected him with more partial truth. "We have an information-sharing arrangement with Morte Noir. No one who comes to our memwriting academy will be allowed to use their new skills to harm innocent bystanders, no matter how profitable."

Augustus turned inscrutable as he tried to connive a workaround for this requirement. It would disqualify at least half the Extreme Risk division.

Cassie leaned close to him and spoke with authority. "I

don't care if they've done these kinds of jobs in the past, but if they come to us, they must never do them again."

Augustus raised an eyebrow. "Or?"

Cassie chuckled. "Or I'll call on Morte Noir for her breach of contract services. You know how she handles a breach, right?"

3

MEETING OF MINDS

Fenya sat in her van, watching the patrons, mostly men, drift into the Maxim Club past the showgirl silhouettes that covered the building's façade. She shivered, turned up the heat, and wrapped her plush sheepskin coat around her more tightly. She hated northern Russia. Even Siberia had better weather.

When she looked at her watch, she realized the group of men she had expected to show up must have been waylaid by some misfortune and would not arrive. She frowned as she put the van in gear to return to her motel.

Just then, a dozen superb physical specimens of manhood sauntered down the street, laughing with the arrogance of alpha males on the town.

Fighter pilots.

As they joked, their breath frosted in the frigid air and caught the light from the street lamps as it formed tiny clouds around their heads. They strode into the club like they owned it.

Fenya rolled her shoulders to loosen up. Time to go to

work. She picked her way carefully through the snowy slush that covered patches of slick ice on the sidewalk. Every time she had the chance to jab the stiletto heel of her shoe into packed snow, she exploited the opportunity to get a firm foothold.

The journey ended and warm air from the club's entry blew across her face, bringing her cheeks back to life. For a moment, she stood on the edge of the main room and wrapped herself in her role—a slightly tipsy, very annoyed cover model—and identified which set of recessed couches the pilots had landed on.

A limber woman wearing a sequin-covered cherry-red g-string dropped to her knees on the tiny stage, then arched up into a handstand. Her legs wrapped around the sky-blue stripper pole covered in glowing white polka dots.

Fenya stared, not at the woman but at the pole. She'd seen it earlier when she'd come in to bribe the management and the girls to give her free rein this evening, but the pole still bothered her. She couldn't remember ever working on such an ostentatious piece of equipment back in the day. Poles were supposed to be silver or gold, metallic and shiny. Where was their sense of tradition?

Men's voices, muffled by the ubiquitous red velvet drapes, floated to her over her shoulder. She turned to see her marks in the largest of the private booths, slouching on blue velvet couches. While they watched the dancer, they sipped their first round of drinks and exchanged lewd comments.

Fenya carefully stumbled over to her marks, reached overhead to grab a handful of the drapery, and rolled her hips sideways. If the drapery ripped, she would fall and make a fool of herself, but she took the risk.

Most of the men lost focus on the pole dancer and fixed their gazes on her. She licked her lips. "You boys fighter pilots?"

The man farthest from her, probably the leader, threw his arms onto the back of the couch and spoke with smug confidence. "We certainly are. You want to strap on my engine and take a ride?"

Fenya swayed on the drape. "I just broke up with my old boyfriend. I need a new one." She swept a hand casually across the couches. "I'd like to interview you all."

Any man with a lick of sense would have guessed he was being played—but then, if he had a lick of sense, he wouldn't have been a swaggering jackass. She owned them now.

The leader leaped to his feet. "At your service, Miss."

Fenya sighed heavily in relief. "Thank heavens. We need to hurry. I am in serious need." She unbuttoned her coat and held the flaps askew. "As you can see, I forgot to wear any clothes."

All the eyes in the booth widened with joy. The leader hurried to maneuver around the men and the tables to get to her first, his grace impaired by urgency. She slid into the empty booth next to the pilots, separated from them by more plush red drapes.

As the first pilot pressed up against her, she unroped the curtains across the front of the booth to let them fall. "Privacy," she whispered as she kissed her mark and let the coat slide to the floor.

One by one, she brought the pilots to her booth for a

tête-à-tête. With each one, after they fulfilled their primary mission, she spent an extra fifteen minutes letting them tell her about their histories, passions, hopes, and dreams. She finished by collecting their contact information.

One fellow proved unable to perform and shook his head. "I'm sorry. Too much to drink."

Fenya doubted that since he didn't smell like an alcohol fire about to flare. She hypothesized he played for the other team. That might make him the winner of the evening's festivities. If he refused to do her bidding and his preferences were ever revealed, they wouldn't just make fun of him or take his fighter plane away. They would put him in prison.

However, both she and Morte Noir preferred happy, well-bribed assets to angry, blackmailed operatives. Either way, he needed her help right now. She leaned over and kissed him on the cheek. "Let me make this okay." She started to moan with pleasure. When he stared at her, she whispered, "Groan a little for me."

As he groaned, she walloped pillows and moaned louder until she was screaming his name in ecstasy. In the end, she leaned over and kissed him again. "See how easy that was?"

She led him back to the boys' booth and slumped against the drapes. "Wow. Whoever's next has his work cut out for him. Anyone ready to take the challenge?"

They were fighter pilots, so they were *all* ready.

Long hours later, Fenya completed her mission. She had trouble standing, much less walking, but she was a professional. She held it together.

Fenya stood next to the pilots' tables one last time.

"Thank you, everyone, for a delightful evening." She blew them all kisses. "I promise to get back to whichever one of you I choose as my new boyfriend." She gave them a sidelong glance. "As soon as I make up my mind."

The men cheered and recommended themselves once more. It took her last remnants of slinky strength to escape into the frigid outdoors without revealing weakness.

Back in the van, she called the Dark Mistress. "I found the right man for our needs."

The Mistress answered with warm sympathy. This was all a routine part of the job, but it was still hard work. "Delightful. Spend tomorrow in your motel room's hot tub. I'll brief you on your next mission the evening after that. Meanwhile, we'll move on to the next phase of the operation here."

Usually, Evgeni's office, with its vast array of bookcases filled with dusty tomes, had a calming effect on Grisha. Not today.

Today, Grisha sat on the edge of his seat, clenching and unclenching his fists. He really needed Evgeni to embrace the mission. "I'm telling you, Andrey is in Rivendell."

Evgeni leaned back in the chair behind the desk and steepled his fingers. "And yet you do not have a single piece of solid intel to confirm that."

Grisha clenched his fists again. "It's the only logical possibility! We need to go in and —"

Evgeni leaned forward, exasperated. "And what? Violate Orinoco territory on the off-chance of finding him? Need I mention that we are now partnered with them on the cobalt mines?"

Grisha struggled with his frustration. After a couple of deep breaths, he decided to withdraw from the direct attack and maneuver around the flank with a seemingly new topic. "Max is back in action."

That stretched reality, based on the report he'd gotten on Max's performance during the home invasion of the Italian trade deputy. The poor fanatic still had trouble moving faster than a walk.

But Max claimed to be ready for anything. Good enough.

Grisha pushed forward with his proposal. "We have a new team of sturmers. A much bigger team, ready for action."

He went to the antiquated whiteboard in the corner of the office and drew a skeletal sketch of Rivendell. "We can use our meat bombs—" Evgeni drew a breath to correct him, but Grisha corrected himself. "That is, our heroic kamikazes. They can blow holes in the outer wall here and here and take out the gate. Once we've ruptured the walls, the sturmers will do the rest."

Evgeni frowned. "I like the deniability. After it's all over, our ambassador in Orinoco can apologize for the whack jobs who attacked them. He'll explain that there's really nothing we could do about it because Ruby Rage has nothing to do with us. They're just conspiracy nuts. Who could possibly control them?"

He frowned. "Can the sturmers really beat an entire fortress full of soldiers?"

Grisha smiled. "Ah! Let me bring you up to date. The

Orinoco troops have left. Cassie and Remy brought in a gaggle of EStormers to run the place and defend it."

Evgeni looked bemused. "EStormers? How did they wind up there?"

Grisha shrugged. "Cassie or Remy invited them. For some reason, the EStormers think one of our thieves is the Emerald." Grisha left the whiteboard to stand across the desk from his boss. "Remember, we faced them once before, and our Ragers rolled over them, even though the EStormers had us massively outnumbered."

Evgeni frowned. "Until one of the Ragers got overzealous and destroyed our target." Anger edged his next words. "If you're trying to persuade me this is a good idea, you're a couple of points short."

Grisha made a chopping motion. "Ancient history. The days when our sturmers thoughtlessly wrecked missions have passed. They are now an elite fighting force."

Evgeni looked unmoved, and Grisha spread his arms in a helpless gesture. "This is the way to go. How can I persuade you to get on board?"

Evgeni spun his chair to look out the window. "Prove Andrey's really there. If we're going to try a brute force approach and create so much blowback, we need to be confident that our target is in the right place."

Grisha slumped but recovered. "I can task more satellite surveillance. Several people around Rivendell always wear clothes that obscure their features when they're outside. We can continue to watch in the hope that he'll slip up." His voice held weariness. "It could take months."

Evgeni sighed. "Have you asked Morte Noir where Andrey and the Quantum Key are?"

Grisha sat back down and folded his hands. "I thought about it but decided against it. Honestly, I'm afraid to ask."

Evgeni raised an eyebrow.

Grisha grimaced. "I don't think she knows about the Quantum Key. Or Andrey. I don't want to clue her in."

Evgeni, who had not contemplated the matter as extensively as Grisha, continued to look puzzled.

Grisha growled, "Dammit, she might decide that the Key is so valuable she'll steal it for herself."

Evgeni winced. "You win. There's no amount of money we could offer her as valuable as the Key."

Grisha nodded. It was more important to keep Morte Noir from learning about the Key than to retrieve it.

Morte Noir sat in a cozy circle with Remy and Laurie near the window of the sitting room. She looked sideways through the glass at the clear fields of fire around her mansion, and tension ran up her back. She had a dark suspicion that she would soon need them.

She sipped her tea.

Remy wrapped up her explanation. "So, the Quantum Key is the reason Grisha and Gamma are after us."

The Dark Mistress grimaced. "Let me try to sum up the players without a scorecard. Gamma wants the Key but doesn't know about the Memwriter. AID and Dread Nought want the Memwriter and would love to pick up the Key while they're at it."

Laurie shook her head at her daughter. "Dearest, you sure have gotten around since we lost you." She looked wistful. "If only we could go back to the days when I just worried that you'd fall off the top of the pyramid when you were cheering the football team."

Morte Noir turned a stern look on Laurie. "Ignorance might be bliss, but it doesn't get the job done."

Laurie glared back. "It's fine for you and me to face this darkness, but my daughter is a *cheerleader*."

Morte Noir responded tartly, "No more. She's a killer." She smiled at Remy. "A damn fine one, too. I'd hire her just for her ninja skills."

Mother and daughter rolled their eyeballs. Remy responded softly, "I'm done with killing."

The Mistress replied as softly as Remy. "But is killing done with you?"

Laurie intervened with a change of subject. "Enough. I need to go see what I can do for my husband." She leaped to her feet. "Mistress. How do we get to Orinoco?"

Morte Noir held up her hand. "A couple of final things." She turned to Remy. "Can I cut a deal with you for the occasional decryption and a few memwriting sessions for my people? Like your deal with Dread Nought?" She chuckled. "You know, if you agree, the only major covert player who won't be using your tech will be Gamma. How sad for them."

Remy had joined her mother pacing, eager to get home, but she stopped to consider. "Okay, deal. Same qualifications. We'll only translate messages that lead to defeating Gamma and AID."

Morte Noir interjected. "And terrorists. We do terrorists too, and I think you'll want to support us."

Remy waved her agreement. "Fine, but we'll only use

the Memwriter for people who have been firewalled so they only take the kind of cases we'll use the Key for." She stared hard into Morte Noir's eyes. "If you violate these rules, we'll know. Believe me."

The cheerleader's confidence that her information sources could root out any attempt at deception gave Morte Noir pause. Sure, Remy had the Key, and she could decrypt any message she could get her hands on. However, in a world full of comm systems, Morte Noir felt sure she could find channels Remy wouldn't know about and couldn't locate. How would Remy decrypt a message she couldn't find?

None of that made a difference right now. She could up her game and make truly staggering profits, even with the restrictions.

Who could she compartmentalize for doing only the work of the angels? Fenya and Dave were out. This would require some thought.

Morte Noir held out her hand. "I'll start a "noble goals only" subdivision immediately. We have a deal."

A short time later, Morte Noir saw her guests to the door.

Laurie looked puzzled. She whispered so Remy didn't overhear. "We're not taking the, uh, you-know-what?"

Morte Noir laughed. "Do you see black helicopters coming in, guns blazing? The you-know-what is for emergencies only. I really shouldn't have told you about it. I only did because…well…" Morte Noir admitted to herself that she had only done it because she liked and trusted

Laurie far in excess of what was appropriate for an asset. "All you need is," she waved her hand at the long, sleek black vehicle coming up the drive, "a limo."

Laurie grabbed her backpack like a lifeline. "I guess I forgive you for kidnapping me. And thank you for saving my life and protecting me all this time."

Morte Noir stepped in and gave her a full-body hug, then kissed her on the cheek. "My pleasure," she murmured in Laurie's ear.

Remy hugged Morte Noir more gingerly. "Thank you for taking care of Mom."

Morte Noir nodded. "Just answer when I ask for information." She turned back to Laurie and handed her two passports. "This one you'll use for the flight to Paris, and this one you'll use for the flight to Orinoco." She turned to Remy. "You sure you don't want any help with the trip?"

Remy shook her head. "I have my own ways of getting around."

Morte Noir laughed. "I'm sure you do."

The Mistress sighed after waving to them as they departed. Oddly, she was going to miss them.

4

SHOOTING MATCH

Armchair political strategists often thought of Kaliningrad as West Berlin in reverse. This chunk of Russia had been cleft from the bosom of Russian territory when the Baltic states departed during the breakup of the Soviet Union. Thereafter, to reach Kaliningrad, a Russian traveler had to pass through either Lithuania or Poland.

So, from a geographical perspective, the territory looked a little like Berlin when it was surrounded by Russian-owned East Germany. From a military perspective, the two could not have been more different.

Long before this geopolitical twist occurred, Kaliningrad had grown into one of the three largest and most important naval ports in Russia. It had bristled with weapons long before the breakup of the Union. Ironically, because of the desperate escape of those now-independent nations from Russia's loving grasp, that harbor had become even more important.

So, whereas West Berlin had been stripped of soldiers as part of the original deal to break up Germany, Kaliningrad had been reinforced with every kind of war machine. On its own, Kaliningrad would rank as one of the ten most militarily powerful countries in the world, even if it was just a city. A better analogy would be Switzerland when it was surrounded by Nazi countries if the Swiss had had a nuclear arsenal to go with their other arms.

The nukes of Kaliningrad held no interest for Bryce Wester. His attention was wholly focused on the non-nuclear Kinzhal hypersonic cruise missiles stored at Kaliningrad Chkalovsk, the air base.

Bryce listened to the road noise as he lay next to Morte Noir, sandwiched between the fake roof and the real roof of a cargo container on the back of a semi-truck. Below the fake roof, several tons of explosives accompanied them through Lithuania, and Bryce and the Mistress shared their crawl space with several hundred pounds of cocaine, which the enterprising Russian truck driver brought along when he made these trips into the military sanctuary.

Bryce should have been freezing, but Morte Noir was snuggled up against him, writhing erotically in his arms. Her perfume dazzled his senses, leaving him able to think of little except what he would do if he was warm enough to remove some clothing without risking frost forming on his more sensitive parts.

Morte Noir gave a low laugh. "Hold it in, lover boy. I've booked a room from which to run surveillance on the airport."

The truck stopped for the checkpoint when they reached Kaliningrad. The guards waved them through without even checking the back of the truck. Bryce sympathized with their disregard for normal inspection procedures for this cargo. Loads of explosives like this one had been known to spontaneously explode, and the guards wanted any such explosion to occur far from them.

A few minutes later, the driver pulled to the side of the road and opened the back. Bryce and the Mistress hopped down. Morte Noir wrapped herself around the driver much as she had wrapped herself around Bryce earlier and kissed him on the cheek. "Thank you so much."

Bryce handed him a suitcase full of rubles, to which the driver replied, "And thank you so much as well."

As the truck vanished into the distance, Bryce used his cell phone to get a Yandex, the Russian version of an Uber. "Where is this hotel we're staying at?"

Morte Noir gave him the address. As they waited for their ride, Bryce worried about two things. Foremost, he worried that his nose might freeze off. Secondly, he worried about the part of the mission he had no clue how to complete.

He had no doubt about their ability to break into Chkalovsk and find a Kinzhal missile. However, once they found it, how the hell would they get it out of Kaliningrad? If the Russians realized they'd lost one, all trucks leaving the province would face zealous inspections, and they couldn't hide a two-ton missile in a false truck ceiling designed for half a ton of drugs.

When he'd suggested to Morte Noir that a little more planning might be in order, she'd laughed at his silly concerns and patted him on the cheek. "Don't you worry your little head over it. I have taken some preparatory steps."

What magic trick could she have up her sleeve?

When Bryce went to the window, his breath crystallized on the glass. Stepping back, he gazed outward. "You're right. We can see everything on the airfield from here." He peered at one of the hangars. "Could you bring me the binoculars? I think I see a plane with a Kinzhal slung beneath it—a huge white missile almost as big as the plane."

Morte Noir silently stepped up beside him. She held the binoculars out too far for him to grab them. When he turned to her, he learned that she had slipped out of her clothes. He lost focus on the glasses and the Kinzhal.

She waved the binoculars. "You don't need these. That *is* a Kinzhal over there. No need for further confirmation."

He started to interrogate her, but she kissed him, then murmured, "I really want to learn more about the world's Number Two assassin." She ran a finger across his chest. "Don't you want to learn more about Number One?" She nibbled his ear lobe. "We have to wait for nightfall to take the next step anyway."

Bryce reacted with irritation at Morte Noir's denigration of his professional skills, but after a moment's reflection, which took more than a moment because the warmth of her body infused him and made concentrating difficult, Bryce concluded that he could soften her mood and interrogate her more easily with a dedicated seduction. He praised himself for coming to such a carefully analyzed decision.

Though he also realized, quite analytically, that the risk that she could kill him was rising rapidly. She was, after all, more deadly stripped nude than most men with full tactical gear.

He let Morte Noir pull him over to the bed. She closed her eyes as she gave him a languid kiss.

That was not fair. She could close her eyes, confident he would not kill her. How many ways could she kill him? He had to keep his eyes open in case she used her hands for a killing blow. Or poison under her fingernails. Or under her toenails. Or... He would have to stay alert to every risk during this entire encounter. It would be exhausting in more ways than one.

But he was a healthy male, and she was an extraordinary and beautiful woman. How could he fail to do his best?

Bryce had not yet reached the climax of his investigation when darkness fell and an alarm went off on Morte Noir's wristwatch. She slid out from under him like a well-oiled eel, leaving him to wonder whether she could escape with comparable ease in a hand-to-hand fight. He grimaced in frustration. "I thought we were learning about each other."

She shrugged. "I've learned what I wanted to know."

That didn't sound ominous. He dared not ever let her get into his head like this again.

Morte Noir hurried to the window. "There she goes!" she cried in exultation.

Bryce caught up with her in time to watch twin streamers of flame accelerate down the runway. He thought he glimpsed the long white outline of the hypersonic missile on the plane's belly as it tipped sharply up and accelerated into the sky. "That's our missile?"

Morte Noir chuckled. "Uh-huh."

Bryce cleared his throat. "Might I ask who's flying it?"

The Mistress leaned into him, warming his side. "A Russian fighter pilot of mine."

Bryce gave her a quizzical glance. "*Your* fighter pilot."

Morte Noir turned to the second suitcase she had brought and ran through the combination to unlock it. "The major flying that jet has an unfortunate history. His Chechen mother was raped by his father, who took a liking to her and brought her back to Moscow after his tour. His father was devoted to the Motherland, which is how my pilot passed his loyalty tests. His mother, however, hated the Russians, which is how he came to be...open to negotiation."

Bryce saw the glimmer of an explanation. "So you seduced him—"

"I sent Fenya to seduce him, actually. She gave herself to him and offered him a new life of wealth in the country of his choice if he would do me just one little favor." Morte Noir tapped her chin as she considered. "He might have done it for free, but why take chances?"

The flicker of more jet engines on the airfield caught Bryce's eye. "They're going to send every fighter and missile they've got after him. Can he really get away?"

Morte Noir opened her case and pulled out the components of a sniper rifle. "He should be fine with a little help from his friends." She stood nude in the soft glow of light from the bathroom, holding a weapon of staggering destructive power. Bryce had never seen anything so erotic.

She cocked her hip. "Are you going to join me or what?" She moved to the window and set up to acquire a firing solution on a plane on a distant runway.

Bryce jumped to his gear and hastily put together his rifle. "Hang on."

The Mistress fired. The blast left his ears ringing. They were firing from such a great range that they didn't dare impair their accuracy by using suppressors.

Bryce rushed to her side. "I said, hang on."

"Slowpoke." She fired again.

The first chase jet exploded after it left the runway.

Bryce grumbled in frustration.

Morte Noir explained the plan. "If we can nail this next one on the ground, we can block the field's lone runway and trap the rest of their forces."

Bryce pointed his night vision scope at the far end of the runway, searching for the next plane to start its take-off. "Can't hardly see anything."

Morte Noir leaned over and spoke in a teacher's soothing tones. "Catch the light from the exhaust. Aim at the engine in front of it." She turned to him with a wicked glint in her eyes. "Remember to lead the target."

Bryce grumbled again.

The two of them traded shots. Their naked hips touched once.

Bryce decided that if he was given a choice between going to heaven or staying in this room with this woman, he would pick her.

Another engine exploded.

Bryce frowned. "Whose shot was it?"

Morte Noir laughed. "Boys and their competitions. Who cares?"

She turned to the pile of clothes she had left by the bed. "We have to boogie out of here *now*. The cops will be here any moment."

Bryce joined her frenzied transition to escape. "What about fighters from the other airfields?"

As she reclaimed her bra, she chuckled. "He's flying an Su-57."

Bryce's jaw dropped. "A stealth fighter? So they have no way of tracking him."

He started laughing, and she laughed with him. They continued to laugh until his stomach hurt.

At that point, Bryce realized how silly it all was. "We didn't have to come here at all, did we? The fighters we just blew away couldn't have found him either." He offered an amused accusation. "You just wanted to get me into a shooting match. Who's competitive now?"

Morte Noir shrugged. "The contract stipulated I had to accompany you to Kaliningrad." She rubbed herself across his back and whispered, "Was there any problem with my performance as your partner?"

5

INSIDE TRACK

Grisha stared out his office window. It was located high in the Kremlin in a hallway adorned with a small sign stating Closed for Renovation. He could see the Moskva River beyond the outer wall of the complex. The water flowed with steadfast calm.

He turned away, still agitated. He *knew* his Key resided in Cassie's and Remy's jungle fortress, but how could he prove it?

His phone chimed when a request for a voice chat came through the TOR onion routers to hide the caller from prying eyes. He accepted the request, and Max greeted him with, "Grisha. We've succeeded."

Grisha winced. Despite his dour demeanor, Max often became overly enthusiastic over victories Grisha barely regarded. Evgeni might delight in hearing that they now controlled the Congo, but for Grisha, it barely deserved a yawn. Still, his job required him to encourage the leader of his teams of Ruby Ragers. "Max. What's the news?"

"One of our double agents inside EStorme got an invite.

He's in the second group of interviewees."

Grisha stopped pacing as he tried to grasp the context of Max's assertion. An invite to where? Oh, of course. "Rivendell?"

Max continued. "Yes. His Western name is Michael McKinney. Good man. Dedicated. I considered him for either the kamikaze teams or the sturmers but reluctantly gave him this mission because of his excellent English."

Grisha allowed his own excitement to enter his voice. "That *is* exceptional news. Any way we can help him with the assignment?"

Max hesitated. "I would like to reward him."

Grisha looked at the phone, puzzled. "We don't pay salaries or bonuses, Max. Too traceable. You know that."

Max cleared his throat. "That's not what I meant. I'd like you to give him a personal pep talk. He'd be honored to speak with the Ruby's personal representative and to get any special instructions you might have directly from you."

Oh, yes, Grisha had some personal instructions for their new agent. The original plan had been to get a couple of people into Rivendell on general principles. Now, he needed specific intel. "I'd be equally honored to speak with such an exceptional disciple."

Max tapped his cell phone. "I'll loop him in on this call."

A new voice came on the line, speaking American with the perfect lack of accent of a person from Ohio. "Max? How can I help you?"

Max introduced Grisha as the right hand of the Ruby. He did not use Grisha's name since even Max didn't know his real identity.

Grisha could almost hear Michael come to attention.

"Sir. I am at your disposal."

Grisha closed his eyes. He still felt vaguely guilty about using these vulnerable, clueless people, but he focused on the job. "Michael, consider me to be at your disposal as well as you go into the heartland of our enemies." He paused. "I have a special assignment for you."

Michael's voice quivered. "Yes, sir!"

Grisha continued, "I'm going to send you a photo of a man who has betrayed us—a Russian named Andrey. I believe he is hiding in Rivendell."

Michael answered with zeal. "Thank you, sir. I'll find him and execute him for you."

Grisha brushed his hand over his eyes. "No, no. We need him alive."

Michael sounded puzzled. "Sir?"

"He has the codes we need to unlock several databases with the plans of our enemies around the world."

Michael remained uncertain. "I'm not sure I can kidnap him and get him out of the jungle on my own, Sir. I'd be honored to try, of course." His voice stumbled. "But I fear I might fail you."

Grisha clarified, "I just want you to find him and get a photo of him as proof of presence. I'll send a team to collect him."

Michael sounded relieved. "That I can do, sir."

Grisha continued in a commanding tone. "Don't blow your cover for any reason. We need you to maintain your secret identity and continue your surveillance on Rivendell."

Michael sounded worried again. "Sir, I need to remind you that I'm just here for the interview. I don't know if I'll pass. I haven't picked up a single clue about what they're looking for, how to pass, or how to avoid failing."

Grisha spoke soothingly. "Take every opportunity to prove your dedication. You're one of Max's top men. If you do your best, how could they not take you?" He turned commanding again. "You must succeed. You are now one of the most important followers of the Ruby in the world."

Michael replied with absolute devotion. "I won't let you down, sir."

Evgeni quietly snuck to a corner of the bunker's conference room. The president sat at the far end of the table, a ten-meter-long piece of furniture that left five meters between him and the people who reported to him.

The paranoid official leader of the nation had been living in this corner of the Nuclear Sanctum since the war with...Evgeni had lost track of which war. Anyway, the president lived here now, never leaving except to see his mistress.

The president explained the next war. "A correct reading of history shows that Nigeria has always been part of the Russian empire. Its recent independence is an affront to the harmony of our lands. Dozens of Russian speakers face persecution there every day. It must be brought back into the fold."

A general cleared his throat. "Shall I send advance members of the Wagner Group?"

The president's implacable face showed implacable disdain. "I was thinking the army could handle this."

The general gulped. "I can deploy a force in about a month."

The president stared at him. "Stop fooling around. Next week."

The general gulped again.

Evgeni listened with growing irritation. The president had clearly forgotten whatever management skills he had learned as a mid-level KGB bureaucrat. Promising unbound vengeance for missing a deadline might guarantee the schedule was met, but it could not guarantee a high-quality delivery. The troops could deploy in a week, but the ammo and the spare parts for the old trucks that would inevitably break down would not get there for a month.

Evgeni was only here to observe, yet some forms of idiocy cried out for a response. He forgot that although he was the most powerful man in Russia, he still needed to pretend that clown was the top dog. He cleared his throat. "Mr. President, why not just let our covert ops teams handle this? We can take control there the way we took control of the Congo."

The president didn't move or change his expression. "But we don't really have control in the Congo, do we? We have a vassal state. That is quite different from a proper part of the Russian empire." He looked around the table. "Who is that person, anyway?"

A deputy director of Alfa Group, who knew the small man in the corner could kill him in an eyeblink if he got upset, answered, "He's one of my assistants. Just here to listen." He glared at Evgeni as if he were angry rather than terrified.

Evgeni did not blurt, "What sort of a moron goes around conquering countries when we can just control them?" He just looked stoically at the floor.

The president grunted. "Next topic."

The ringing of his phone forced Grisha to awaken. He started to swear but realized the call came from Michael in Rivendell. He rose from the bed, excited. "You have information?"

Michael whispered, "I found Andrey. I'm sending you his photo now."

A message with a photo attached arrived. Andrey stood by a window in a living room, staring out at the scenery, seemingly at peace with the world.

Grisha vowed to change that. "Exceptional work. The Ruby thanks you." He paused. "How is the interview going?"

Michael hesitated. "I think it's going okay. It's a week-long process. I'll be undergoing a lie detector test tomorrow."

Grisha grimaced. "If you fail, it's my fault. I should have arranged for training so you could control your heartbeat and breathing. Or given you medication that would suppress your reactions."

Doubt crept into Michael's voice. "It's not like that, according to the interviewees who completed that phase of the testing. They put a balaclava on your head with a bunch of electrodes wired into it. Are you familiar with it?"

Grisha frowned. "I've never heard of anything like it."

He spoke authoritatively. "Pay careful attention to every detail of the procedure. Even if you are rejected, the information you collect about the machine will be extremely valuable."

Michael whispered, "As you wish. I have to go," and hung up.

Grisha sat on his bed. Were Cassie and Remy using advanced electroencephalography for lie detection?

He had thought more than once that the other people chasing the girls were less interested in his Key than something else. Could this be it? Would an infallible lie detector be more valuable than the Quantum Key?

He would suggest to Evgeni that he should mention it to the PSYOPs scientist who had engineered the Ruby Rage conspiracy system. Might the Doc have an idea?

Cassie found her prey on the bank of the river leading away from the Kerepakupai Meru, the tallest continuous waterfall in the world, which was an easy walk from Rivendell.

Tina sat cross-legged, poking stones with a stick. Cassie crouched next to her. "I was about to leave for Ciudad Bolivar to meet Remy and her mom when they told me you'd come this way, acting really upset." She rubbed Tina's shoulders. "You okay?"

Tina stuck her stick into the bank and jabbed deep into the mud. Each jab seemed to make her angrier. At last, she looked at Cassie. "Remy isn't the Emerald, is she?" Her anger softened to irritation. "You aren't either."

Ah. Tina was responding to the memwriting as Cassie had hoped. "Why do you say that?"

Tina snorted. "All that critical thinking stuff you've been pouring into us. Like apophenia, the clinically extreme version of illusory pattern recognition."

Cassie nodded. The human mind worked overtime, all the time, to identify patterns. If there were no patterns, the mind went wild inventing them. The results could lead one to astonishing but incorrect conclusions.

Tina continued. "And then there's the illusory truth effect."

Cassie forced herself not to smile. Illusory truth arose when a person heard the same lie over and over. Even when warned that they were hearing a lie, sufficient repetition would often compel people to believe the deception anyway.

"Burden of proof reversal." This time, Tina explained it. "If you tell me I'm wrong about someone drinking babies' blood, I'll demand that you prove they don't."

She snorted again. "And all the others. Causation versus correlation, and holy hell! Confirmation bias on steroids." Her sigh sounded painful. "Those are the forms of self-delusion upon which EStorme is based."

Cassie could no longer contain her smile, though she did not grin. "If Remy isn't the Emerald, who is?"

Tina jabbed the stick into the bank harder, then threw the branch into the river. The current rapidly carried it away. "There is no Emerald." She glared the accusation at her mentor. "You were using us."

Cassie turned her face to the sun and allowed her grin

to emerge. "Most excellent!" She leaned back on her elbows, which got soaked in mud. "It's okay to hate us."

Tina cleared her throat and spoke with sorrow. "But only a little bit. Really, Brett and I were using ourselves." She sighed. "With the Emerald showing the way, the whole world really did make sense. Simple sense." Her head sank. "But in reality, the things that make real sense don't fit on bumper stickers. Life is complicated."

Cassie levered herself up and turned serious. "You're only allowed to blame yourself a little bit too, Tina. Let me tell you who *has* been using you and millions like you." She described the Analytical Intelligence Division and the mysterious scientist called "the Doc." "We're all vulnerable to misinformation and mental trickery. The Doc is the one who weaponized our weaknesses and designed EStorme to exploit them."

Tina looked at her thoughtfully. "How do we take them down?" She looked away. "Never mind. I guess since I no longer worship the Emerald, I'm disqualified for a place here." She wearily struggled to her feet. "I loved the Emerald because she gave me a sense of belonging. Now I'm a castout even among the castouts." Sorrow washed over her. "I'll go pack my things."

She turned to leave, but Cassie grabbed her wrist. "You've got it backward. You aren't cast out. You're cast *in*. You just passed the interview, Tina. Recognizing the truth is the *only* way to pass the test."

Her smile dazzled the whole jungle. "Welcome to a *real* Awakening."

6

RAGE AGAINST THE CRITICAL MIND

Hunching, Grisha surreptitiously looked around the landing field one last time. He chided himself for foolishness. If Evgeni had eyes on him and decided to stop him, he would not know until the hammer fell.

He leaped lightly onto the borrowed Venezuelan black helicopter, a Russian Halo troop transport. The engines revved, and the *chop-chop-chop* of the blades accelerated until the helo lifted into the air and tilted forward. A fleet of identical vehicles formed up behind him, then surged south to cross into Orinoco airspace.

Max yelled over the noise of the engines and the props, "It's good to have you back with us, sir."

Grisha yelled back, "It's good to be here." He breathed a sigh of relief. He was now committed. Evgeni could not stop him from seeing this mission through.

He respected Evgeni's reasoning in demanding that the Ragers operate independently. Gamma needed the deniability, especially when attacking targets within the national boundaries of their allies. Under most circumstances, Grisha agreed with him.

However, assaulting Remy's fortress did not in any way count as an ordinary mission. Given that the Ragers had reached superior levels of effectiveness, if Grisha could get his hands on Andrey, Gamma would effectively own the world.

Currently, deprived of Andrey and the Key, Gamma faced its enemies deaf and blind.

The helos crossed the river separating Venezuela from Orinoco. Grisha spent the next fifteen minutes fighting anxiety, clenching his teeth 'til they ached, but as expected, no opposition arose. The Orinoco army had been adequate to defeat the Venezuelans when they were protected from direct ground assault by the river, but the nation had no Air Force.

Soon, the helos approached the target. One sturmer slid the hatch aside, and another dropped a drone out the opening. The formation slowed almost to a hover while the drone scooted forward to assess the threat.

Everything looked quiet. A guardhouse by the main gate and a pair of sentries in each of the towers on the four corners of the outer wall, afforded the only evidence of defense. A handful of men and women tended plots of pale white orchids while others lounged by the pool. Wheeled white tables—robots, actually—wove among the loungers and the gardeners, delivering drinks and snacks.

The robots looked familiar. Ah, yes...Morte Noir had utilized similar machines at the Auction. One had been used for the cake-slicing competition.

Grisha took a deep breath. The scene before him

exuded a pastoral peacefulness. In the assassin's experience, this level of lazy unawareness generally denoted a trap.

What kind of trap could Remy have set? He worried because he could not visualize a serious risk. She could have a small army of troops hidden in the basement levels, for which Michael had not yet sent complete information. However, reliable intel informed him that the Orinoco troops had all departed and their slots had been filled with EStormers.

He still couldn't identify anything to worry about. His sturmers were hardened vets. Even if Remy had EStormers stuffed in every closet, he would prevail.

His lack of worries worried him.

Grisha signaled Max to begin the assault. The helos accelerated to full speed. Grisha kept his eyes glued to the feed from the drone as they darted into visual range. He found himself clenching and unclenching his fists.

Max looked at him with puzzlement. He spoke in a calming tone, or as calming as could be achieved when he had to shout to be heard over the props. "Problem, sir? Everything's going according to plan." He pointed at the drone feed. "We caught them completely unaware. They still have no clue that we're here. We have achieved perfect surprise."

Grisha's head tried to explode. He yelled back, "That's the problem, Max. It's too perfect." He pointed at his ears. "They've been able to hear us for the last five minutes. A thundering fleet of helicopters is bearing down on them, and they're still sunbathing by the pool! Doesn't that strike you as unlikely?"

In the deepest level of Rivendell lay Andrey's lair, known to all as the Vault. Despite the name, on a typical day, it was not particularly secure. Andrey delighted in having visitors come to see him after years trapped underground with little human contact, so on most days, he left the blast door open as he worked. Not today.

Tina sealed the door behind her and patted Andrey on the shoulder. "You're a good man, Charlie Brown."

Andrey, still hunched over his keyboard, answered distractedly, "Thank you, I think."

Tina stared at the twin displays as the action proceeded. "How long before they figure out the truth?"

Andrey sat back, finished with his part in the upcoming conflict. "They should be figuring it out about now."

Max barked to the pilot, "Stay in the lead. Bring us down right by the Welcome to Rivendell sign." He pointed at their landing zone.

Grisha shook his head. "Belay that. Max, pick another team to take point. You and I need to hang back until we have a secured area."

Max grunted in grudging acknowledgment. "As you command."

They were so immersed in watching the attack via the drone that they reacted with surprise when a fireball burst outside the helo's front window.

"We have incoming!" someone desperately shouted on the radio.

When Grisha looked at the physical world, he saw a remarkable change in the scene. The people who had been sunbathing by the pool had transformed. They now wore combat armor and carried rifles.

Grisha looked at the view from the drone. Several of the sunbathers jumped into the pool, splashing the people near the edge. A couple reached up from the water to grab drinks from the robot waiters.

Somehow, Andrey had performed a marvel of real-time video rewriting with the Key, transforming soldiers into sunbathers on the fly. The blasted engineering genius had developed a novel application for his tech, one which Grisha would never have allowed. How irksome.

Grisha now understood how dangerous the Key could be in the wrong hands. He screamed, "The drone's been hacked! Look out the window!"

Max pointed at the top of the Keep. "Stinger missiles!" Another contrail left the rooftop and tore across the sky as they watched. Another fireball ensued.

All the sturmers, and Max in particular, had been reprogrammed after their first lost battle to recognize a hopeless situation and preserve themselves. He followed that programming now. "Abort! Abort!"

Two more fireballs blossomed.

Grisha groaned. "Too late."

Max realized that as well. The only way out was through. "All helos down, down, down!"

The pilots of the helos had already deduced their only safe course. Helicopters hit the ground as fast and hard as they dared and bounced. Then the troops scattered lest another Stinger find its mark.

The lone Hind gunship that had not been obliterated by Stingers closed on the Keep and fired a pair of missiles into the top floor, destroying a roof filled with men and missiles. The helo hovered, pinned in position by the need to maintain surveillance lest the survivors find another way to use the tower for tactical advantage.

Grisha spoke sternly to himself. *Stay calm.* His only chance to help his men required him to think strategically. What else could the enemy do since they had the Key?

He reeled when he identified the obvious threat and shouted over Max's continuing stream of commands, "Our comms have been hacked! Trust no radio communications! Proceed as independent units!"

He prayed the enemy had not had the foresight to replace that message with their own.

Andrey pounded on the edge of the desk. "Damn! Almost had 'em."

Tina raised an eyebrow. "What did you almost have?"

Andrey leaned back in his chair and spun it around. "I matched their leader's voiceprint, and I was about to start giving them orders." He grinned at her. "Or rather, *you* were going to start giving them orders, O Mighty Leader."

He spun his chair back to the keyboard. "But we missed. They've all gone to local control."

Grisha squinted so hard his eyes closed. He was afraid to watch.

Max hesitantly touched his shoulder. "Do not worry. Our men are all trained to operate without higher command. Having battlefield communications was a luxury." He shrugged. "We are Russian. We endure."

Grisha forced himself to watch again.

Half the helos had landed outside the main wall. The handful of sentries in the corner towers opened fire on the troops as they rushed to the main gate, knocking sturmers to the ground at a surprising rate. Grisha peered at the towers. "Snipers." EStormer snipers. When had they acquired snipers?

A handful of Ragers peeled off and rushed the towers as another small team rushed the gate. The main body of troops slowed down, and Grisha smiled.

He knew what that meant.

Tina cursed as she watched the situation outside the gates evolve. She snapped orders to the men in the towers. "Kamikazes coming at you! Priority targets." She gave the men descriptions of the most important enemy soldiers to hit.

The tower guards did their best, but the Ruby Rage kamikaze fanatics proved too hard to stop. Even fatally wounded, they continued the attack. A couple blew up when the sniper fire struck the explosives packed in their abdomens, but the kamikazes were trained to keep enough distance from each other to avoid setting off a chain reaction of detonating men.

One by one, the survivors reached the bases of the towers and exploded. The buildings shook, and the sentries had no choice but to race for the stairwells as the towers toppled with slow grace.

A team of kamikazes reached the gate and blew themselves up against the hinges. When the sturmers reached the archway, a slight push caused the gates to topple.

The sturmers surged onto the main plaza, where the main battle had already commenced.

On the Vault's largest screen, the action on the main sward played out in high resolution. Tina watched with admiration. "That's a really nice camera on that Russian drone."

Andrey nodded. "Isn't it, though? Better than ours, actually. I've pulled all our drones in to keep them safe. Who needs them when the enemy is watching this for us?"

Tina focused on the action. "Okay, work with me to highlight all the Ragers who have sniper rifles and all the ones who act like team leaders and officers. Those are our targets."

Andrey nodded and started highlighting candidates in red. Tina pointed out several priority designations as well, then rattled off the targets to EStormers spread across the southern part of the sward between the main residence and the Ragers.

A Rager ran across the field and exploded when he reached the line of EStormers.

Tina cursed. "Damn! How do we catch those bastards?"

Andrey grimly answered, "Answer fire with fire."

Tina pursed her lips. "All right." She broadcast the command. "Everyone withdraw into the building." She touched Andrey on the shoulder. "Get ready to light 'em up."

Grisha watched as the sturmers' progress across the lawn faltered. He couldn't discern why.

Max made a guttural sound. "Half the enemy troops are snipers."

Grisha blinked, then turned his attention to the enemy lines. The EStormers had broken up into two-man teams. In each team, one member held a sniper rifle. Max had told the literal truth—half the opponents were snipers. Judging by the results as he matched enemy fire with friendly deaths, they were also good snipers. Really good.

Training a sniper took hundreds of hours, yet there had been no reports of endless sniper training. Neither satellites nor Michael's on-site human intelligence had hinted at any such thing.

Thinking about Michael distracted him for a moment. Grisha had hoped to speak with him during the final days of preparation for the assault, but Michael had missed two check-ins. Could he have been caught learning about Rivendell's weapons training and strategies and executed? Would Grisha ever find out if he had been?

Back to the problem of the snipers. Grisha couldn't

imagine having enough teachers to train that many people in the fine art of one shot, one kill. How had they done it?

That reminded him that he still didn't know why AID and Dread Nought wanted those women except for the Key.

One of the kamikazes reached the enemy line and blew up, taking two fire teams with him. Grisha ground his teeth. Once again, the meat bombs were proving to be the most valuable elements of the Rager repertoire.

More meat bombs surged forward as the EStormers retreated into the main building.

Grisha frowned as a hiccup occurred, another error in the programming of the sturmers the Doc needed to correct.

The Doc had specified the day the attack should take place since his conspiracy-management systems could not keep the sturmers at maximum fury constantly. Rather, he allowed the anger to ebb and flow to give the sturmers' hormonal responses a rest between flooding their brains with rage opioids. The current rage cycle peaked today.

Unfortunately, maximizing rage also maximized irrationality. A number of the sturmers were clustering about the badly wounded EStormers to mutilate them. The loss of focus was slowing down the assault.

Fortunately, it did not take long for the Ragers to satisfy their needs and run to catch up with their peers.

Now the only things moving in the space between the Ragers and the building were the robot waiters. The poor machines milled around at surprising speed, like they were as confused and panicked as human beings would be.

The main body of sturmers moved up fast, though they

remained careful not to overtake the kamikazes lest the explosion of one of the meat bombs take them out. Meanwhile, the enemy focused on the kamikazes and killed them in large numbers.

However, too many of the suicide Ragers raced forward for the enemy to get them all. A group ran to the wall between the main door and the closest bay window.

Their explosions blew out not only the door and the window but also every inch of the concrete wall between them. The huge opening would allow sturmers to enter the building without running a gauntlet of withering fire.

Grisha thought he saw some of the sturmers cheering as they charged past the weaving robots toward the breached building. Soon the advantages of his veteran Rager army would *shine*.

Andrey complained, "I really wish we didn't have to do this."

Tina sympathized but rolled her eyes. "Inferno time. Now."

Andrey sighed and pressed the button.

As his men rushed into the breach, Grisha saw a couple of the robot waiters scoot to new locations. A pattern emerged after he studied their seemingly random gyrations.

The robots were distributing themselves so that each

clot of Ragers approaching the building had one in their midst. Grisha's eyes widened when understanding came.

He screamed a warning. "Stay away from the robots! They're bombs!"

He realized as he said it that even if the men had time to react, they would pay no attention to a warning they heard on the radio. He had issued that order himself.

A string of explosions coalesced into an ocean of red-orange flames. Whirls of smoke rose from the barbecued corpses.

A few clusters of attackers who'd arrived late to the party survived, the rage-hypersaturated men who had paused to torture their victims.

With only zealous suicide bombers and the over-amped sturmers to continue the mission, no sanity remained.

Andrey looked at the drone images of the dead and grimaced. "I think I might be sick."

Tina hugged him. "I know. But hold on until we're finished. Okay?"

Andrey swallowed hard and nodded.

For Grisha, one bit of good news formed the one silver lining: the bots' explosion had enlarged the already substantial entry hole created by the first kamikazes. His sturmers now had the equivalent of an eight-lane California highway for their final assault.

Max demonstrated a flash of insight. "If they would take a moment to think through the situation, they would realize that their best bet is to retreat to the helicopters outside the wall. With the Stinger launchers taken out by the Hind, they can escape." He turned morose. "I fear the interior of that building holds nothing but death, skilled though they are."

The Ragers dashed madly into the building and out of sight.

Grisha watched in despair. "But there's no chance to think things through in a battle like that. They believe the only way out is through." He shrugged. "The EStormers are battered as well. Perhaps our men can win after all."

He pondered the matter. Time to take a risk. "Let's bring our helo down to the front door. If our men come out, hopefully with Andrey, we'll pick them up and get out of here."

Max looked concerned. "It's not safe."

Grisha pointed at the only other helo still in the air. "With the Hind gunship holding the Keep at bay, it should be safe enough." After all, he wouldn't have to explain this disaster to Evgeni if he died.

Andrey cursed as he watched the surveillance cameras strewn throughout Rivendell. "They must have a map of the layout. They're coming straight for us."

Tina slung her M-4 over her shoulder and walked to the Vault's blast door. "Lock this behind me."

Andrey stared at her. "Are you crazy? Stay inside and lock it yourself."

Tina patiently explained, "If they still have enough kamikazes when they get here, they can blow this door."

Andrey yelled. "*Those people are crazy! You won't be able to stop them!*"

Tina drew her M1911 Colt .45 from its holster and caressed it. "They think they know what they are fighting for, but it's just a fantasy. A delusion." She stepped outside the bunker. "Whereas we understand the stakes and the reality. We'll see what happens when truth collides with fiction. Which prevails?" She turned away.

Andrey grumbled but sealed the door.

Tina started down the hall and had almost reached Rudy Ross's compute center when heavy running footsteps echoed down the stairwell. Tina raised her Colt with cold determination. "Come to Mama."

A big bruiser of a man burst through the stairwell's fire door.

Tina pointed the pistol up and away. "Brett, you nearly gave me a heart attack."

Brett shot her a lopsided grin. "Great to see you too, darlin'." He briefly hugged her. "Two kamikazes in the lead. I'd swear they were hopped up on drugs if I didn't know better."

She smacked his chest. "They're hopped up on fury. Better than drugs." She raised her Colt. "But I have the cure."

Brett's smile widened. "You know I only married you because you have such good taste in weapons."

She blew him a kiss. "I love you too."

The fire door flew open with no warning patter of feet. Brett muttered, "They're quiet, too. Practically cats."

Tina stepped away from her husband. "No prob." She fired her pistol repeatedly.

The 1911 Colt and its .45 caliber rounds had been developed to cope with the fanatical Moro warriors of the Philippines. Like the Ruby Rage kamikazes, they were high on rage opioids when they charged across the battlefield. No consideration of consequences distressed them. Smaller caliber bullets could kill them, but not before they killed their assailants.

The Colt stopped them dead.

Would Tina's century-old firearm still succeed against the latest technology for overclocking the hypothalamus and drenching the brain in fury?

Tina's first shot struck the first suicide bomber in the shoulder. It slowed him not at all.

The second shot fared little better.

She tried a headshot and missed.

Brett opened up with his carbine, seeking the smaller target of the attacker's abdomen—the one vulnerability that accompanied the near-immunity of the rage.

Tina and Brett hit the mark at the same time, and the cache of C-4 exploded.

The lead Rager's blast lit off the second Rager. Brett swept Tina into his arms and turned his back to the concussive blast that hurled them both to the floor. When Tina recovered her senses a few moments later, she found herself buried under her husband's bulk. "Blast it, Brett! Get up."

Brett did not hear her. She pushed him aside and came up into firing position, panting.

Fortunately, the sturmers behind the kamikazes had caught up with the bombers by the time the explosives detonated. They lay strewn across the hallway.

Tina turned back to her husband. "Brett?"

He didn't move.

Tina knelt to examine him. The body armor on his back was battered beyond repair, and blistering burns covered his neck. Tina smacked out flames on the remnants of his pants and heaved him onto his back. "*Brett!*"

Her husband coughed. "Ugh. Roll me back, darlin'." His voice fell. "Hurts."

Grisha was quietly brooding when someone he recognized spoke on the radio. The speaker's voice trembled. "Grisha."

Grisha chuckled. The kid still feared him down to his toes. It was impressive that his asset had made the call himself. Grisha responded, "Andrey. So good to hear your voice."

"I'll bet. We have some wounded down here that belong to you. Send the Hind away, and we'll give them to you."

Grisha pursed his lips and put anger into his voice when he spoke. If he couldn't grab the kid, he could at least reinforce the terror he had worked so hard to instill in him. "Deal."

7

GOAL ALIGNMENT

Cassie watched in the Hummer's mirror as Remy's head banged into the back-seat headrest. The banging continued in synchrony with the banging of her mother's head on the front-seat headrest. Neither woman roused from the stupor into which they had fallen.

The ditches and bumps on the long, winding road to Rivendell made for an exhausting trip, and Remy and her mom had already been exhausted when they'd arrived in the Orinoco capital by separate routes. Cassie had suggested they relax a day or two before heading out, but Laurie desperately wanted to see her husband, and Remy desperately wanted Laurie to be in the safest place she knew, so they departed immediately.

Cassie pulled through the gate checkpoint and up to the sign welcoming visitors to the main building, on the green sward where helos and eVTOLs landed.

Remy spoke with a smidgeon of her normal energy. "Mom, wake up. We're here."

Laurie squinted blearily and staggered out of the

Hummer. She stopped at the sign. "Rivendell. Merely to be there," her voice faded. "Too many bullet holes to read the rest."

Cassie grimaced. She hadn't yet seen the wreckage, but Tina had told her about it.

Remy's belief that this was their safest place needed some adjustment. Cassie answered the unasked question, "We'll be fixing the sign soon."

Laurie's querying gaze fell upon the blown-out wall of the main building.

Cassie confessed, "Fixing that will take a little longer."

Tina rushed out, and Brett lumbered behind her. "Welcome!" She approached Laurie. "You must be Remy's mom. We've all looked forward to your arrival." She gestured for Laurie to follow her. "Let me take you to your room so you can freshen up."

Laurie sagged but shook her head with determination. "Take me to my husband."

Cassie, Tina, and Brett frowned. Cassie spoke first. "But—"

Remy took her mom by the elbow. "Let me show you where he is." She looked at Cassie. "Any change in his condition?"

As Cassie tried to figure out something encouraging to say, Remy started to lead her mother away. They got five steps before Andrey ran out. "Remy! Cassie! I figured out who AID's Doc is!" He continued less enthusiastically. "Sort of."

Cassie followed Remy and Andrey down to the Vault. He proceeded to the unusually comfortable conference room, which he had insisted on installing adjacent to his command center.

The conference room was reconfigurable to a bunker-barracks for twenty people if things went badly.

Remy slumped in a chair. Words croaked from her throat. "Tell us what you know about the Doc."

Andrey gave her a smug geek smile. "The most important thing I've learned is why we know so little about him."

Cassie glared at him. "That's it? You know why we don't know?"

Andrey huffed defensively. "Hey, it's an important breakthrough." He placed a large tablet that showed a map of the world with curved lines crisscrossing continents on the table. "You know there have always been messages in the UDC that I couldn't decode. A trivial fraction of the stuff there, of course, but I ran into them whenever I tried to follow a thread that led to AID's psyops research."

Cassie interpreted. "You couldn't decode messages about Camp No outside Guantanamo or messages in and out of the camp."

Andrey nodded. "Exactly."

Remy had her head cradled in her arms on the table. "So, the Doc uses a form of encryption that defeats even the Key."

Cassie twitched her lips. "How can that be? Is he using some exotic new form of quantum encryption? Tech more advanced even than yours?"

Andrey laughed despite the seriousness of the problem. "The Doc went old school. Old-old school. One-time pads."

Cassie rooted through her extensive knowledge of encryption systems and gasped. "So, they combine every byte of data with a byte of pure randomness, but it's a random byte the recipient knows as well, so he can separate out the data with ease."

She shook her head. "One-time pads were never popular because you had to lug books of random numbers around with you. Then, when people ran out of numbers, they had to physically exchange new books. It offered a prime opportunity for someone to steal the encoding data."

Andrey gave her a fist pump. "Everyone abandoned one-time pads when they invented modern encryption systems." His expression held amazement and appreciation. "The last people to use this stuff might have been a handful of Nazis working on secret projects that are still a mystery today."

He pointed at the map. "Though I can't decrypt the messages, I *did* decrypt the envelopes that carry them through the onion routers. Here's the traffic analysis."

Cassie studied the pattern. "It looks like there are two major clusters, one set centered in the States and one set circulating around Russia."

Andrey affirmed that excitedly. "Exactly."

Cassie spoke up. "Two different people or two teams of people?"

Andrey frowned. "Perhaps. Maybe one person with a team." He pointed to streams crisscrossing the southern hemisphere. "Sometimes the streams meet down here."

Remy raised her head as curiosity overcame her exhaustion. She stared at the tablet. "Tierra del Fuego and the Cape of Good Hope?"

Andrey grimaced. "Relays from satellites is my best guess."

Cassie shook her head in disbelief. "The Doc has his own satellite system?"

Silence met this suggestion. Another oddity occurred to her. "Two patterns of unbreakable crypto in America and Russia. Two patterns of conspiracy theory, EStorme and Ruby Rage in America and Russia."

Remy channeled Cassie's sarcasm into a question. "Coincidence?"

Dale arrived at Rivendell long after dark. He had officially made the trip to negotiate the next tranche of training sessions for Dread Nought agents. In reality, he had come to discuss matters that made him restless as he sought sleep.

Early the next morning, in the shade beneath the east wall of the fortress, he sat quietly, watching the grass tremble in the breeze. The murmurs of workers repairing the blast damage at the far end of the compound barely reached him. As long as he kept his eyes down, he could not see the shattered west wing of the main house.

He could pretend all was right with the world.

He turned his head and stared into his coffee cup as if he could read the swirls of cream and therein divine the plan, the future, and his place in it.

Cassie silently walked up and sat down across the small table from him. "You're even more pensive than usual."

Dale finally put his finger on the problem. "We've lost our momentum."

He took a sip of coffee. "First we stole the Quantum Key. Then you tapped into the Utah Data Center and created the nation of Orinoco." He used his spoon to swirl the cream into new patterns to shape new prophecies, but they provided no insight. "Finally, we got Remy's father back, and her mother joined us."

Cassie saw his point. "Now we're standing still while our enemies take shots at us."

Dale slumped. "No one has ever won a war playing defense."

Cassie pulled out her phone. "Remy. Strategy time. Now. With tea at the east wall."

Dale's eyes twinkled. "Since when did you start giving orders?"

Cassie retorted. "Since Remy went all mushy now that she's reunited with her mother *and* her father." She sighed. "Though her father's condition does remind her to be angry. That's a plus."

In a few minutes, Remy joined them, carrying a tray with mugs of tea. "Hey, Dale. I didn't know you'd be here, or I would have brought you tea too." She glared at Cassie. "She's not very forthcoming when she's being bossy."

Dale held up his coffee cup in a peacekeeping gesture. "I'm fine."

Cassie snorted. "No, he's not." She explained his concerns.

Remy blew on her tea. "He's right, of course. My entire plan revolved around getting my mom and dad back."

Dale marveled at his benefactor. She'd planned the Quantum Key Heist and the Utah Data Center wiretap as mere incidental requirements for solving a kidnapping.

He offered his best observation. "We need a new strategy to stop Gamma and AID." He nodded at the blast damage throughout the facility. "And simple blunt attacks like theirs won't work for us. If Remy had blown up Congress or Fort Meade with her boron reactor bomb, it wouldn't have made any difference. AID would have been reconstituted with new players, stronger than before."

Cassie's eyes twinkled over her mug. "And let's not forget about Dread Nought. Our arrangement with your company is working for now, but Augustus is a greedy SOB. He'll eventually get tired of following the rules."

Dale looked down in despair. "I can already see it. He wants the Memwriter without constraints. He's just biding his time until he sees his chance."

Remy looked at him with alarm. "When he moves, he'll kill you. You're far too much of a..."

Cassie finished, "Boy Scout."

Dale's expression went sour, then he grinned. "True."

Cassie spoke sharply. "It's not a laughing matter. Dread Nought has plenty of operatives who are unabashedly depraved."

Remy whispered. "Curtis." She and Cassie unconsciously touched their scars.

Dale turned defensive. "I can't help believing that Dread Nought should be easier to deal with than the others. They're not as...drenched in evil. It's mostly good people working to improve things for their customers." He shrugged. "Unlike AID, which doesn't have customers."

Remy's eyes widened with enlightenment. "Of course."

Cassie leaned forward. "Watcha thinkin'? Spill."

Dale joined Cassie in peering at her. He had his own insight. "It's all about the customers, isn't it? Crucial difference."

Remy nodded. "The world of covert operations is zero-sum. One group benefits only when another loses." She got excited. "But corporations live in a non-zero-sum world."

Cassie offered an example. "Like when Morte Noir stepped outside the bounds of covert ops to negotiate our mining deal. Orinoco got royalties, the mining company got revenues, and all the people in the world got cobalt for batteries. Everyone profited."

Remy pointed at Cassie. "Most excellent."

Dale waited for more information, but Remy remained wrapped in her own thoughts. He tried to stumble forward on his own. "So, Dread Nought profits when their customers profit. If we can figure out a more profitable way of helping more customers, we win."

Remy's eyes gleamed. "I see how to do it." She explained her proposal.

Dale shared her excitement. "Win-win-win for everyone. Not zero-sum." The Boy Scout's features clouded with guilt. "Well, it's zero-sum for a few people."

Cassie smacked the table with satisfaction. "Oh, yes. Zero-sum for the people who deserve it most."

Dale raised an eyebrow at Remy. "So, what's our first step?"

Grisha sat back in his chair with his legs up on another chair in Evgeni's office. He had his eyes closed.

Normally, he kept his attention on his boss, but his boss was not the main person to worry about in this conference. He had closed his eyes to improve his focus on the person speaking on the phone.

The Doc continued in his usual monotone cadence. "It will take some time to bring another batch of Ruby Ragers up to the level of fanaticism needed for kamikaze operations." He paused. "I can deliver more sturmers sooner, but they'll be raw. Regaining the skill level of our veterans will take time and bloodshed."

Grisha winced.

Evgeni muttered darkly, "We'll have to pare back our offensive operations while we replenish our organic munitions. I'll reprioritize the sturmer missions so we give them a graduated series of increasingly more difficult ops as part of the training process." He glared at Grisha. "I know we talked about using the Ragers as disposable units, but even with paper cups, you can use too many too fast."

Grisha offered a few words in defense. "If we'd gotten the Key back, it would have been worth it."

The Doc supported him. "High risks, high rewards."

Evgeni couldn't help one last bitter observation. "Still, the new director of AID must be laughing his guts out. Whoever he is." One new problem they faced was that they still didn't know the AID director's identity. He sighed. "Moving on."

The Doc returned to a detail of the assault that he

seemed unable to get past. "You said you lost contact with this Michael McKinney in the days before the operation."

Grisha rolled his head. "I don't know what happened to him, and we've had no contact since then. I've assumed they found him out and put him down." He reflected on their last conversation. "I should have pulled him out when he told me they were going to put him in a lie detector."

The Doc asked sharply, "What kind of lie detector?"

Grisha sat bolt upright as he dredged this part of his conversation with Michael out of memory. "Something with a cap and a bunch of gold wires sticking into your head. At the time, I thought I should ask you about it. I've never heard of anything like it. Have you?"

The Doc remained silent for such a long time that Grisha wondered if the call had dropped. When he came back, testiness infected his scholarly calm. "I need you to forward everything you have about Michael McKinney. I don't suppose you recorded that conversation. I would like everything, word for word."

Grisha offered apologetically, "I'll write you a detailed report on every word I can remember. Is this as important as it sounds?"

The Doc returned to a coldly scientific mode of operation. "We have to hope he died. Much worse things could have happened to us than a simple execution." He hung up.

Grisha raised an eyebrow at Evgeni. "He's not a team player, is he?"

Evgeni frowned back. "He has his own agenda. I've been trying to get a line on his background since he showed up and demonstrated his Ruby Rage system." He shrugged. "For now, our goals seem to align."

Grisha stood up and shook the circulation back into his legs. "When it's time for our paths to split, let me know. I'll take care of it."

A chilling thought came to him. Did the Doc also plan to "take care of it" when their goals no longer aligned?

The Doc studied the little old woman strapped to the table with neither compassion nor malice. This retired housekeeper was just another tool.

He had not had to harm her or coax her to tell him everything she knew about her ex-employer's house. She'd talked about her years of work quite happily, with no other incentive than to have someone to talk to.

He could not take everything she said as the truth, of course. She was suffering from early-stage dementia, which was why Morte Noir had let her go—so she could spend the rest of her days in a comfortable assisted living facility on the Scottish coast.

The nursing home reminded the woman of the Mistress's home. She had talked about it incessantly, which, through a series of lucky breaks, had led to her acquisition for interrogation.

The Mistress's home also lay close to the Scottish coast, and it was grand, with beautiful landscaping and a series of gardens so exquisite that speaking about them brought tears to the woman's eyes. She described all the different kinds of flowers and shrubs the Mistress maintained at length, especially the bright yellow cowslips she remembered very clearly.

The woman didn't know where the house was since she had been driven to work in the back of a windowless van. But with a little help from the analysts of the NSA, the director of AID thought he could pinpoint the location.

When he had the data, he would have to move fast. He could not count on Morte Noir to sit still.

He waved at one of his assistants, who asked in a bored tone, "Dispose of her body?"

The Doc shook his head. "It will be less suspicious if we just return her. Let everyone think she went on walkabout and miraculously survived the outing."

The assistant shrugged, still bored. "Very good."

As the assistant unstrapped the woman, the Doc allowed himself a small smile. Morte Noir's death, or preferably her capture, would alter the balance of covert power. Combining her intelligence-gathering with a conspiracy cult's actionable skills would give him a whole new level of force projection possibilities. He thought he could use that synergy to destroy Gamma's Ruby Rage.

He'd get his players into position immediately. They'd move the moment the NSA supplied the missing pieces.

8

ALL GOOD THINGS MUST PASS

Morte Noir was lying on a sofa in the sitting room when a loud explosion shattered her catnap. As she leaped up, alarms wailed throughout the house. "Well, all good things must come to an end."

She ran to the window and saw the smoking ruin of the bicycle shed, whose domed roof cloaked the building's anti-aircraft missile battery. More explosions marked the deaths of other outbuildings that contained remotely controlled machine-gun emplacements.

Unless the enemy had an inside man, which she doubted, they had clearly made shrewd guesses as to the layout of her defenses.

The stutter of a thirty-millimeter cannon drew her attention. An American Apache helicopter was laying down fire, trying to catch a small person in a burqa darting across the garden to the obliterated shed.

Morte Noir swallowed a futile scream at her undaunted young employee. "Esin, you idiot! You're not immortal!" She ran to the fireplace, and the mantle popped open to present a sniper rifle. She ran back to the window and struggled to open it. She would have shot it out, but the damn thing was bulletproof.

By the time she had set up for a shot, the situation had evolved. Esin had made it into the shed, which afforded a little protection. The rubble could not protect her from a direct shot, but it hid her well enough that the Apache could only spray bullets and pray.

Morte Noir turned her attention to the helicopter, which was escorting a Black Hawk full of troops. This surprised her only in that they had sent only one Black Hawk.

The Apache remained fixated on Esin's position. The Black Hawk's troops represented the greater strategic threat, but the Apache presented an immediate danger to one of Morte Noir's people.

The major question was how she could take it out. The thing was fully clad in armor capable of stopping her .50 caliber rounds.

The contrail of a missile distracted her as she lined up on the Apache.

Esin! The young woman had rooted through the bike shed and found a Starstreak, a British handheld surface-to-air missile. The idiot girl had stepped into the open to fire it, then ducked back into the building.

The Apache launched another missile at the building, maddened by its desire to destroy the assailant.

The Dark Mistress heaved a sigh of relief as she watched the missile scoot through the air. Esin had saved herself. "Good girl."

Except she had *not* tried to save herself. She, like Morte

Noir, had realized the bigger threat was the Black Hawk. She'd designated the troop carrier with her laser when she'd fired.

"Idiot girl!" Morte Noir shouted.

The Black Hawk disintegrated as it dove for a landing.

Now, all Morte Noir had to do was save Esin.

The situation evolved again. A dozen Hummers raced down the country lane that led to her mansion.

One thing at a time. Save Esin, then kill the Hummers.

The Apache pilot had concluded that he had killed the missile-launching enemy and turned to the main house.

Morte Noir finally saw a vulnerability she might be able to exploit if she was very, very good.

Esin ran back across the garden, waving her arms wildly, to draw the Apache's attention away from the house.

The pilot saw her and rotated toward the young woman.

Morte Noir swore, then set up the shot far too fast and fired a whole five-round magazine in a desperate effort to save the girl.

This once, Lady Luck stood by her. One of her shots struck the face of the cylindrical Hydra-70 rocket pod hanging from the Apache's portside weapons pylon. It lit off one of the hydras and involved the entire pod in a blast large enough to crack the helicopter.

Esin reached the house as the Apache spun down in a semi-controlled landing.

Morte Noir's people had trained the surviving remote machine guns on the Hummers, but every time a gun revealed itself, a combat vehicle responded with a TOW missile.

Morte Noir was not surprised that the enemy had come in overwhelming force. She only had one question. All this American gear clearly proved this was a covert AID operation, which meant the British government had no clue.

How had AID secretly gotten all this gear into the country?

The co-pilot of the Apache shook his head to clear it after the helo smashed into the ground. He quickly unbuckled and turned to his captain.

The captain's head lolled. The co-pilot shook him, but the captain did not respond.

A *whump* from the engine compartment suggested haste might be required lest they get caught when the fuel exploded. The co-pilot experienced the thin edge of panic as he unbuckled his pilot.

The mission had been carried out under strict radio silence and emissions control. They had been warned to assume that the enemy could listen to their every transmission and decrypt anything they heard.

This assertion seemed ludicrous to the operatives participating in the assault. No one had that kind of capability unless the NSA had it in a secret basement. The assault team nevertheless operated as if it were true.

But when the co-pilot discovered that both cockpit doors had jammed shut between the explosion and the crash, his panic flared, and he forgot the rules. "We're trapped in the helo, and the engine's on fire!" he shouted on his radio. "The doors are jammed! And Morte Noir's got us pinned down! Help!"

High above the conflict, a satellite code-named Vortex orbited. The unobtrusive platform was tasked with the continuous collection of electronic emissions on behalf of the Echelon surveillance network. The Five Eyes intelligence consortium, comprised of Australia, Canada, New Zealand, the United Kingdom, and the United States, monitored Echelon and Vortex continuously for signs of trouble.

At the speed of light, Vortex distributed the co-pilot's radio signal to listening stations in the participating countries.

The recording Vortex forwarded to the United States quickly found its way to the Utah Data Center. The computers there logged the transmission and examined it for red flags that might trigger the curiosity of myriad NSA analysts watching for different threats to American interests.

The brief encrypted message on a military channel set off no tripwires, and the computers stored it with petabytes of other data that had no immediate use.

However, a handful of the computers at the UDC also watched the streams for messages that might trigger Andrey's curiosity as he monitored for threats to Rivendell's interests.

When Remy had called from the mansion to tell

everyone at Rivendell she was okay, Andrey had traced the conversation through the onion routers to its point of origin in Scotland. Since Remy's life was always under threat, he followed his normal routine and augmented his filters to flag anomalous electronic emissions around Morte Noir's home.

After Remy left, Andrey had kept his filters in place. Morte Noir was a person of considerable interest in the world he inhabited.

Consequently, his automated servants in the UDC came to alert when they picked up a military transmission at the house. Decryption of the scream for help followed with nary a pause.

When Andrey's voice translation software heard the name "Morte Noir," it forwarded an alarm to him.

Morte Noir moved into the command center adjacent to her bedroom and removed the failsafes on the house's self-destruct systems. She also set a long timer to destroy the data center room in the basement.

All her data was encrypted. The only place the decryption keys for the data were stored in the clear was in the transient RAM of the servers, and logging in to decrypt the decryption keys required using a constantly changing passcode on a two-factor authentication dongle. So just killing the power and forcing a reboot would render it useless without the dongle, which she kept on a chain tucked into her blouse.

Morte Noir understood this techie solution and even

some of the math. However, her real security involved bricks of plastique seeded throughout the server room.

Esin ran in, wild-eyed. "How can I help, Mistress?"

Morte Noir scanned the surveillance cameras and listened to the patterns of gunfire. She hosted several hitters in the house at all times, and they had grabbed weapons and moved to positions where they could take the enemy under fire.

The battle had not yet been lost, but that would change when the AID troops gave up on trying to grab the people and computers intact. Then they would use heavier weapons to breach the building. For now, however, the firefight seemed evenly matched.

Morte Noir pointed Esin to the bedroom. "Grab your sniper rifle and see how many men you can pick off."

As Esin obeyed, Morte Noir's phone rang. Unsurprisingly, the enemy had not yet taken out her satellite connection, which was housed in an armored box beneath the roof.

She considered shutting the phone off, but the call had come in through the odd piece of software Remy had given her. Could Remy's people have useful input for her?

Reluctantly, she answered.

An excited young male with the merest trace of a Russian accent rushed into speech. "Morte Noir, this is Andrey. I work for Remy and Cassie. AID might be about to attack you."

The Dark Mistress suppressed her laughter. "Already underway."

Andrey sounded taken aback. "Sorry. How can I help?"

One thing continued to bug Morte Noir. She had

sources throughout the world, but this attack had been a surprise. "Unless you have a fighter-bomber you can send, I only have one question maybe you can address. Where did these guys come from?"

Andrey sounded remorseful. "Sorry, no bombers available at this time." His tone picked up. "But I sure ought to be able to tell you how they got to you." The sound of keys furiously clacking bounced across the continents. "Meanwhile, I don't know if this makes a difference, but there's apparently a helo with people trapped by jammed doors and an engine fire."

Morte Noir looked out the window. She saw the fire, a pale face in the cockpit, and a fist pounding on the hatch. It looked like they'd cook in a moment. Excellent. "I see it."

Andrey muttered. "Let me get back to you in a few." He hung up.

A sound from the doorway made Morte Noir turn with a sudden rush of adrenalin. "Esin." She relaxed. "How's the firefight going?"

Esin looked sheepish. "I think we're doing all right. I couldn't find a good window that we didn't already have covered, so I thought I'd make sure you were okay."

Morte Noir smiled. "I appreciate the thought."

Esin entered the room. "I heard the phone call about the fire." She looked out the window. "Should we shoot them? It would be kinder."

Morte Noir shook her head. "The hatch is armored. We couldn't kill them if we wanted to. Besides, they're irrelevant. Even if they get out, they're pilots, not troops. Harmless."

Esin winced. "If they can't hurt us, can we save them?"

The Mistress stared at her. Esin wanted to save the guys who'd just tried to kill her?

Morte Noir suddenly knew what she had to do with Esin if they got out of this alive. In the meantime, how should she respond to the girl's request? Morte Noir closed her eyes, praying to whatever gods might be to protect her from Girl Scouts.

Then she had an idea. She could turn the question into an educational exercise. "Very well." She pointed at the windowsill. "Set up for a shot."

As Esin got into position, Morte Noir took the spot next to her. She zoomed her scope on the cockpit.

A terrible explosion came from the south side of the building. The AID troops had lost patience with the exchange of fire and were blowing out the walls.

Morte Noir fiddled with her phone. A new and shriller alarm went off, telling everyone to undertake their last resort. *Evacuate.*

Esin had lined up on the target. "Mistress, I have them in my sights, but I don't see how this will help them."

Morte Noir re-acquired the target in her scope. "Ok, you see those thin cylinders on the side of the hatch? Those are the hinges."

Esin shifted slightly. "Got them."

"Shoot them out."

Esin fired.

The hinges disintegrated, and she tapped Esin on the shoulder. "Good enough. Now we run like hell."

The co-pilot cringed as bullets slammed into the hatch. He was still trying to get himself and his partner out. He realized it was over. If he kept the hatch closed, they would cook. If he got the hatch open, the enemy fire would turn them both into Swiss cheese.

Bullets continued to slam into the door. The pattern of smoke and dust from the impacts suggested they were striking in a precise line along the edge between the door and the frame.

Suddenly, the door gave way. The forces that had jammed it now blew it away from the helo. The co-pilot knew the next shots would come through the opening and finish him and his partner.

The firing ended.

The co-pilot jumped from the helo and dragged his partner clear just before the fuel tank exploded. He looked at his hands and touched his chest with wonder. "I'm alive," he said with surprise.

Morte Noir ran down the steps to the basement two at a time. Esin passed her early in the journey. She was taking the steps three at a time, which was crazy since she was carrying a rifle almost as big as she was.

They both reached the basement without breaking any bones. Morte Noir paused long enough to use her cell to reset the timer on the explosives for three minutes before following Esin into the tunnel that led to the sea.

They soon reached the boat slip next to the beach. A dense growth of trees and bushes hung over the water.

Beneath the vines, a pale blue torpedo-shaped vessel peeked above the water. Dave waved at them from the hatch. "What took you so long?"

Morte Noir sloshed through the shallow water to the narco-submarine. "Training exercise."

Dave grinned. "In the middle of a firefight?"

Esin climbed the side of the boat and put a foot on the ladder in the hatch. "The Mistress helped me blow the door off the side of a helicopter. It was really cool."

Esin disappeared into the boat, and Morte Noir climbed up.

Dave raised an eyebrow. Morte Noir shook her head. "Don't ask."

Her phone rang—Andrey. "I'm still trying to backtrace the Hummers, but I figured out where the helicopters came from."

Morte Noir heard the low rumble of her house blowing up. They had to leave. "Good. That's the big mystery anyway."

Andrey continued. "There's a container ship straight out from your house off the coast, probably just beyond line of sight from your location. The helos crossed the ocean tied down on board."

The answer struck Morte Noir like a punch to the gut. She had planned to take the sub straight out to lose all observers as quickly as possible. If she had gone that way, she would have taken her people directly to the enemy ship. And the sub had no weapons.

Morte Noir took a deep breath. "Thank you. Your information has been quite helpful."

9

SUBS AND SUBTERFUGES

While cruising down the coastline of Europe in her narco-sub, Morte Noir dropped off her operatives in twos and threes. Usually, she came within half a mile of the coast and had them snorkel to shore. When they landed, they disappeared into towns and villages to await further instructions.

They all had safe houses of their own, and they could easily telecommute, so a central location was not really necessary. Morte Noir's home had become a de facto headquarters only because everyone enjoyed the companionship of a place that was not only safe but also full of lively people like themselves.

The Mistress continued south past Gibraltar and came close to the shore again in Morocco. Dave hugged her and Esin. "Take care, you two," he admonished before sliding off the side of the ship, "Let me know the moment you're ready to start up operations again."

Esin faced Morte Noir, worried. "What about me, Mistress? Where will you drop me?"

Morte Noir smiled at her. "What would you do if I just launched you into the void like Dave here?"

Esin gulped. "I'd survive."

The Mistress's smile became a grin. "I'm sure you would." She closed the hatch and steered the sub out to sea. "But one of the aspects of your training I've neglected is teaching you how to disappear and survive in comfort and style. I'd hardly be a good mistress if I tossed you out of the nest just yet."

She brushed her hair back and allowed a mischievous tone to enter her voice. "Besides, I have a job for you."

Esin's eyes lit up. "I'm ready."

"You're going to help me with a break-in."

The thump when Esin jumped in place echoed oddly off the curved fiberglass hull of the sub. "To sneak up on our enemies?"

Morte Noir shook her head. "Our friends."

The ringing of Morte Noir's phone interrupted the discussion. Someone was calling on that odd app again. Someone from the group Morte Noir now thought of as Remy's Consortium. She hoped it wasn't Andrey with more bad news.

Cassie's voice filled the sub. "Hey, what's happening with—*static*—guys? I've been trying to—*static*—days."

Morte Noir yelled at the phone for all the good that would do. "You're breaking up. Let me move to a better location." She turned the sub around and headed back toward land to get a better signal. Then she let Esin take the wheel and climbed up to stick her head and her phone out the hatch.

Cassie's voice was stronger when she spoke again. "Can you hear me now?"

Morte Noir laughed. "Loud and clear."

Cassie sighed in relief. "I've been trying to contact you for days."

Morte Noir explained. "We've been running under strict EMCON since we escaped from Scotland."

Cassie voiced her concern. "I've seen the sat photos of your home in the aftermath. If you didn't know already, your mansion is a total ruin." She hesitated, afraid of the answer to the next question. "Did you get all your people out?"

"More or less." Several had been badly wounded, and she had dropped them off first in France, where a team of black market doctors would patch them up. "Most of the damage occurred after we left. I blew the place up myself. Leave no secrets behind, I always say."

Cassie paused. "Obvious in retrospect. Where are you now?"

Morte Noir told her the next step in her current plan.

Cassie greeted the scheme with approval. "That should work for my request as well. I need your help." A note of mystery entered her voice. "And now that I know where you're going, I have a nice housewarming gift for you."

Cassie gave Remy's French passport to the Customs official as she entered the Gran Canaria Airport near Las Palmas, the largest city in the Canary Islands. Since she wore her blonde hair today, the official easily matched her to the photo.

She stepped out into a beautiful day in paradise. A cool breeze greeted her, and then trouble found her. Morte Noir charged across the street and passed the cars parked in front of the airport, loading the luggage of arrivals or unloading luggage for departures.

Cassie sidled down the sidewalk until she was close to the largest group of innocent bystanders in the vicinity.

Morte Noir leaped at her, shouting, "Remy, you bitch!"

A furious hand-to-hand fight ensued.

Cassie observed as she gave ground that Morte Noir was astonishingly good for someone who had never had MemWriter training. It was just as well that they'd refused her request to get some indoctrination on the machine. She did *not* meet the Rivendell requirement that only people doing good deeds need apply.

Ow! The bitch snuck in a strike to her ear. Cassie veered back. "Get off me, you cow!" She put her foot into Morte Noir's gut, eliciting a satisfying grunt.

A pair of policemen ran toward them. Cassie broke off and raced to catch a bus that was just pulling out.

Morte Noir yelled as she ran back to a car on the far side of the street, "I'll get you yet. Later!"

The police concluded that they'd succeeded in breaking up the fight. Instead of pursuing, they returned to their previously scheduled activities.

Cassie rubbed her damaged ear and looked out the window of the bus. "That went pretty well."

Bryce resisted the urge to hurry when he received the summons to his boss's office. He didn't want anyone to get the impression that the new master of AID intimidated him.

He found the Doc contemplating the mold growing on the walls. He lightly tapped the door frame to break the director's concentration. "You called?"

The Doc turned to him. "I need your assessment of a matter that has come to my attention."

Well, this should be easy. Bryce gave his boss a half-bow. "At your service."

The Doc waved him over to the wall of monitors. "Is that Remy or Cassie?"

Bryce watched Morte Noir assault the target individual with zeal. He had the Doc pause the video a couple of times and rewind a couple more. In the end, Bryce grunted. "Her martial arts are very smooth, either from years of training or months of memwriting. I would guess it's Remy since she's had more time with the machine than Cassie, but I can't be sure from these videos."

The Doc handed him excerpts from the comments the witnesses had recorded on social media and transcripts from lip-reading the participants.

Bryce studied the documents. "Of all who have studied these two, Morte Noir seems to have the best handle on recognizing which is which. If she thinks it's Remy, we can be pretty sure it is."

He finally put his finger on another thing that bugged him. "And if it were Cassie, she would have yelled at Morte Noir for attacking the wrong person." He smiled as he thought about the pithy words of wrath Cassie would have unleashed on her misdirected assailant. "That would have ended the fight at the outset."

A hint of happiness entered Doc's cold eyes. "Excellent. I can proceed with the next step in our attack."

Bryce raised an eyebrow. "What's the new plan? Where am I going?"

The Doc waved him out the door like a servant who asked too many questions.

Bryce left filled with anxiety. If the Doc wasn't willing to brief the man who'd been in charge of the hunt for Remy for so long, what horrific things was he planning?

Dale stood outside a low-slung Palo Alto office building nestled in thick, clinging shrubbery. The doors, which were glass with wooden frames, beckoned him into the future. Or into abject failure, all according to the whims of the mortal gods who lived behind those doors.

The harsh beeping of his phone interrupted his philosophical thoughts. "Hey, Augustus."

Augustus sounded peeved. "Not just me. I've got Joyce on the line as well."

Dale smiled. Talking to Augustus was always exhausting. Talking to Joyce was a joy. "Joyce, good to hear from you."

Augustus interrupted the pleasantries. "Bring him up to date."

Joyce explained the call. "Remember those French passports we gave Remy and Cassie on our first job together?"

Dale closed his eyes and inhaled the aroma of the carefully tended purple flowers—wisteria?—surrounding him. "That was such a long time ago."

Joyce continued. "Well, I just got a hit on Remy in the Canary Islands."

Dale spoke with alert concern. "What's she doing there?"

He could almost hear Joyce shrug. "I have no idea." She continued before he could ask the standard question. "And I'm pretty sure it's Remy. When she went outside, she got into a fight with another woman. An amazing woman.

"Wow. You should see the surveillance footage. If I could fight like that and looked like her, I'd be running the whole covert ops world. Anyway, I don't have confirmed ID photos of the suspected attacker, so I can't verify, but we're pretty sure—"

Augustus interrupted. "Morte Noir. Unquestionably."

Joyce agreed. "Yeah. Back to the point. Morte Noir called our girl Remy, according to the witnesses we tracked down and asked. I would expect Morte Noir to know which one's which."

Dale pondered a moment. "What do you think Remy's doing in the Canary Islands?"

Augustus spluttered, "I should think the answer's obvious, but more to the point, you're in charge of keeping track of these people. And why would she make a scene? Now every covert asshole in the world knows where she is."

Dale sighed. "I'll leave at once."

Augustus made a last request. "When you catch her, ask her why on earth she's buying a submarine."

Dale blinked. "A submarine?"

Augustus growled, "What else could she possibly want in the Canary Islands?"

Dale pocketed his phone and turned to his partner in his current double-covert operation. "So, Remy, *do* you have any idea why Cassie's buying a submarine?"

Remy swept back her blonde hair. Dale had had a long discussion with her about who she'd be for the impending meeting. She had agreed that it would be safer for her to attend as Cassie, but Cassie had done such a good job directing all eyes across the Atlantic that Remy figured it was pretty safe. If the wrong people spotted her in California, they'd figure she was Cassie pretending to be Remy.

Besides, Remy was tired of not being herself. "I have no idea about the sub, but at least we have confirmation that everybody thinks I'm out of the country."

Dale nodded absently, fixated on a related question. "More fundamentally, why is Augustus so sure she's looking for a sub in the Canary Islands?"

10

FUN AT THE FAIRE

As Esin gently beached their sub on the soft sand, Cassie held onto an overhead grip and addressed Morte Noir. "So, why *do* you want a better sub, anyway?" Her words bounced around the fiberglass hull of the craft, producing an eerie echo.

Morte Noir popped the hatch and sighed. "Honestly, Cassie, I'm a little gun-shy about showing up on land right now. I have no idea how they found my Scottish home. I need some time in a secure location to think and plan." She started to climb out. "And I need mobility as well. No trains, no planes, no passports. What could be better than a sub?"

Cassie followed her out and got her first look at the Faire.

Years earlier, the world's major smugglers had established a narco-submarine graveyard in the Canary Islands. When the collection of obsolete boats grew, inevitably, someone poked through the corpses and found a couple of vessels worth retrofitting for resale.

As time passed, they established a storefront in this inlet close to the graveyard—a dealership for used subs. Here, customers could inspect, evaluate, and haggle over the merchandise.

Unavoidably, mechanics put up rude repair bays for fixing the subs when they broke down and customizing the purchases of discerning clientele.

What could have been more predictable than that someone would bring a factory to this slice of paradise to build next-generation narco-subs for high-end operators? Some of the people in South America who were already building fully submersible boats joined the others in this pastoral haven, and they started rolling out limited-production runs of diesel-electric boats more similar to Swedish or Chinese coastal submarines than the narco-subs of the early twenty-first century.

Thus, the Sub Faire was born. The beach was filled with canopies and tents where you could buy or sell just about anything. You could not only acquire a sub, you could also kit it out with recon drones or install a Stinger missile launcher in the back under a radar-absorbing dome.

Of course, working this hard to select the perfect submarine made people hungry. You could also buy every kind of finger food to enjoy while browsing the possibilities. Food stands offered hot dogs from America, caviar from Russia, and steak and ale pie from Britain.

As a result of her spiking paranoia, Morte Noir had already marched down the walkway by the time Cassie and Esin splashed ashore.

Esin had dressed for the occasion in a black bikini and

gold sandals. She reveled in opportunities to leave her burqa behind.

Cassie wore jeans, now soaked with seawater, and a tank top that read, *Sarcasm is one of the services we offer*. She held her oversized backpack above her head to protect it from the water.

A dark-skinned man hurried up to them and bowed. "Mistresses. I, Hassan, am your humble servant. Are you interested in selling your submarine today? I offer the highest prices at the Faire for any boats that are well-maintained and seaworthy."

Cassie shook her head. "We probably *are* selling the sub today, Hassan, but you'll have to ask her." She pointed at the golden-haired vixen disappearing behind a large tent advertising rebuilt diesel engines.

Hassan squinted at the woman. "I caught a glimpse of her before she took off. Is that..." He seemed afraid to speak the name and whispered, "Is that who I think it is?"

Esin explained brightly. "My Dark Mistress, Morte Noir."

Hassan had trouble closing his jaw. He bowed them good day once more and rushed off to speak to a number of small clusters of close friends.

Cassie and Esin reached the food court without further interruption. Moments later, Cassie was enjoying a bowl of paella at a picnic table with Esin, who was watching the people go by. Some were sub runners in grungy blue jeans, some were sub owners pretending not to sweat in their three-piece suits, and some were skinny teenagers in shorts running parcels to and fro.

They all strode or strolled beneath the various walkways' canopies. Unlike at traditional fairs, the operators of these facilities made sure their customers could move about forever under cover to protect them, not from rain, but from the prying eyes of surveillance satellites.

A disturbing number shot surreptitious glances at Cassie and Esin as they hurried past.

Cassie scowled. "What's their problem?"

Esin answered with a giggle, "They've heard we work for the Mistress. We are elite here."

A dapper fellow with an English accent came over, placed two wine glasses and a bottle of Corton-Charlemagne Grand Cru before them, and bowed. "The sun is very hot here in the Canaries. I thought the members of Morte Noir's crew might need refreshment."

Esin looked at the bottle in dismay. She had embraced the idea of living in a world with alcoholic beverages, but she had not embraced drinking.

Cassie reached for the stem of the bottle. The fellow was right; dining on this beach was thirsty work. She struggled for a moment to pop the cork, poured half a glass, and took a sip. "Thank you." She then allowed her runaway paranoia full rein and turned on her strongest scowl. "Why?"

The fellow placed a business card on the table. "I thought I'd offer my services. Very discreet deliveries worldwide, including two-day delivery of extremely sensitive packages to the most challenging places on earth."

Cassie picked up the card. A sub, a jet, and a rocket raced each other across the stiff rectangle.

She supposed that since Morte Noir had helped her mislead Dread Nought regarding Remy's whereabouts by smacking her on the ear for the surveillance cameras, Cassie should play the role everyone seemed eager to assign to her—Morte Noir's sub commander. "Your service sounds like something that might interest her very much. I'll pass the card along."

The Englishman bowed and departed.

After much internal deliberation, Cassie concluded that she could drink the wine she had poured and still take any five people at the Faire, including the guards hired to keep the negotiations civil. She indulged herself for a few moments before Esin got itchy and wriggled in her chair. "We should go find the Mistress."

They had barely started to amble down the main walkway when a thug with a flattened nose accosted them. This interloper wore shorts and combat boots and showed off his rippling arm tats in a muscle shirt. He glowered at them and spat, "I hear you work for Morte Noir."

Esin scowled back at the intruder. "Back off. We're in a hurry."

The man stood his ground. "I wanted to let her know that if she needs someone good at intimidation who has the strength to back her threats, I'm available."

Esin stepped into his personal space. "You need to get out of our way."

The thug looked at the girl with a blend of humor and anger. "You need to listen when someone good makes an offer."

A handful of guards started casually working their way toward them.

Cassie ran her hand over her face.

Esin seemed to have decided that in Morte Noir's

absence, Cassie was the commanding officer. "May I have your permission?"

Cassie peered at the sky in search of a sign. None came. She waved for the approaching guards to hold off and turned to the thug. "Let me give you a quick interview."

She pointed at her companion. "Esin, plant him on the ground. No permanent damage."

Esin stepped out of her sandals and approached.

Cassie pointed at the thug. "Knock her down."

The thug stared at her, then laughed. "That tiny thing?" He laughed again.

Esin whirled and planted a foot in his gut. He staggered back. She followed up with a jab to the throat, but he pulled back far enough to block. He countered with a roundhouse swing that Esin dodged with little visible motion.

Deciding to stick with what worked, Esin struck him in the stomach again. And again. The third time, he landed on his butt.

Several onlookers clapped.

Esin muttered, angry at herself, "That took too long."

Cassie put her hand on the girl's shoulder. "Taking out a much bigger man without crippling him is always hard. You did just fine."

They eventually tracked Morte Noir down at the largest and sleekest factory. Through the open bay doors, they could see a submarine that looked like a half-size version of a United States Los Angeles-class hunter-killer. Cassie checked to see if it had torpedo tubes. Their absence surprised her.

They heard Morte Noir before they saw her. It was the first time Cassie had ever heard her sound anything less than cool and collected. Now, she sounded like the wrath of the archangels. "I'm telling you, I must have this submarine. It's the only vehicle at the Faire that meets my immediate needs."

The factory owner took another step back. He had clearly tried stepping back before and was now trapped against a metal lathe. "But I only have this one, a custom job for a very important customer. I can have another for you in just six short months. It will be even better and certainly worth the wait."

Cassie thought she could see steam coming from the Mistress's ears and embraced her adopted role. "Mistress, I take it you found a new submarine?"

Morte Noir, realizing her efforts at intimidation would not yield a positive outcome, whirled on Cassie. "I certainly have." She pointed at the sub, then at the display screen that listed the features of the vessel. "Look at this!"

Unlike most of the other submarines at the Faire, this one did not focus on a threadbare interior into which smugglers packed as much cocaine as possible for a single run. Rather, this was someone's dream getaway vessel. Comfy bedrooms for six plus a large master suite were the highlights of the video.

Cassie thought that was nice but was much more impressed by the hybrid diesel-electric power system that would allow them to cruise all day on batteries, then pop to snorkel depth at night to recharge using the diesel engine. Cassie could work with that power train. "I'm sold."

Morte Noir had calmed down but still scowled. "Now all we have to do is convince *him*." She pointed at the owner.

Cassie went over to the owner, wearing a big smile and offering her hand. Having gone through so much trouble to make AID think Remy was in the Canaries, she had to keep up appearances. She turned bubbly. "Remy Tambook, commander of Morte Noir's submarine fleet."

The owner stared at her while shaking hands. "Fleet?"

Cassie nodded solemnly. "This needs to be our flagship."

The owner looked at the ground. "My customer is very demanding." He swallowed hard. "*Very* demanding."

Cassie believed this readily. "Not a problem. Let me talk to him."

The owner's eyes widened. "You can't threaten him." He gulped again. "I don't want to get in the middle of anything."

Cassie wrapped her arm around his shoulders. "Trust me. This is going to be a friendly business deal." She coaxed him into providing the number, though not the name.

Morte Noir came up to listen in, as did Esin. Cassie sighed and put her phone on speaker. A gruff male voice answered, "Yes?"

Cassie pulled out the sales pitch mode she used for most of her marks. "Hi. My name is Remy Tambook. I work for Morte Noir. I'm hopeful that you know who she is."

The man suddenly sounded both alert and respectful. "Of course."

"We've been looking at your beautiful submarine here at the Faire. My Mistress has realized she really needs it."

The voice turned hostile. "I really need it as well." Remembering who he was talking to, he tried conciliation. "I'm very sorry. It's mine."

Not unexpected. Cassie would offer incentives. "Morte Noir understands, but your builder promised he can make a new one, much better, in six months. Let him tell you about the advanced features it'll have."

She nodded at the factory owner, who waxed poetic about the one he had planned.

Before the man could respond, Cassie added, "Let me sweeten the pot. My employer will pay the difference in price between your current boat and the next-gen one." She stared at Morte Noir as she said it. The Mistress glared at her, then nodded.

The voice sighed. "I really need my boat now."

Cassie could tell she was close. "Did I meet you at the Congressional Auction? I don't recognize your voice, but I expect you were there."

A wistful note infused the speaker's next words. "I can't say I've been there. Always wanted to go."

Gotcha! "Then why don't you let my boss import you, all expenses paid, for the next Auction? I promise you'll make contacts that are worth far more than just money." Cassie looked at Morte Noir again, and the woman rolled her eyes. Cassie interpreted that as consent.

The man was silent for a moment, then, "Deal."

11

LAND OF OPPORTUNITY

Dale self-consciously straightened the maroon tie that accented his three-piece navy blue suit while he studied the corporate battlefield before him.

The nondescript conference room offered no hint that he had landed in a space in which *wealth* was created. Real wealth, not to be confused with mere money, which was just paper printed by governments. Wealth, not money, delivered better lives in the form of better stuff, better services, and hopefully today, greater security.

Dale watched Remy bring up the slide show. The first slide showed the Dread Nought headquarters, a vast complex of squat buildings connected by elegant cylinders that rose between them like trees caught between rocks.

Lee Gurley, a partner in Anderson Perkins Venture Capital and the host of today's discussion, snorted at the picture. "That is our target? The first thing you could do to increase profits is sell that complex, distribute everyone to smaller suburban offices, and telecommute."

Caught off-guard, Dale opened and closed his mouth, realizing he'd already lost the initiative.

Remy channeled Cassie and glared at the VC. "Security is a business like accounting. An important part of the marketing is persuading the customer you are strong, capable, and reliable." She pointed at the photo. "That bespeaks power. Impregnable security."

Dale could not decide whether to wince or laugh. One of the first things Remy and Cassie had done upon meeting him was break into the aforementioned impregnable HQ.

He saw an opportunity to use Remy as a foil. "While my partner is correct, your suggestion might fit well with our new business plan, which will be much less dependent on customers."

The colonel, a retired Marine representing a small financial company from New York, pursed his lips. "No customers? You lost me already." He looked at his watch impatiently.

Remy discarded Cassie's confrontational style and offered coaxing words. "I promise it will make sense when we're done. First we need to bring you up to speed on the market."

Buddy Warwick, the CEO of one of the biggest reinsurers in the world, shook his head. "Are you really going to try to explain the world of AID, Gamma, and Morte Noir to these muggles?"

Dale was not surprised that Warwick knew about the agencies pitted against Dread Nought's Extreme Risk division. The reinsurance industry, which insured insurance companies against unpredictable catastrophes, was the only major industry with an intimate knowledge of the covert agencies that largely ruled the world. Anyone who entered the reinsurance game without knowing the truth was doomed since so many of the unpredictable catastrophes were caused by covert action.

Rafael Barton, a retired deputy administrator from the CIA, had earned the money he now invested by playing the stock market with the insider knowledge he acquired via agency eavesdropping. He turned sharply to Buddy. "Hold up. Morte Noir, I know. What are AID and Gamma?"

Dale started to answer, but Remy put a hand on his arm. "Care to explain for everyone, Mr. Warwick?"

Buddy laughed and gave a short song and dance about the covert world. "It's hard to take in, I know, but it's the reality I live with every time a container ship goes down in the middle of the sea for little or no reason. Or a hacker clobbers a town's automated water chlorination plant and poisons everybody."

Dale's heart skipped a beat. He had been responsible for one such ship and one such town. How much did Buddy know? He kept his face smooth and gave a short, sober nod. "Exactly."

Rafael from the CIA shook his head. "I don't believe it."

The colonel had been frowning, but his face cleared. He looked like he'd just seen Jesus. "It explains so much."

Gurley stared at him. "Are you crazy? What does it explain?"

The colonel looked at him with an expression free of a chronic tension Dale suspected he'd suffered from for years. "It explains the success of the crazy conspiracy theories on the crazy conspiracy websites. EStorme. Ruby Rage." His laughter sounded carefree. "We don't have millions of whack jobs out there. We have a handful of secret agents and psyops engineers transforming ordinary people into whack jobs."

He looked into the distance. "It restores my faith in humanity."

Gurley tried to bring him back to mundane reality. "Do you hear yourself? Covert mind engineers? The world can't be that insane. Impossible."

The other investors looked amused and smug. Remy took sympathy. "As Mr. Warwick—"

"Buddy," the CEO interrupted with a soft smile.

Remy brightened and returned the smile two-fold. "As *Buddy* pointed out, it's hard to take it all in in a single sitting. If you'd like, after this session, I'd be happy to go through a few of the past year's headlines that don't make sense and explain the real background for each event." She swept back her hair with a laugh. "After all, you have to understand the market to understand the opportunity."

Gurley took a breath, then replied unsteadily. "That would be good."

Buddy smiled at her, but his voice cut like a knife. "I understand why Dale knows about the world's secret operators. He's with Dread Nought. He's in the game. Why do you know so much?"

Dale held up a hand. "Remy has been the target of multiple agencies for a long time. She learned about them as a part of the process of surviving." He leaned forward. "The reason they've wanted her is one of our secret advantages."

Gurley took the dodge as an opportunity. "I think we've all had enough secrets revealed for the moment. Let's take a refreshment break. Anyone who thinks we've entered the Twilight Zone is welcome to depart." He muttered, mostly to himself, "Except I'm hosting, so I guess I'm staying anyway."

That got a chuckle from the room. He continued, "For the rest of us, I recommend that when we reconvene, we assume this alternate world is real and explore the market and some numbers."

He looked around the table. "Deal?"

When they came back together, Gurley observed cheerfully, "At least I now understand why the non-disclosure agreement we signed was so over-the-top. Even startups with brand new tech don't have secrecy clauses in their contracts with so many forms of punitive damage." He frowned at everyone. "Whether these agencies and technologies are fantasy or real, we can't let these discussions loose on the street."

Rafael from the CIA scowled at Buddy. "It's all verified by our friendly reinsurance expert here." He pointed at the CEO. "I concluded you had to be a shill, planted to help these two," he gestured at Dale and Remy, "put one over on us, so I did some investigating."

Gurley leaned forward. "And?"

Buddy chuckled. "Do tell."

Rafael clenched his fist. "You're legit, which probably means you're telling the truth." He shook his head. "The Analytical Intelligence Division of NSA. The Gamma branch of Alfa. Psyops engineers. Dead internets. Rage opioid addicts. Conspiracy websites creating suicide bombers." The CIA agent pounded the table. "Even *I* didn't know. *Jesus*!"

Dale coughed to get everyone's attention. "Shall we turn to the market opportunity?"

Gurley steepled his fingers on the table. "Oh, absolutely."

First, Dale brought up a page of numbers from Dread Nought's quarterly filings and additional notes on unreported details Andrey had scooped out of the UDC. Dale explained key items. "So, as you can see, today, Dread Nought generates about half its profits by protecting ordinary businessmen from unscrupulous governments and corporations."

The colonel added, his anger only partially suppressed, "They get the other half by supporting those unscrupulous governments and corporations."

Rafael shrugged. "So? They're like arms dealers selling weapons to both sides in a war." He pretended to yawn. "Not a lot different from the CIA when you get right down to it."

Dale shook his head. "I like to think both Dread Nought and the CIA do a little better than an even split, but regardless, their business plan leaves an immense amount of money on the table."

Rafael tapped the table thoughtfully. "Of course! You could expand your work with the corrupt and powerful against the ignorant. The ignorant *are* the biggest targets on earth, after all."

The colonel bristled. "Not on my watch."

Gurley's eyes gleamed. "Let's not be hasty. Stay focused on the prize. The profits, that is."

Buddy crossed his arms. "You're planning to force me to raise reinsurance rates? I don't think so."

Dale put his hand over his eyes.

Remy waved her hands and exclaimed, "No, no! You've got it all wrong. The easy money is in going after the bad guys."

Silent skepticism filled the room. Dale stepped into the opening. "Everybody in the game is out there competing to chew up the poor chumps who play by the rules. It's the other side of the equation that offers the expanded market."

He licked his lips. "The play-by-rules guys are *radically underserved*. Let me show you some of our targets." He brought up another slide. "This is a sample of thirty thousand accounts at Credit Suisse held by clients who engage in kidnapping, torture, drug trafficking, money laundering, and other serious crimes."

Remy stepped in, bursting with enthusiasm. "Every dollar here can be targeted for lawsuits and punitive damages recovery."

Gurley ran the numbers in his head. "Billions."

Dale flipped to the next slide. "Eighty billion, to be more precise."

Remy laid out the math. It was a superfluous exercise for this group, but everyone listened nonetheless. "With a ten percent finder's fee, this one bank offers an eight billion dollar revenue potential."

The colonel pointed out the obvious. "And there are lots more banks with that kind of exposure. My God."

For a moment, everyone in the room shared the vision

of gold bars raining down from the heavens, burying them in wealth.

Then Gurley coughed. "If this is such a great opportunity, why aren't there other players?"

The CIA man surmised with dark confidence, "Easy to guess why. These accounts are owned by people who take their money seriously."

Dale bowed his head, clasping his hands soberly before him. "Rafael is correct. It was tried. Back in the eighties and the nineties, there was a company that identified corrupt companies in Russia, forced massive reorganizations, and boosted share prices as diverted revenues reflowed to the bottom line."

Buddy remembered more. "They made stellar returns. I was considering investing in them myself."

Gurley pursued the big question. "Why didn't you? What went wrong?"

Buddy sighed. "Critical members of the company started dying."

The colonel clenched his fists. "The bosses got away with it." If thoughts could kill, a round of global assassinations of corrupt executives would have started then and there.

Gurley gulped.

Remy spoke triumphantly. "That is why you need *us*."

Dale continued. "Dread Nought has the combat power to provide vigorous deterrence and, when necessary, the whole gamut of fully effective responses."

Rafael chuckled. "You can blow them away."

The colonel sighed. "You can't build a startup company

to enter this field? You need an organization the size of Dread Nought just to launch the market?"

Buddy nodded. "The targets could wipe out a startup company with a single bomb." He continued thoughtfully, "From my perspective, it's just as well to start with a fully formed corporation. A startup company would be too small for me to get involved. I can't afford deals with investments less than two billion dollars."

Gurley returned to skepticism. "Even with all Dread Nought's resources, can you really defend against these people? Not just your own executives, but the judges and juries and witnesses who deliver the punitive damages?"

Rafael supplied part of the answer. "Dale and Remy would only need to take out a few targets as examples. The rest would choose legal battles over blood fights. Even those people prefer keeping their skins intact to their money." He paused reflectively. "Most of them, anyway."

The colonel pointed at the list of targets and voiced his doubts. "Some of these people have their own armies."

Buddy echoed this worry. "Good point. To my knowledge, even Dread Nought does not have the resources to tackle them."

Dale smiled. "This is where I bring up a radical new approach that Remy and her team bring to the table."

Remy played a video of the recent battle between the Ruby Ragers and the EStormers at Rivendell. "We have developed a new process for the rapid training and deployment of elite warriors." She gave a brief discussion of the speed and effectiveness of the training of the defending troops without mentioning the Memwriter.

The colonel watched, amazed. "Both sides in this battle

are exceptional in skill and dedication." He frowned at the Ruby Ragers as they finished off the wounded EStormers. "Though the attackers are barbarians. It breaks their discipline and makes them vulnerable."

Dale paused the tape when the robot waiters exploded. "Colonel, you have the expertise here. Once we adopt this training regime at Dread Nought and bring in employees like these, will we be able to take on the armies you fear?"

The colonel nodded, but Rafael went back on the attack. "This is all very well, but none of it will stop a well-placed assassin." He coughed. "As I have proven on numerous occasions."

Dale flipped to the next slide. "An excellent point, which brings me to the next topic. The core competence for success will be superior intelligence, both for protection of assets and identification of targets. We need to be able to maintain and evolve target lists like these Credit Suisse accounts I showed earlier.

"If a target tries to corrupt a jury, we need to be able to counter-corrupt the target's target. Thus, we need not just intel excellence or even intel superiority. We need intel *supremacy*. How do we achieve that?"

Dale explained the basic tools for information-gathering already in place at Dread Nought: AI search algorithms integrated with social media feeds, contractual arrangements in critical locations around the world for vidcam access, and numerous non-consensual arrangements in which Dread Nought hacked other vidcams. He mentioned the electronic intrusion opportunities on strategically placed Alexas, Assistants, and Siris.

Dale shrugged. "We also use traditional commercial information collection, achieved by posing shell companies as vendors working through advertising agencies. These allow us access to both raw and processed data from all the major corporations. It might be important to know, for example, if an at-risk judge's wife is pregnant. Walmart and Target know a woman is pregnant, often before the woman knows herself, based on advanced analysis of the data they collect on purchases and web searches."

He summed up, "There is no question but that we have the most sophisticated and successful intelligence collection systems in the business world."

Rafael yawned. "All very well, but you still aren't in a league with the NSA."

Remy followed the traditional advice for persuading someone with whom you disagree: agree with them first, then explain why they're wrong as a series of nudges. "You're right that the NSA has some advantages, but it's not as true as you think. By integrating our algorithms with the algorithms of numerous other corporations as described earlier, we can extract a surprising amount of intel from ordinary behavior without needing surveillance satellites and networks of human assets."

Rafael looked set to offer a tart reply, but Dale picked up the ball. "Furthermore, as part of the new plan to redirect the company, we have a number of other advanced arrangements for intel. We have a connection that allows us to use Pegasus, for example." Pegasus was an Israeli virus, a zero-day attack that could wholly subvert a cell phone if you got within Bluetooth range with your phone. Andrey had made it a priority and snatched Pegasus long ago.

Dale gave the audience a moment to be amazed that Dread Nought could now access this very tightly held cyberweapon, a nuclear missile of digital warfare. Then he raised his hands dramatically. "But I have something even better."

Rafael stared at him. "What could possibly be better than Pegasus?"

Dale gave him an insider's smile. "I also have a contract to put Morte Noir on retainer at very favorable rates."

Rafael's eyes widened. "Favorable rates? For *her*?"

Remy's enthusiasm made her bounce once in place. "It's an intel-sharing agreement. We help her, she helps us."

Dale expanded. "Think of it as a version of the multinational Five Eyes consortium on the commercial side."

Rafael looked awed. "That changes things."

Gurley changed topics. "What other investors do you have lined up?"

Dale flipped through the slides until he found the right one. "When you join us, you'll be joining a global investment fund. We have interested parties from all over the world."

Buddy twitched his lips. "I've never heard of these companies. I'm afraid to ask. Shell companies?"

Dale acknowledged the point. "Probably. We suspect several intelligence agencies are interested in our success." He pointed at one. "We suspect these people are with Mossad, though honestly, we haven't investigated."

In fact, the name he'd highlighted was one of the shells

through which Andrey was funneling money they'd stolen from drug cartels and dictators. Andrey, Dale, Remy, and Cassie had all agreed that the Quantum Key and the tap on the Utah Data Center needed to remain a secret from the investors, so the shells pointed in lots of different directions no matter how many layers you peeled off the onion.

As a purely financial matter, Rivendell could have funded the entire takeover of Dread Nought with its own resources. They needed the others in this room as a source of legitimacy, not money.

Gurley pointed at one organization with a recognizable name. "The Orinoco government is one of your investors?"

Remy cheerfully answered, "They certainly are. The battle we showed you on video earlier took place on their soil, so not only do they appreciate the profit potential here, but they see our goals as aligned with theirs in other ways. Notably, they want to make a world with fewer players trying to corrupt their nation."

Buddy added pensively. "I understand their position. Even if your new, improved Dread Nought merely broke even, my company would profit from the elimination of risk exposures. The information about, and intervention against, future planned disasters would pay for the ride."

He frowned. "I can't help worrying that you're eating your seed corn, however. Sure, going all in on sucking the life out of the fraudsters, thieves, and grifters among the world of power players might provide a number of very profitable quarters, but then what will you do?"

Gurley snickered. "Who cares? Rake in the profits at full speed, pump the stock, then sell out. There's always a sucker willing to buy at the peak of the market. Even if Dread Nought somehow wiped greed from the planet—"

Rafael and the colonel snorted.

"We'd still come out reeking of money."

The colonel gave them a serious answer. "More fundamentally, there will never be a shortage of evil. Like the drug cartels, take one out, and another will step up to take its place."

"Amen," Rafael agreed.

12

GOING HYPER

The missile felt itself falling as the latches holding it to the belly of the fighter released. As it embraced its newfound freedom, it knew what it had to do next. Its programming and circuitry dictated only one course.

The missile fired its engines, and enormous g-forces smashed into its components. The missile shrugged off the pressure. Its components had been designed to take it, so they survived.

A tweak to the fins guided the projectile up, up, up into the stratosphere. It leveled off before it reached the vacuum of space. Vacuum would kill its engines. It did not want to go there, because its designers had decided it should not.

Time to compare its current location to its destination. The fighter plane had pointed the missile in the right direction, sending it west and a little south from the launch point in the equatorial Atlantic. It would now endlessly refine its flight parameters.

The missile queried its inertial guidance systems for the

changes in acceleration it had experienced since launch, computing in tiny fractions of meters per second its changes in velocity and the consequent change in location compared to its target. Everything from the roaring of the engine to the flow of the jetstream to the fluttering eddy of a moment's gust fed into the computation. The missile twisted its fins by fractions of a degree to bring itself closer to the programmed course hundreds of times a second.

Meanwhile, the missile's second location computing system continuously listened to the broadcasts of the GLONASS satellite constellation. GLONASS supplied the same functionality for Russian military systems that GPS supplied for Western civilization.

GLONASS confirmed, second by second, the correctness of the inertial guidance systems.

All was well.

It finally reached full speed ten times the speed of sound. Its nose heated up, and as some of its systems watched and worried about the heat, other systems, the parts involved in dodging anti-missile missiles, relaxed. The fiery heat wrapped the missile in radar-absorbing ionized gases, giving it a property its developers called "plasma stealth."

Onward, the missile soared. The flight did not last long by human standards. By computer standards, it continued for a considerable length of time.

The moment came to descend once more to Earth. The engines shut down, and the missile glided lower and slower.

Its velocity fell below Mach Five, the minimum velocity specified in the missile's glossy advertising brochures. The weapon did not understand that its Russian developers had exaggerated its capabilities to win the contract. It also did not know that the quality control personnel had been invited to an elaborate party at the Ruki VVerkh! Bar on the day of the final testing and had rushed through the signing of the certification papers at the behest of their bosses, who had already pocketed the rest of the testing funds. The missile's speed declined until it was barely traveling at Mach Three.

Without the hypersonic velocity to maintain it, the immense heat around the nose faded, and the plasma stealth dissolved. The programming intended to protect from anti-missile missiles went into overdrive to identify threats it would need to dodge.

The inertial guidance and the GLONASS positioning systems continued to work in harmony, depicting the path to the target. No anti-missile missiles disturbed the serenity of the defense systems.

All was well.

The patches Andrey had inserted into the UDC to listen to the flow of realtime data picked up some chatter from an early-warning radar plane looking for drug traffickers in the Gulf of Mexico. Since the plane belonged to America, the NSA had the decryption keys, so they conveniently stored the messages in the clear. The chatter suggested that someone had launched a hypersonic cruise missile off the coast of South America. That was unbelievable.

A number of governmental agencies leaped into frenzied action to understand what was happening. Another group started searching for the right people in Orinoco to inform, though the missile flew much faster than the bureaucracy.

Meanwhile, when Andrey's AIs saw info on a Mach Ten missile launch and its direction of flight, they recognized an impending disaster and alerted him on his phone, his tablet, and his computers. He activated the Rivendell Emergency Broadcast System. "Red Alert! Everyone into the bunkers now! *Missile incoming! Red Alert!*"

Andrey left the blast door to the Vault open for anyone coming his way. He would close it at the last moment. For now, he focused on trying to defeat the missile, which was, according to a hasty examination of the ongoing stream of American radar reports and glide path signature analyses, a Russian Kinzhal.

He felt helpless. He couldn't jam the missile's radar since it didn't use radar to home in. He couldn't hack the control signal for the missile since it flew autonomously without a remote operator. He couldn't interfere with the inertial guidance system since it was internal.

Shucks, the blasted thing had no contact with the outside world except for listening to the GPS signal from GLONASS.

Nothing but GLONASS. *Of course.*

He had one long shot at saving the base and started typing furiously at his keyboard while wondering, *Could this really work?*

With no anti-missile missile interference, the Kinzhal continued straight ahead until the GLONASS system showed that the inertial guidance had drifted north. The missile corrected its course to the south, which seemed to fix the problem.

However, according to GLONASS, the inertial system continued to drift at an alarming rate. A more sophisticated software system might have thought this a bit odd and used something like a leaderless Byzantine consensus algorithm on all its readings to ascertain which, if any, of its instruments were defective.

In fact, such a consensus algorithm had been a part of the original software design. However, since the schedule for the fundamental elements of the system had slipped, the manager had been under the gun to cut less critical features—and the gun he feared was literal. If he did not finish on time, he would be marched to a gulag with an assault rifle at his back.

Therefore, the manager cut a number of secondary modules from the final implementation. The Byzantine algorithm was the first one to go. The inertial sensors had never failed a test, and no one had ever hacked GLONASS, so why spend time and money on eventualities that would probably never occur?

The consensus process had been replaced by a single line of code that averaged all the readings. So the missile arced farther and farther away from its original flightpath until finally it collided with the planet.

At its point of contact, its speed and mass afforded it considerable kinetic energy. It released four kilotons in a fraction of a second.

Andrey pulled the Vault door closed behind the last EStormer to join him. "Any minute now," he said loudly enough for everyone to hear.

"Will we survive here?" one asked in panic.

Brett spoke in calming tones. "Fear not." He rapped a knuckle on the blast door. "Cassie and Remy built this place to protect Andrey even from a nuke."

That got a chuckle. Then the lights went out.

Brett spoke again, more loudly this time. "It's okay, folks. Andrey, was that it?"

Andrey's voice squeaked in relief. "It missed us."

Someone attempted humor in the pitch-blackness. "That was a miss?"

Brett guffawed. "Good one."

Andrey thought out loud. "I guess it struck close enough to shake the above-ground buildings. The power plant is buried as deep as we are, but the wiring is vulnerable. Probably blew some breakers." He turned on the flashlight app on his cell phone and pawed at the door. "I'll go see what happened and get the power back on."

The lights came up on their own, and the computers rebooted.

Andrey laughed. "See? I told you I'd get the power up really quick."

Everyone rushed out of the Vault to go see what had happened.

Andrey burst out the front door with everyone else and looked around. At first glance, nothing seemed amiss.

However, when he looked at the top of the Keep, the south side of the roof had suffered considerable damage. Chunks of concrete had been ripped from the top two floors, and rebar stuck out at odd angles.

Suspecting he knew what had happened, he ran back into the main building and up the stairs.

On the top floor, the southern windows had been blown out. He looked out through the missing rear of the building to see that the south side of the outer fortress wall had been blown into stone and concrete rubble. Beyond the wall, a cone of devastation had flattened trees as it expanded away from Rivendell into the jungle.

Tina stepped up next to him. "Glad it missed."

Andrey looked at the scene, mesmerized. "Well, it was smaller than the Tunguska event but bigger than I ever want to see again."

Tina raised her eyebrows. "Tunguska?"

"A meteor disintegrated in Siberia at eighty times the speed of sound in 1908. It created a twelve-kiloton blast." He pointed at the center of the cone. "If we'd been on that side of the hit rather than this side, the fortress would have been leveled."

Tina decided he needed a hug and embraced him. "But we would have been safe in the underground bunkers."

Andrey shook himself. "Yes."

Tina asked the obvious question. "I thought they wanted you and Remy and Cassie alive. Who did this?"

13

HOMELESS

The transcontinental video call included four different locations: a venture capitalist's conference room in Palo Alto, an old missile silo in Arizona, a submarine sales office in the Canary Islands, and a fortress in the jungles of Orinoco.

Cassie peered at the lapping waves on the beach, studiously avoiding the shrimp taco. It would look delicious if Andrey wasn't making her head ache and her stomach hurt with his description of the missile attack.

He summed up, "So, we didn't lose anybody, and the buildings mostly survived. Again."

Grandma sputtered with rage. "The Russians did this? Remy, do you still have that wiffle ball you upgraded into a low-yield nuke to drop on the Capitol? How about we drop it on the Kremlin instead?"

Remy covered her eyes with her hand. "I disassembled it already."

Grandma growled, "Well, *re*assemble it."

Cassie made another attempt to reroute the conversation. "Grandma, we don't have a stealth Gobi to deliver it, either."

Grandma's eyes gleamed. "So what? It's small. Let FedEx deliver it, or have an Uber driver drop it off."

That was a disturbingly reasonable strategy. Grandma must have given this a lot of thought. She could not be outmaneuvered on technical grounds.

Andrey offered more opposition. "I'm not sure the Russians even launched it. This missile was fired under very strict EMCON. I didn't get a whiff until an American radar plane picked it up."

Grandma still wanted to throw a big bomb at the issue. "So, what's the problem nuking them?"

Andrey countered, "The problem is, they might not be the ones to blame. The Russians don't have the kind of discipline for that kind of EMCON."

Remy looked puzzled. "Who else could have shot a Kinzhal?"

Andrey bobbed his head. "Exactly the right question. According to a series of encrypted ELINTs captured by the NSA a while ago, somebody stole a Kinzhal missile. That could be the one that showed up here."

Dale chimed in. "Let's back up and think about motives. I can't think of anyone who would want Rivendell and all its people killed. Grisha and Gamma still want Andrey alive. Bryce and AID still want Remy for the Doc unless the director who replaced Ferris has completely flipped their policies."

Andrey interrupted. "I still don't know who that is, by the way. AID has managed to keep all data on the new director out of the UDC." He muttered, "Very disturbing."

Dale returned to the main thread. "The shooter wasn't Morte Noir. She's now on our side, more or less."

Andrey interrupted again. "Could we ask her what she knows about the missile?"

Cassie answered, "She's at sea at the moment, literally. She's cruising in her luxury submarine while she figures out her next move. Plans uncertain, destination unknown. At least, that's what she said to me."

Dale coughed in irritation. "As I was saying. I just went through the whole list of players in our world, and they all want something they'll lose if they make Rivendell a smoking crater. Outside our world, there's even less motivation to hit us. Consider that the Russian government owns all but one of those missiles. What would they have to gain?"

Cassie sighed. "They don't even know we exist, do they? And they wouldn't have any reason to care even if they did."

Grandma grumbled, "Blowing the Kremlin up is still a good idea. Even if they didn't shoot the missile, some good would come of it."

Andrey, annoyingly identifying the pluses and minuses of every decision, offered support. "Evgeni's office is in the Kremlin. If we made sure to blow the nuke while he was there and Grisha was with him, a great deal of good would come of it."

He swallowed hard. "Of course, I might be too biased in favor of killing them to make an objective assessment."

Cassie snorted. "You think?"

Remy clapped for attention. "That's it! Andrey, you're a genius!"

Andrey peered at her uncertainly. "Uh, sure."

Grandma, reviewing what Andrey had said, figured it out and cackled. "Oh, Remy, *you're* the genius." She turned her attention to the others. "If you want to kill Remy with an explosion at Rivendell, first you have to make sure she's *at* Rivendell."

Cassie shook her head. "We made sure everybody thinks Remy's here, in the Canaries."

Remy took the analysis to the next level. "Whoever tried to destroy Rivendell didn't want to kill me. They wanted to destroy our safe house. Put us back on the run to make it easier to catch us."

Dale noted a detail. "And they didn't care if Andrey died, so they're not interested in the Key. Just Remy."

Grandma clenched her fist. "AID again."

Grisha stewed as he stepped over the light chain across the corridor that held a red sign warning, *Do Not Enter. Under Repair.*

The sign had been warning people about repairs underway for years. You'd think someone would catch on to the sign's lack of veracity, but no. Here in Moscow, repairs *always* took years.

He paused outside Evgeni's door to smooth his features, then knocked politely and swept inside.

Evgeni watched him with his usual mild amusement. He answered the question before Grisha could ask it. "No, we did *not* shoot a missile at Andrey."

Grisha blew out a breath he hadn't realized he'd been

holding. "What about our so-called government? Or our current flavor-of-the-day president?"

Evgeni sighed. "No evidence leads to them. I'm still checking, but why would they?"

Grisha sank into his usual chair. "Then who? And where'd they get the missile?"

Evgeni leaned forward. "That I can answer. They stole the missile from Chkalovsk Airfield, along with a stealth fighter to carry it and a pilot to fly it."

Grisha stared at him, goggle-eyed. "This happened a while ago?"

Evgeni nodded.

Grisha scowled. "And you didn't tell me?"

Evgeni shrugged. "Need to know. And need to care. If they'd shot it anywhere but at Rivendell, would you have had one whit of interest?"

No, he would not. "So, who took it?"

Evgeni steepled his fingers. "We have a chain of clues leading to Morte Noir."

Grisha heard the doubt in his voice. "Let me guess. Convenient clues. Too convenient."

"Maybe. It doesn't make any difference, however. Bottom line is, we don't know who the end buyer was."

Grisha pondered that. "It had to be someone from our world. But whoever it was either didn't know or didn't care about Andrey." He chuckled. "Sometimes we're lucky our nation's equipment doesn't work very well."

Evgeni joined him in laughter. "As it happens, a lot of the money for the Kinzhal development got diverted into our accounts, so in some sense, we saved Andrey's hide. You might mention that when you finally catch him."

Grisha grinned. "Promise." He went back to brooding. "Apparently, they didn't know or care about killing Remy, either."

Evgeni gave him a puzzled look. "I thought you told me she was in the Canaries?"

Grisha put two and two together. "You're right. They probably knew as well as we did that Remy was away. After we saw that video of the fight, I sent an agent over there. He had eyes on her when the missile struck."

Evgeni frowned. "And you didn't grab her?"

Grisha shook his head. "The Faire has too much security." He paused. "My man said he was willing to try, except he was pretty sure she'd made him and was *eager* for him to try."

Evgeni rose to pace the room. "These people are very annoying." Before Grisha could agree, he continued, "At any rate, this explains who took the shot."

Grisha raised an eyebrow.

"As you've said, AID has never shared our eagerness to get the Key. Sacrificing Andrey to make Remy vulnerable fits their operating parameters."

Grisha grunted. "AID again."

Cassie dropped her phone on her chair and ran across the beach to take a quick dip in the ocean. After everyone on the video call agreed that AID was responsible, they'd also agreed to take a break before discussing the next steps.

The swim did not offer as much relaxation as a romp in the surf should. Cassie periodically squinted across the sand to keep an eye on the Gamma agent Grisha had presumably assigned to her. He seemed to have accepted his current job as a watcher only, but you could never trust those kinds of people to stick to their roles.

She thought about having a drink delivered to his table but decided against it. No reason to stick a finger in his eye. Who knew when she might have a use for him?

When the conference call resumed, Andrey offered the first morose recommendation. "We'll have to abandon Rivendell."

Remy responded with an upbeat denial infused with the cheery confidence she had mostly lost since she'd brought her father to the fortress. "Nonsense. I thought so too at first, but it's quite unnecessary."

Cassie gawked. "You think they won't try again?"

Grandma chortled. "You have a plan."

Remy's hair bounced as she bobbed her head. "They want us on the run. Very well. We'll promise them we won't go back to Rivendell."

Dale responded with slow care, "Then there'll be no need to blow the fortress."

Andrey saw further motivation. "And if you stay on the run, not only do they not need to blow this place up, they won't want to. They still want me, after all."

Grandma chimed in. "And I already sweetened the pot. I'm using Andrey to decrypt the occasional message for them for some substantial bucks. They don't want to blow the fort since they don't want to blow the arrangement."

Cassie shook her head. "That's all good, but it still means Remy and I are on the run. I confess I sort of like having a place to go home to." She sighed. "Can we go back to Grandma's? They could lob missiles at her all day long without much effect."

Grandma frowned. "They could destroy my beautiful dome. Though I do miss having company."

Remy responded softly, "We miss you too."

Grandma turned gruff. "Oh, I don't miss *you* two! I meant all the agents they had on surveillance that I could force to go to town and buy me coffee."

Cassie winced. Remy chuckled. "We just need another, better place. Someplace in Russia might be a good idea. After all, they're the ones who supplied the missile, no matter who fired it."

Grandma clapped. "A little poetic irony does seem in order."

Andrey asked innocently, "Where in Russia?"

Remy squinted. "It's not *exactly* in Russia."

Dale laughed. "You're going to steal a new home. Am I right?"

Remy let the suspense build until Cassie broke and screamed, "*Give!*"

Remy displayed a photo of a gleaming white megayacht on the shared screen. "As you know, for years, it's been open season on the high seas for grabbing the yachts that belong to Russian oligarchs. Everybody else is stealing their ships. Why shouldn't we too?"

Dale grimaced. "Are there any left? I'd expect that all the good ones were taken."

Andrey was feverishly pounding his keyboard. "I found the one you're showing on the screen. The *Glory*. It belongs to the president of Russia."

Remy clapped. "Exactly. He lost the missile. What could be more fitting than for him to give us a new home?"

Grandma laughed again. "What did I say? Genius."

Cassie gawked. "You sure we want to make yet another enemy who wants us dead?"

Dale choked, he laughed so hard. "What difference does it make at this point? With AID and Gamma on our tails, the Russian president would be the least of our problems."

Grandma identified a possible upside. "Could we get the president to blame Gamma? Confess, Cassie; it would be fun to give Grisha a hard time. Maybe even get him executed."

Cassie had to admit that that sounded eminently satisfactory.

Andrey interrupted their delightful daydream. "Ah, folks? This might not be the easiest heist in the history of Russian yachts. I think I know why the *Glory* alone of all the yachts once owned by the president has not yet been picked off by anyone."

Remy remained upbeat. "By all means, Andrey, tell us the catch."

Andrey grimaced. "He has a Russian frigate continuously hanging out just over the horizon. The *Admiral Gorschkov*, as it happens—the lead ship in the newest and most powerful class of frigates in the world. By some measures, it's about half as powerful as an American guided missile cruiser."

Dale whistled. "Not something to mess with lightly."

Cassie hardly blinked at the description of the danger. She'd done so many heists that she had become alarmingly blasé about guns and bombs and missiles, and, apparently, top-of-the-line naval combat vessels. "Not a problem," she asserted. "I'm not yet sure *why* it's not a problem, but I'm sure it won't be."

Remy agreed, "Cassie and I can handle it."

Andrey added a complication. "Meanwhile, I'll see if I can track down its location."

Cassie shook her head. "Don't all the big ships have transponders so they don't run into each other?"

Andrey waved off the question like a mosquito. "Oh, they all have transponders, but all the ships sailing covertly reconfigure the things to deliver false positions. According to the *Glory's* transponder, she's just off the coast of Miami in the middle of a regatta. Does that sound likely to you?"

The meeting broke up shortly thereafter. Remy's last words were, "Remember, we have to get the word out that Cassie and I won't be returning to Rivendell."

Cassie looked at the Gamma agent surveilling her. "Don't worry about that. I'll get right on it."

She ordered two margaritas from the nearest bar and sashayed over to her mark. He watched her approach with rising surprise and discomfort.

She watched him watch her approach as she wriggled in her bikini. As she got closer, he looked more like a man watching a woman and less like an agent watching a target. She licked the salt from the rim of her glass with a sensuous flick and put his margarita on the table in front of him. "Tell Grisha we won't be going back to Rivendell."

His hand automatically went to the drink though he remained fixated on her. "What?"

Cassie leaned close, giving him a good view of everything she had. "We won't be going home. Ever. Promise."

She straightened. "And tell him he's going to be very sorry about that."

As she turned away, an evil laugh emerged from her throat. "Very sorry. Promise."

Bryce took a calming breath as he stood outside the director's office. He had to stay cool and try not to kill a man he suspected might kill him first.

The assistant waved him through. He found the Doc lying back in his desk chair with his eyes closed. His nostrils fluttered like he might start to snore at any moment.

Bryce relaxed as he abandoned his thoughts of assassination. The director's pose was perfect—if he was setting a trap and Bryce was an amateur.

The Doc might have many skills, but professional assassination was not among them.

Bryce sat in a chair across from the director and tapped on the desk.

The director opened his eyes, yawned, and stretched. "Sorry. Long night."

"Mine too." Bryce leaned forward, letting anger seep into his voice. "Would you mind telling me why you're trying to kill my target?" More heat filled his next words. "With a missile I acquired for you?"

The Doc steepled his fingers. "Seriously? You assured me she was on the other side of the Atlantic."

It took a few moments for the assassin to understand.

The Doc continued, "I told you I'd use the Kinzhal to set

our enemies against each other. Here they go." He rubbed his hands together. "Now Remy and Cassie are mad at Gamma for trying to kill her people, and Gamma is mad at the Russian president for trying to blow up the Quantum Key. When Remy and Cassie retaliate, the triangle of retribution will be complete."

Bryce thought his boss seemed entirely too smug and satisfied. "You do realize you didn't manage to kill anyone, right? The missile missed."

The director shrugged. "It worked well enough. Remy and Cassie can't go back. They'll probably have to evacuate, and with their people intact, they'll have more resources for their counterpunch against the Russians, whatever they do. Should light up quite the war. Snatching Remy in the midst of the chaos should be much easier."

Bryce reluctantly admitted some admiration. "Not a bad plan. Very different from anything we've tried before. It might even work." He let his mind explore the consequences, problems, and potentialities. "You might be underestimating their ability to see through this series of subterfuges, however. Cassie in particular has a very suspicious nature."

"Perhaps," the Doc acknowledged. "But it seems unlikely."

A polite knock on the door interrupted them. The director raised his voice. "Come in."

The admin peeked in, then hurried to Bryce's side. "A message for you," she explained. "It came in on a secure line with a max priority signing key." She shook her head. "I don't know what it means, but the cover said you had to see it immediately." She handed him a sheet of paper and rushed out of the office like a rabbit being chased by a bobcat.

Bryce scanned the handful of words. His suppressed chuckle became an ironic chortle. "You might want to reconsider." He held the paper out to the Doc.

Tell your boss there's no need to blow up the base. We won't be going back. Scout's honor. Jackass.

14

HOT AIR

The intruder looked at the incredible waterfall so close to her target.

Beautiful but irrelevant.

The sun slid behind a thin wisp of cloud, which broke the light into splinters of red and gold. She stripped off her clothes and pulled her wetsuit from her backpack. She squeezed into the tight neoprene skin, stuffed her thick hair into the thermal hood that left only her eyes and mouth uncovered, and jumped into the water. The beams of sunlight bounced and interlaced with the cresting foam of the waterfall for her entertainment.

Beautiful but still irrelevant.

She let the water soak through her suit until she reached full saturation. To an infrared sensor, she would look like a damp spot on the ground.

When she came to the sharp edge where the jungle yielded to the manicured land surrounding the fortress, the intruder paused to pull a small dish from her pack. She slid on the companion headphones and listened for the locations of the surveillance drones as they whirred hither and yon.

She timed her approach to the outer wall to match the moment of least drone coverage near her chosen route.

The wall merged with the brick and mortar of the corner tower at a right angle. The two surfaces splayed at too great an angle for crack-climbing, but enough imperfections marred the surfaces to allow a strong, skilled climber with good grippers on her hands and feet to find purchase.

A lone sentry watched the world from his tower perch, counting on overlapping video surveillance as his backup. Both failed to see the dainty pair of hands catch the lip of the parapet.

The intruder swung back and forth as she relocated the fingers of her left hand farther from the tower. Her right followed, and she moved slowly and invisibly toward the center of the wall. She carefully anchored a grapnel on the outer side.

Next, she peeked over the ledge and watched the sentry until she understood the rhythm of his scanning eyes. As he looked away, she flung herself over the parapet and rappelled down the inner side of the wall, sliding so fast she looked like she was falling.

Still wearing her wetsuit, she dashed across the sward, popped the front door lock using a thumbprint that was not her own, and lunged down the stairs, taking them three at a time.

Andrey often slept in the Vault, though he had a comfy bedroom many floors up.

Often, people who'd been traumatized by being kept prisoner for years in the basements of their kidnappers had trouble letting go. Sometimes, after their captors were captured and the victims were freed, they would buy the house where they'd been kept and live there, a horrific iteration of Stockholm Syndrome.

Andrey figured he was doing better than them.

Regardless, he was catching a nap in his conference room when something tapped his face lightly. He brushed at it and wriggled his nose to avoid sneezing.

A giggle forced him to open one eye.

A petite woman in a wetsuit stood over him, struggling to pull her neoprene hood off.

Andrey looked around wildly for a weapon.

The woman achieved victory over her headpiece and yanked it free. Her black hair fell wetly past her shoulders to disappear against the backdrop of black neoprene. Her dark eyes blazed with excitement. She grinned. "Hi. You're Andrey, right? We're here to help you improve your security."

Andrey sputtered, "Our security is exceptional."

Another lovely female voice laughed around the corner. "You see an impregnable fortress. We see a candy store."

The woman the voice belonged to halted at the door and pulled off her wetsuit's hood with the ease of long practice. Honey-gold hair glistened as it spilled over the black neoprene. "Consider yourself officially kidnapped. As a thank you for saving our lives."

Cassie stood next to Remy, examining the T. Rex towering over them. Her hand itched to grab her katana off her back, which would have worked poorly since the katana was packed in a suitcase at the moment. "I don't think we could take this bad boy with the batons."

Remy chuckled. "I'd be more inclined to use a cannon if it sprang to life."

Cassie looked at the lions in the distance. "Those guys, on the other hand, are too fast to take on with a cannon."

The partners were hanging out at the Yorkshire Wildlife Park, killing a few minutes before they went down to the airfield to negotiate for the craft Remy had identified as the perfect solution for their next mission.

A short time later, they strolled onto the airfield, and a man in a suit waved at them. "Ms. Tambook? Ms. Parker? I'm here to answer your questions about the Airlander 10."

The salesman looked at them expectantly, but Cassie and Remy ignored him and gazed at the immense machine behind him. The salesman smiled. "She *is* impressive, isn't she? Behold the *Glorious Horizon*."

Remy muttered, "We'll have to fix that name. Too many glories in our lives."

A white double-dirigible bigger than a 747 floated a few feet off the ground. It rotated in the breeze, and Cassie saw propellers in the back.

Cassie chortled. "I see why it's called the 'flying buttocks.'" The Airlander had the shape of two dirigibles mashed together, Siamese twins conjoined down most of their length, leaving two rounded tail sections in the shape of a derrière.

The salesman took offense. "The ship is too distinguished for that."

Remy clapped. "I told you, Cassie, it's perfect." She pointed at the ship. "Can we see the cabin?"

The salesman hesitated. "Your pilot trainee and his wife seem unhappy with the current furnishings. The decor was designed to the specifications of Air Nostrum, the buyers of this particular ship."

Cassie shrugged. "The interior can't be too bad compared to our last aircraft." Though she had loved the Gobi eVTOL, using a bucket to pee and sleeping in the chairs had left much to be desired.

The airship filled the sky while the salesman continued to fret. "Your people were most interested in the configuration with eight double en-suite rooms." He led them up the steps into the vessel. "This is configured for a sightseeing dinner flight for twenty."

An elegant wrap-around sofa with twenty pillows encircled a pair of glass-topped tables. Cassie immediately visualized herself stretching out on the sofa and taking a nap.

Tina came out of the cockpit, rolling slightly as the craft swung in a gust of air. "This is going to be so much fun," she drawled.

Brett lowered his head to get through the door behind her. He had a Go-Pro strapped to his head, and he carried a Memwriter balaclava. "I could use more time and more memwriting, but we're ready to go."

The salesman looked at them in alarm. "Go where? This belongs to Air Nostrum, as I mentioned earlier."

Remy handed him a sheet of paper. "No longer. We offered them a premium equal to the profits they hoped to make on the ship for the next year. It's ours now." She tapped the frame of one of the windows that wrapped around the compartment. "And since we'll soon have another ship named *Glory*, a name change is in order. I hereby christen thee the *Faithful Renegade*."

The salesman stared at the paper. "But you don't have a qualified pilot."

Brett stared at his feet. "It's true. There are only a couple dozen qualified dirigible pilots in the world, and it takes over a year to get certified. Flying these babies is much harder than flying an airplane."

Tina wrapped herself around his arm. "Relax, lover-boy. We aren't going to be flying down the streets of New York, smacking skyscrapers on both sides. We're sticking to the ocean. What could go wrong?"

Brett held up his hand to list potential disasters. Tina stepped on his foot.

The salesman was adamant. "He's not certified. I cannot let you just fly away, heedless of consequences."

This was Cassie's cue. "It occurs to me that you haven't received a sufficient commission on this sale. Let me fix that for you." She held up her phone, which displayed a wire transfer app. The amount to be transferred contained many zeroes.

The fellow looked at the offer with a blend of desire and sorrow. "But—"

Cassie took the phone back. The salesman watched it go wistfully.

Cassie had to confess that she enjoyed solving problems with money. It was so simple compared to the workarounds she had navigated in her hard-scrabble days. Though she did notice that her problems were now even bigger than her very big bank account.

Every solution had limits, apparently. She tapped the phone and added a zero to the amount.

The salesman's eyes bulged.

Remy leaned close, filling the air around him with sweet perfume. "Surrender to victory."

He closed his eyes, and a look of decision filled his face. He nodded.

Cassie transferred the money.

The salesman checked his cell phone, then addressed Brett. "You have the keys already, right?"

The *Renegade* had barely ascended over the city of Doncaster when Cassie heard Tina offer a regretful observation. "I've heard so many stories about your adventures. I was kinda hopin' this would turn out to be a heist."

An obscene oath emanated from the cockpit.

Remy giggled. "Well, we *did* take it without a certified pilot. I think it qualifies as a heist."

Cassie tapped her foot impatiently as she watched the scenery drift below. "If this is a heist, we're making the slowest getaway in the history of thieving."

Remy turned serious. "Tina, did you load the paint?"

Tina pointed at the back.

Cassie asked eagerly, "And the flyboards?"

Tina pointed at a closet. "Can I come along? I've been practicing and memwriting, and my flyboard's in there too."

Cassie and Remy spoke in unison. "No!"

Remy continued apologetically, "We're going to be handling a paint sprayer, wearing a paint canister, and working with wind gusts on an uneven moving surface. It's dangerous."

Tina pouted but stayed silent.

In a few minutes, Remy and Cassie were flying above the dirigible. Between the wind from the *Renegade's* passage and the occasional blast of air from nowhere, the paint they sprayed hit everything, including each other.

Remy offered a redundant caution. "Remember, no matter what, we don't dare get too close to the airship's skin. If we hit it with a blast from the jets on our flyboards, who knows how bad the damage will be?"

Cassie attempted to wipe paint off her face. "Yeah, yeah."

"On the other hand, we don't have to do a great job. Just cover most of the top with paint. It'll be fine."

"I know, I know. It's not like anybody is going to be doing a close inspection." Before Cassie could continue in this vein, a third person on a flyboard scooted up and over the airship.

Tina asked cheerfully, "So, is the painting as hard as you thought it would be?" She scrutinized them. "You two trying out for Blue Man Group? I didn't know they had an opening."

Remy sighed and pointed at the nose. "Since you're here, start spraying up there."

Cassie added, "And don't—"

Tina interrupted, "Don't get close enough to blast the ship with the flyboard's jets. I heard you."

They worked in silence for a few minutes, then Brett spoke on their earbuds. "Hey! You're getting paint on my windshield."

Tina winced. "Sorry, babe."

Another interruption cracked over their ear buds. Andrey shouted triumphantly, "*Hey, folks! I found the Glory! You're going to love it!*"

They forced Andrey to wait offline while they finished the paint job, re-entered the airship, and showered. By the time they sat down at the dining room/conference table, he had nearly exploded several times. "What is *wrong* with you people?"

Tina answered soothingly, "Settle down, friend."

Remy cooed, "We're so sorry. We painted as fast as we could."

Cassie rolled her eyes. "Spill."

Andrey threw a map on the tablet they were using as a woeful substitute for a communications setup. A dot blinked northeast of Caracas.

Cassie blinked. "The *Glory's* heading for Venezuela?"

Andrey was calmer when he answered, "I think so. I decrypted some traffic just stored at the UDC as a helicopter took off from a deserted part of the ocean and headed to the capital. The NSA analysts think it's the Russian president's chopper getting him to the airport to fly back to Moscow."

He flipped up a low-res satellite photo of an area with a phosphorescent white wake that might have been made by a megayacht. "Additional comm indicates the ship is running low on fuel and heading for the Port of Sucre."

Cassie's paranoia kicked in. "That's quite a coincidence. The ship we want is moving toward the country where our people live."

Remy gave her a bright-eyed look. "There's a point at which paranoia becomes delusional."

Tina snorted.

Remy spread her hands. "I'm just saying it's not that big a surprise. Where else can the *Glory* go for fuel? A place where nobody would dare try to hijack or impound her? Remember, Russia owns the Venezuelan dictator from the top of his head to the heart of his black soul."

Cassie smiled as she considered those points. "Okay, then. If it's not a trap, it's wonderfully convenient." She rubbed her hands together. "How soon can we hit her?"

15

SEVEN WAYS TO DIE IN THE SEVEN SEAS

Morte Noir sat next to Andrey as he called the dirigible. They got Remy and Cassie on a video call.

Cassie gave Morte Noir a piercing stare. "What are you doing with Andrey?"

He cheerfully answered, "Oh, she kidnapped me."

Cassie looked like she would explode.

Morte Noir chuckled. "Relax. It's just a little kidnapping."

Andrey explained. "She and her trainee Esin broke in to study our defenses."

Morte Noir interrupted. "Let's be clear. Esin planned and executed the break-in. I just followed her." She nodded off-screen. "Esin, come take a bow."

The very young woman came over holding a croissant in one hand and waving fiercely with the other. "Ms. Cassie, Ms. Remy. Nice to see you again."

Morte Noir pointed her back to the breakfast table. "I have decided to help you with your security here."

Cassie shouted, "*We don't need—*"

Remy put her hand on Cassie's shoulder. "What did you have in mind?"

Morte Noir laid out several key items in succinct sentences. She had perfected a crisp patter through years of performing similar services for other clients.

Andrey supported her argument. "I really think we should let her do this. I mean, if Grisha had hired her to take me..." He gulped.

Cassie remained suspicious. "How much is this going to cost?"

Morte Noir laughed gaily. "Cassie, sometimes you can be so silly. As if you needed to care about money anymore." She turned serious. "Actually, I was hoping you'd let me do it for free."

This time even Remy looked skeptical. "What's the catch?"

Morte Noir wrinkled her nose. "Ahem…it's like this. I'm currently living on my new submarine." She pointed at Cassie. "Thank you for helping with that, by the way."

She continued, "And it's very comfortable. Very serene beneath the ocean waves. No fears of raiders." She grimaced. "But it's claustrophobic. I was wondering if I could share your delightful little fortress here."

Cassie blinked, then barked a laugh. "You want to move in with us?"

Andrey clarified. "Technically, she'd be moving in with us, but not you. You're not allowed to come here anymore, remember?"

Cassie glared at him.

Remy looked concerned. "Morte Noir, I hate to say this, but you have as many enemies as we do. Maybe more."

The woman nodded. She did have more enemies since she had been accumulating them far longer.

Remy made her point. "If you move in, you'll endanger everyone there." Her eyes glistened. "Including my mom and dad."

Morte Noir gave her a warm smile. "Which was why I discussed it with Laurie first." She nodded off-screen again.

Laurie joined them on camera. "Hey, kiddo. Cassie, good to see you."

Remy looked at her in astonishment. "Mom, you're okay with this?"

Laurie winced. "I wasn't at first." She cast a sidelong glance at Morte Noir. "But she's quite convincing. We might be safer with her here. And her people."

Cassie's eyes bulged. "And her *people*? Murderers and blackmailers?"

Morte Noir jerked forward and defended her team. "Hey, they're just doing their jobs."

Cassie held her throbbing temples. "Their jobs as murderers and blackmailers!"

Morte Noir patted the air to calm her. "There'd only be a handful here at any one time. It would be like my mansion in Scotland. A place to unwind between jobs, a stress-free environment in which to take a break. Unless Rivendell is attacked, in which case they'd be some of your best defenders."

Remy chimed in with another worry. "We're not letting them use the Memwriter."

Morte Noir decided to exploit this opening to shift the topic. "Which reminds me. Before all the trouble with AID destroying my home and shooting cruise missiles at you, we talked about doing some memwriting for several of my people."

Cassie opened her mouth to object, but Morte Noir pushed on. "Only ones dedicated to ethically sound murder and blackmail, of course."

Remy sighed. "I remember."

Cassie glared at Remy. "You agreed to that?"

Laurie interjected, "It was a good offer."

Morte Noir waved off more objections. "Anyway, I've picked my first candidate for my Memwriter-augmented noble warrior team." She gestured off-screen again. "Esin, come here."

Esin returned with a big grin. "I would be deeply honored to be the first memwritten assassin and blackmailer for Rivendell and for my Dark Mistress."

Cassie opened her mouth and closed it several times. She could not think of a single valid objection.

Remy recovered with hardly a blink. She replied, her voice as bubbly and effusive as Esin's, "What a delightful choice! Most excellent!"

Cassie looked at everyone on the call. "Are you all nuts? With two high-value targets like Morte Noir and Andrey, we're looking at twice as many attacks with twice as many attackers."

Laurie gave her a stern look. "As the Mistress and Andrey have said, our defenses will be twice as good as well."

Remy was upset. "We can't expose you to this kind of firefight, Mom. You shouldn't be put in that much danger."

Laurie glared at her daughter. "Young lady, let me

assure you I am more than able to handle a gun. I *am* your grandmother's daughter."

Remy looked dazed, and she sounded younger when she spoke. "How come I never knew you could handle a gun?"

Laurie sighed. "Let's face it. I love my mom, but she's over the top on the paranoid side. I never thought guns were that important, so I encouraged you in other directions."

She turned contemplative. "Turns out she was much more correct about how the world works than I was."

Cassie cleared her throat to return to the topic at hand. "The problem's bigger than just ground and air assault." She turned her gaze once more on Morte Noir. "I asked you before about the risk of being targeted by cruise missiles. At the Auction, everyone who had advanced weapons also had a stake in the meeting. At Rivendell, you're just a target."

Morte Noir raised an eyebrow. "You think I'm the only reason someone might shoot one at us? You think your promise to remain on the run will keep everyone's missiles leashed indefinitely? We all need a more robust solution than a gentlemen's agreement."

She explained her proposal. "I'll need Rudy's help."

Laurie chimed in, "I already talked to him, and he's on board. Frankly, he's deliriously happy at the idea of a road trip." She remembered another point. "Oh, and Esin would like to go, but she's worried about whether it's allowed."

Morte Noir put her hand over her eyes. "I told her it would be fine." She sighed. "But I suppose I should formally request authorization to take her along." She stepped to the side. "Esin!"

Esin hesitantly stepped into camera range. "Yes, Mistress?"

Morte Noir chuckled. "Damnable ethical sourcing diehards."

Cassie pumped her fist. "Tell me about it. Remy and Grandma—" Her voice cut off as Remy poked her. Laurie scowled.

Remy focused on the topic. "Esin, what is your question?"

Esin looked around, shy since she had all eyes on her. "I made you a vow to use my memwriting skills only for projects of great worthiness." She hesitated.

Morte Noir smiled. "Go on, girl. Spit it out."

Esin bowed sharply. "I'm a little worried. Is stealing from the Navy really worthy? Are they not the good guys?"

Cassie opened her mouth to offer up sarcastic wisdom. However, Esin looked so sincere it hurt. She closed her mouth without speaking.

Laurie exploded into laughter, then stopped herself. "Ethics comes to covert ops. I never thought I'd see the day."

Remy gave Esin a thumbs-up. "You have just asked a very important question."

Morte Noir sourly objected with a sour note, "Please tell me you're not going to side with her." She looked at Esin, her face reflecting a complex stew of emotions. "I would be proud of you for taking such a firm stance despite the need for direct confrontation if I wasn't so irritated."

Cassie, having been involved in decisions like this, completed the statement. "And you'd be irritated with her if you weren't so proud."

Esin looked at each, smiling uncertainly, then glanced at Remy. "Help."

All eyes turned to the rigid moral interpreter of the group. However, the rigid moralist had had to face far worse ethical questions than this during her time on the run. She had loosed a prison full of criminals and slaughtered a troop of soldiers. She had come to understand the grand diversity of shades of gray.

What choice did she have here?

Remy whispered, "This is a greater-good decision, Esin. We will leave the Navy a bit weaker, but we will help everyone we know a lot. At the end of the day, this is a life-saving mission."

Cassie breathed a sigh of relief. "Enough with the philosophy. I do have one recommendation, however, based on my own experiences in the field."

Morte Noir rolled her eyes. "Please remember that I have been doing this somewhat longer than you have, but do tell. What is your recommendation?"

"Thermite."

Standing away from Brett as he piloted the *Renegade*, Cassie stared through the cockpit window across the deep blue expanse at a white dot on the horizon. "So, that's the *Glory*?"

Remy nodded. "And the only one of the Russian dictator's megayachts not yet impounded and sold to help rebuild the cities he destroyed."

Cassie put her hand on the glass and leaned forward to see it better. "Once again, we maintain our reputation for ethically sourced heists."

Remy twisted her head to intercept Cassie's gaze. "Come on, confess. It's more fun this way, isn't it?"

Cassie turned away to hide her smile. Okay, it was fun. Gangsters were a little harder to steal from since they used more muscle to protect their stuff, but as long as it worked out, it was great. She walked back to the closet with the wetsuits. "I suppose we should undertake this assault, uh, *gloriously*."

Cassie spoke as Tina helped her wriggle into her suit. "Thanks."

Tina grunted as she pulled the zipper up the last inch. "My pleasure."

Cassie hitched the parachute into position above the scuba tank. As she finished, Brett shouted, "Gotta go now. Soon, they'll be able to see you."

Cassie muttered loud enough for Remy to overhear, "I still think we should have used the flyboards to drop onto the deck."

Remy shook her head. "Trust me. When we get close, all eyes will be on the sky. Machine guns, too. They'd turn us into Swiss cheese."

Cassie grumbled, "Whatever," and launched out the hatch into the blue sky.

As she fell, she could hear Remy in her head, shouting, *Don't open the chute yet! Don't open the chute yet!* Sheesh. Of course they had to do a low open drop to avoid having the guys with the guns watching their parachutes pop.

So Cassie held the rip cord and waited, her anxiety growing but an enormous grin splitting her face. She preferred to think the grin was the wind blowing her skin back, not that it was fun.

Of course, Remy also had the same grin, but she *would* think it was swell.

Finally, Cassie grew so terrified she couldn't bear watching the ocean scream toward her any longer. So blue. So big. So very solid. Aargh! She had to pull the rip cord. She had to pull the rip cord *now*. She shouted, "Remy, you bitch, pull your damned cord!" and her fingers twitched.

Remy popped her chute, and Cassie followed a nanosecond later.

It seemed like only another nanosecond before she slammed into the water like an express elevator slamming into the basement without brakes.

As she rapidly sank beneath the waves, she realized she hadn't taken a full breath when she had the chance. She scrabbled for the mouthpiece on her regulator and jammed it into her mouth as her lungs started to burn. Ah, air!

As she breathed, she took stock. She'd survived two certain deaths in the last few seconds, first by not smashing her body when she crashed into the sea and the second by not drowning. Most excellent.

But she was plunging deeper into the ocean since she had the weight belt pulling her down and hadn't yet inflated her buoyancy compensator. She started to fix that, then remembered it was a bad idea to stop sinking until she'd gotten free of the parachute fluttering above her. It would shroud her like a mummy if she let it fall around her.

Okay, then; ditch the parachute. Easier said than done since she couldn't see a damn thing with the chute blocking the light. Aargh.

One parachute buckle refused to budge. What kind of idiot had decided it should be really hard to get free of a parachute? Probably the idiot who thought it would be a bad idea to get loose while you were still airborne. She started to panic.

Other hands grabbed the buckle, and Remy freed her.

Without the chute supplying drag, she sank even faster. Where had they hidden the damn button to pump air into the buoyancy compensator?

And how deep was she? She remembered the stern warnings about going too deep and replayed them in her mind. *Nitrogen narcosis. Nitrogen is poisonous under pressure. It'll make you delusional. Don't go too deep.*

Ah, there was the button. She heard air spurt into the BC, and her descent slowed, then stopped. She probably wasn't going to die of nitrogen narcosis. Another hideous death avoided.

She added air to start her ascent, but she rose too fast. Her breath caught in her throat as she remembered that when you rose to depths with less pressure, the air in the compensator would expand, causing you to accelerate.

If she rose fast enough from deep enough, the nitrogen dissolved in her blood by the pressure would boil out, causing generalized barotrauma, popularly known as "the bends." The bends killed you painfully. Panicking, she let all the air out of the BC and sank.

After yo-yoing a few times, she got the hang of it and rose more gracefully. Then she realized she was holding her breath. *No!*

She remembered what would happen if she held her breath going up. The air in her lungs would try to expand, but with nowhere to go, it would force itself into the pleural space around her lungs, causing pneumothorax. Or it would drive into the interstitial space of her lungs, causing mediastinal emphysema. In either case, it would tear and destroy the alveoli where the blood picked up oxygen, and she would suffocate as she inhaled vast gulps of air.

She explosively exhaled all the air from her lungs. Inhaling again in a panic, her body desperately wanted to hold onto the air lest it be her last. She exhaled raggedly and wondered how she was likely to die this time.

She broke the surface, spit out her regulator, and sucked in a huge volume of fresh ocean air. But a wave submerged her head, so instead of inhaling air, she inhaled a lungful of water.

No! I made it this far. I am not *going to drown,* she told herself.

Remy, who was bobbing nearby, inspected her partner critically. After Cassie got control of her sputtering, Remy splashed water on her face. "'Tune up your scuba skills,' he said. 'Tune them up.' But did you listen?"

Cassie could not see the yacht, but she could see the airship, which Brett had pointed in the right direction. She pointed into the distance. "That a-way."

Remy nodded. "Let's go." They stuck their snorkels in their mouths and swam in companionable silence.

Captain Belyaev stood on the bridge of the *Glory* and watched grimly as the balloon drifted in his direction. His radarman asked him to speculate. "Who do you think it is?"

The captain was in no mood for either questions or dirigibles. "Somebody doing some kind of publicity stunt."

If the airship had arrived four hours earlier, he would have assumed it was an oddball assassination plot to take out the president. However, the revered madman leading Belyaev's country had already departed on a helicopter. If that airship held assassins, they were in for a big disappointment, even if they survived a firefight with the Spetsnaz on board.

Belyaev considered making the situation even more dire for the dirigible. He rang the lieutenant in charge of the Spetsnaz. "Have you seen the airship plodding toward us?"

The lieutenant grunted. "*Da.*"

Belyaev didn't really like Spetsnaz commandos. The arrogant pricks thought they ran the boat, and it rankled the captain that if they ever disagreed with him, they would teach him that they *did* run the boat.

Under these circumstances, however... "Think it would make sense to bring a couple of Verbas up on the deck?" The Verba was the Russian handheld anti-aircraft missile launcher.

The lieutenant pondered that. "You think the balloon is a threat?"

The captain shook his head. "Better safe than sorry."

The lieutenant considered. "Agreed. I'll have the men on duty keep an eye on it as well." He hung up.

As the captain looked down from the bridge, it appeared that the lieutenant's command for the commandos to keep it under observation would be superfluous. They were all watching the huge airship approach. Half of them had raised their weapons as if they expected to shoot it down with assault rifles. The dirigible presented a big target, so they could hardly miss...except that, even though it was coming in low, it was still quite high.

The captain suspected the Verbas wouldn't do much good either. As big a hole as the missile might shoot in the airbag, it would still take hours or days for the balloon to lose enough helium to fall.

As he considered other far-fetched tactical plans, the airship unrolled a streamer from its tail.

WELCOME TO ORINOCO, it announced as it flapped in the wind.

The *Glory* cruised toward Cassie and her partner with unstoppable grace. Finally, Remy gave the order. "Time to make our final approach." She slipped the regulator into her mouth and sank ten feet.

Cassie followed suit, then unpacked the plastic-coated metal disks she'd brought along, strapping one to each knee and holding one in each hand. Remy struggled with her disks, and Cassie had the smug satisfaction of helping her arrange them properly.

The ship's nose cut past them. Cassie touched the steel hull. She felt rather than heard the clang as her neodymium magnets, the most powerful ones on earth, latched onto the ship's skin.

The current swirled around her, trying to drag her back toward the propellers, but to no avail. Her magnets were too strong. She slid the magnets up the hull one at a time until she broke free of the bow wave to find herself clinging halfway upside-down on the curved prow of the *Glory*.

Remy slid up next to her and spat out her regulator. The bottom of her face under her mask wore an immense grin. "Do I take you to the best places, or what?"

Cassie had to smile. "Enjoy it while you can. We're going to be hanging here until the sun goes down."

Remy remained bubbly. "It's going to be a great sunset."

16

ACROBATIC ROUTINE

Cassie had to admit that Remy had been right. It *was* a great sunset. It was especially great for sliding and clamping the magnets up the side of a ship and climbing onto the deck with the sun behind them to blind anyone looking their way.

Like all the other guards, the sentry at the bow had focused most of his attention on the dirigible floating overhead. When he heard them clamber over the gunwale, he waved his rifle in their general direction as he squinted into the glare. "Who's there!"

Cassie spoke soothingly in the fluent Russian she'd picked up for the Kremlin heist so long ago. "Relax, Comrade."

The guard twitched the gun closer. Remy, who had come up the other side, zapped him with her baton.

Cassie laughed. "After fighting Mother Nature all day long, taking out a heavily armed soldier was the easy part."

They stripped off their scuba gear and pulled on clothes

from their packs. Cassie grabbed the guard's rifle. Remy grabbed his sidearm.

The sun slunk over the horizon as they slunk amidships.

The crews of private yachts work very hard to remain invisible to the passengers until they are needed, at which point they work very hard to appear magically with whatever tool, item, or service the guest requires.

Apparently, Cassie qualified as a guest since no one showed up to challenge her.

Unfortunately, she needed to find the engineering deck and an engineer or two. She halted in the middle of a salon with white couches, purple chairs, and plush pillows everywhere. "Could someone help me?" she shouted to thin air.

A young fellow magically appeared at the end of the room, and Cassie waved him over. "Hey." As he approached, she pointed the gun at him. "Very quietly, I need your help. There is no cause for alarm. If you make a sound, I have to shoot you. Understand?"

The steward raised his hands.

Cassie waved the AK-74. "Put your hands down. You're leading the new guest—that's me—on a tour."

She had an idea. "First, I'd like to see the crew's quarters."

The young man took her on a truncated tour to where the crew hung out. Cassie took a deep breath. "Again, I don't want to hurt anybody. Stay here, okay? And be quiet. Quiet, and everybody lives. Noisy, and everybody dies."

The steward nodded. "I understand."

Cassie threw the door open and zapped the biggest guy she saw. She waved the gun at the rest. "Do I have your attention?"

She presumed the stunned expressions constituted acknowledgment. "I'm going to plant a bomb outside your door. If you try to open the door before I come back, someone will have to gather up your bodies and inform your families. Are we clear?"

One of the women bent over the man she had nailed. Cassie gave her permission since the woman was clearly going to do it anyway. "Make sure he's okay. If not, he'll be the first order of business after I complete my current project. Everyone understand? And my apologies for the inconvenience. We'll get things back to normal very soon. Until then, remember…there's a bomb out here."

She exited and shut the door behind her, then turned to the steward. "Engine room, please."

The steward gave her a puzzled look. "Aren't you going to plant your bomb?"

Cassie gave him a sly smile. "Maybe later." She waved the baton. "Onward."

They ran into one Spetsnaz commando on the way. Cassie gave him a passenger's clueless smile and a jab with the baton on the way past. She had the steward gag and zip-tie the man, then stuff him into an aromatic cedar-lined closet for later retrieval.

Cassie whispered to her guide, "You're doing great. We're going to give you a really big tip when this is over."

The steward muttered bitterly, "A big enough tip to flee to America?"

Cassie laughed. "Perhaps, but if things work the way they're supposed to, you might want to stay."

They reached the engine room. One man sat watching the dials and gauges.

Cassie leaned over him and whispered, "Hey."

The man jerked, startled.

Cassie put her gun on the tip of his nose. "I need you to do several things for me. I'm an engineer, so please do not pretend to do something you're not, or I will make you seriously unhappy. Agreed?"

The steward jumped at her. Cassie had been expecting it for a while and whacked him on the side of the head with the baton. He crashed down, dazed.

Cassie sighed. "I'm still going to give you a big tip, but only if I survive. Understand?"

The steward's eyes shifted to a point behind her and widened. Cassie ducked and spun.

A Spetsnaz lieutenant swung at her with an impressively large knife. Cassie jumped out of range.

He also had a pistol. Cassie guessed he had tried the knife first so as not to disturb the guests, but the situation had evolved. He reached for his gun.

Cassie could have shot him with the AK-74, but she too was intent on avoiding any noisy firefights as long as it seemed like no alarm had been given. She dropped her rifle and leaped at the lieutenant with her taser-tipped weapon.

He parried with his knife.

Every time Cassie backed away to make some room, the lieutenant reached for his pistol again. Each time he reached, she leaped forward again.

Finally, she stayed out of range long enough for him to grab his sidearm.

Retrieving the weapon distracted him. She moved in one more time, swung her weapon to smash the arm with the knife, grabbed the hand wrapped around the pistol, and finished by hammering the baton into the side of his face with all the power she could muster.

He fought to stay on his feet. Cassie touched the taser's electrodes to his chest. "You're already unconscious. Go with it."

He fell.

A movement by the door through which the lieutenant had snuck up on her caused her to spin, weapon at the ready.

Remy crossed her arms. "You about done playing around down here?"

Captain Belyaev sat morosely in his chair on the bridge, watching the sun fall below thin, distant clouds. He let his eyes wander back to the main source of his disgruntlement. The irritating airship had swung and was steadfastly pacing them. How could a balloon waving a banner that read Welcome to Orinoco feel so threatening?

The only thing that didn't seem right was the banner's implication that he was traveling to Orinoco when he was actually heading to Venezuela. It could be a simple mistake on the part of the dirigible's owners. He was close enough to Orinoco to offer some confusion.

He'd had the navigator check with GLONASS to be on the safe side. No problem there.

As the glare of the setting sun subsided, he focused on the forward progress of the ship: the bow breaking the water, the foam sweeping to each side, the sunlight glinting off the body of a Spetsnaz soldier curled on the deck.

He jumped to his feet, shouting, "*Red Alert!*"

A sailor smashed the button to sound the alarm, but no alarms sounded. Belyaev grabbed the intercom. "We are under attack. All hands prepare for combat!"

The pastoral silence continued.

He turned to the radioman. "Raise the frigate. Tell him to come here, fast!"

The sailor sent the message repeatedly while shaking his head. "We seem to have lost all comms."

The captain sank into his chair, trying to figure out his next move. He was not surprised when the Spetsnaz lieutenant stumbled onto the bridge with his hands behind his back and some kind of collar around his neck a few minutes later. The right side of his face was swollen, and his eye was welded shut.

A bubbly female voice came from behind the soldier. "Very good, lieutenant."

Cassie slid around the lieutenant to the right. Remy went left. Remy's baton was attached to an ingenious collar around the soldier's neck. If the man tried anything, she could electrocute him with no muss or fuss. Cassie wondered if they could start a business selling similar setups to women going on first dates.

Regardless, the most important matter now was intimidating the captain and the officers here with him. Cassie swung her AK-74 around the room as if she were an expert with an assault rifle and not afraid to use it.

To be fair, she had some knowledge of the weapon, having practiced with the Orinoco troops and done a little memwriting. She handled the gun better than a typical Russian soldier, though she was sure the Spetsnaz troops had far greater proficiency.

However, she was afraid of shooting the blasted thing. She didn't mind shooting the men. Killing them would disturb her, but she'd bulldozed her private objections to killing during the process of taking out Dallas Ferris.

Lose the men, no worries. But the instrumentation? She was terrified of blasting holes in the bridge equipment since she felt sure they would miss it if they lost it.

Remy addressed the captain. "Sir, there has been a change of command."

Belyaev did not respond immediately.

Cassie took one step forward and leveled her gun at him. "I'm not hearing your acknowledgment." She nodded at her partner.

The captain reluctantly took his eyes off Cassie's gun and turned to Remy. He slowly raised his hand to salute. "Aye aye, ma'am."

Remy's eyes twinkled. "Such a gentleman. Call me Remy. This is Cassie." She looked sideways at the lieutenant. "And this is one of the people who will be leaving the yacht soon."

Cassie zip-tied two bridge officers to their chairs, leaving the captain free. She then zip-tied the lieutenant's zip-ties to the captain's seat.

The commando looked so upset that she patted his cheek. "Don't worry. Everything's going to be all right." Finally, she followed Remy and the captain into a small conference room behind the bridge, an elegant space lined with teak bookshelves.

Remy looked at the bookshelves and shook her head. "So many bookshelves and yet, no books!" She tapped a series of sports trophies won by the president and by his mistress. "This is where the president of Russia works? Where's the reverence for knowledge? The wisdom that makes a ruler great?"

Cassie gawked at her. "You're kidding, right? He's a dictator. What does he need knowledge or wisdom for?"

The captain looked like he might burst a blood vessel. Cassie waved him to a chair. "Captain Belyaev. Please. Sit before you fall over." She realized she should shift personae. Enough with being a high-seas pirate. She should switch to—

Remy sat down across the table from the captive. "Cassie, could you please bring the captain coffee?"

Cassie swallowed an epithet. Apparently, she would now shift to wait-staff. It was just as well that the coffee machine was in one corner. She stumped off to do her duty.

Remy placed her hands on the captain's tightly clenched fists and cooed, "How would you feel about captaining the *Glory* for us instead of the president?" She stroked his wrist. "I can offer you twice the salary."

The captain stared at her. "You want me to be your captain?"

Remy leaned back. "I know you lost your son in the president's last war." She clenched her own fists. "Anatoly had a promising future as an architect. He would have built beautiful buildings, full of light and grace." Her voice thickened with the rage that still mastered her once in a while since she'd seen the atrocities done to her father. "Such a stupid waste of a good man."

Belyaev stared at her. "How did you know?"

Remy relaxed and flipped her hair back. "This is not an ordinary hijacking, Captain. Assume I know everything, and you'll be close to the mark."

The captain licked his lips. "My wife..."

Remy looked at him in dismay.

Cassie had the solution. "I can have her out of Russia in forty-eight hours."

Remy looked sidelong at her, perplexed.

Cassie gave her a sly smile. "The EStormers who helped me."

Remy accepted that and shot the captain a sincere smile. "Believe her. She's done it before."

The captain goggled.

Remy turned the cheerleader charm to full power. "We have people in position, ready to help."

The captain shrugged and moved on to the next problem. "About half the crew is going to be very unhappy to betray the president."

Cassie nodded. "Not a problem. They can leave with the Spetsnaz."

Remy explained, "We're planning to load them on a lifeboat and point them to Port Sucre, where you were going before."

That apparently jogged the captain to another concern. "We're running out of fuel, and we have a frigate trailing us. There's no way we can shake them."

Remy laughed. "The frigate is in for a surprise, and you'll have all the fuel you could ever hope for in a few minutes."

Cassie felt a need to double-check the critical factoid. "According to the specs, you have hybrid engines, right? Diesel-powered electric generators that drive electric motors for propulsion?"

Belyaev nodded. "Why?"

Cassie sighed in relief. "It's too dark to unload now. Let's spend a little time interviewing the officers and engineers. See who wants to stay or go." She yawned. "We'll bring our extra crewmen down with the equipment at first light."

The captain turned puzzled eyes to her. "Crewmen? Equipment?"

Just outside Moscow, Leonid slumbered in his basement bedroom. Despite the depth of his sleep, he heard his mother call, "Time for breakfast!"

He threw back the covers and yelled, "I'll be there in a couple of minutes!"

He groped for his tablet to read the most recent gem drops on the EStorme site. He prayed for something exciting like more news about Rivendell.

When Rivendell had first announced a request for candidates to come to Orinoco to interview, Leonid had submitted his résumé like everyone else. He'd prayed with all his might for an acceptance letter, but he hadn't really expected to be Called. He *was* just an automotive mechanic.

He had, however, included a paragraph about how he had helped an EStorme operative, a woman who personally knew the Emerald, escape from Russia despite a full-scale manhunt. Surely, that would give him a leg up.

Alas, he had received no word. He was still just a car mechanic.

His phone buzzed. Who could be calling him?

"Leonid. Long time no see."

He recognized the voice. "The friend of the Emerald."

She sounded urgent. "Yeah. Is your computer on?"

He never shut it off. "Of course."

"Type this URL as I speak it and follow the link." A string of letters that started with https:// and ended with a huge number of random characters rolled off her tongue. "Click now. Quick!"

The link took him to a page that said, "Redirecting." Moments later, a page with a video panel in the middle appeared. He gave her a shy smile. "Hi."

The woman smiled back. "Sorry I couldn't tell you my name last time. I'm Cassie."

Leonid's blood pounded. Something exciting was going to happen today after all. But first, he better warn her. "All our networks are tapped. They probably followed the link you gave me and are listening in."

Cassie shook her head. "The redirect page was a one-time-only pass-through. If they had gotten there before you did, you wouldn't have made it to this page. Since you did make it, they arrived too late and got redirected to a porn site."

Leonid laughed. "Good. Keep them entertained."

Cassie fiddled with her machine. "I'm bringing up a picture of another person in dire straits." The photo of an older woman named Belyaev appeared on his monitor. An address accompanied the image. "Can you help her the way you helped me?"

Leonid swallowed hard. When he'd helped Cassie, it had been really scary. Did he want to go through that again?

The alternative was being nothing but a car mechanic. "I'll find her and see what I can do."

Some tension in Cassie's face dissolved. "Thank you. If you hurry, you can get her out before anyone starts looking for her." She scrutinized his image. "Oh, Leonid, I'm afraid to ask. Are you still living in the basement?"

Leonid looked around and winced. "Yeah." He pushed his one hope of leaving. "Could I come to Rivendell with Ms. Belyaev? I submitted my application to interview, but I guess I wasn't, well, good enough."

Cassie shook her head sadly. "There's so much wrong with what you just said that I hardly know where to begin. First of all, the lady you're rescuing isn't coming here.

Secondly, I know you submitted your application, but the problem wasn't that you weren't good enough."

Leonid raised his eyebrows. "Then what?"

"Think about it. If you were here, you wouldn't be able to help us now, would you? You're in Moscow because that's where the Plan needs you."

Leonid considered that. "I guess so."

Cassie turned stern. "No guessing. It's the truth." Her eyes brightened. "Hey, I have an idea."

Leonid turned hopeful.

"When I was on the run before, I was pretty broke. We've scored some hits on the Dark since then."

Leonid nodded. "Enough to build Rivendell."

"Exactly. You need to get out of that basement, so I'm going to send you a little money. Enough to get you into an apartment of your own. Sound good?"

Leonid smiled. "That would be beautiful."

Cassie chuckled. "Here it comes." She typed, and a bank name and an account number appeared. "That should do it."

Leonid didn't care how much money there was. He was just thrilled to be acknowledged—to be recognized as a person, not just a mechanic. "Thank you. I'll track this woman down immediately."

Cassie gushed, "Thank you so much, Leonid. I'll call the next time we need you for the Plan." She closed the connection.

Before taking off to find Ms. Belyaev, he logged into the bank and checked the account she'd given him. He gasped. It might have been just a little money to Cassie, but for him, it was transformational.

Dawn crept across the ocean east of Venezuela, striking the *Glory*'s stern. The captain radioed the frigate on a standard check-in, telling them everything was fine despite the annoying balloon and its banner. Cassie watched the *Renegade* descend, dropping ropes and ladders as she approached. Tina slid down the rope onto the deck first, followed by half a dozen Awakened EStorme team members.

Captain Belyaev watched with his mouth set in a grim line. "These are your new crewmen? Have they ever worked on a ship?"

Tina marched up to him and punched him on the shoulder. "I've never even been a passenger, but trust me. We're fast learners." She turned a knowing smile on Cassie and Remy. "We have our Go-Pros coming down right after this." She turned to the cargo line next to the ladder, where a wiffle ball jiggled to a stop.

Cassie grabbed the ball with delight. "Here's your fuel, Captain."

Belyaev stared at her.

Remy chuckled. "You'll see."

Cassie held the ball up. "Can you assign an engineer to me? We need to install this ASAP."

Before Cassie departed for the engine room, the captain broke down and asked, "What is it?"

Cassie smiled gaily. "It's a nuclear reactor. Nothing to worry about."

Cassie and Remy followed Captain Belyaev on a tour of the ship. They came to a door behind which they heard thumping and splashing.

The captain announced, "This is the highlight of the ship." He opened the door to show them a room lined with windows, dominated by the fifty-foot swimming pool running down the center.

Dominating the swimming pool were two young girls butterflying from end to end and back.

Dominating the girls was a young woman going through a gymnastics routine in which back handsprings played a prominent role. As she bounced from places deep in shadow to places lit by beams of morning light, her hair shifted color from mud brown to blood-red.

She flipped and sprang down the side of the pool with no more thought than a normal person would give to rolling out of bed.

Cassie muttered to Remy, "How long do you think it would take us to get that good with the Memwriter?"

Remy gave her a wry smile. "Even with a Memwriter, her skills might be beyond us. She's—"

Captain Belyaev's face broke out in a big smile. "Alina! There you are."

Alina stopped tumbling and approached warily. "Yes? How can I help you?"

The captain made the introductions. "Alina Ocheretnaya, allow me to present Remy Tambook and Cassie Parker. They are, uh, well..." He glanced at his new bosses.

Case stepped in to help out. "We're the pirates who just stole your yacht."

Alina looked incredulous. "Stole the yacht? You?"

Remy walked to the intercom. "XO? Could you turn twenty degrees to port, please?"

The XO answered, "Aye aye, ma'am." The yacht heeled over.

Alina stepped back and spoke with the force of a drill sergeant. "Annika. Vera. Come here."

Two soggy little girls ran into her arms. She glared at Cassie. "Don't hurt my children." Worry crept over her face. "Please."

The captain broke the silent tableau. "Cassie and Remy, allow me to present Alina Ocheretnaya, the—"

Remy interrupted. "The Olympic gymnastics gold medalist."

Belyaev nodded. "She's also—"

Remy cut him off again. "The president's mistress."

Cassie winced. "Goodness. That complicates things."

Remy shrugged. "Does it?"

Alina's lip trembled. "What are you going to do with us?"

Remy gave her a comforting smile. "Relax. We're shipping off about half the crew in lifeboats for Venezuela. You'll go with them."

One of the little girls wailed. "I don't want to go to Venezuela. There aren't any gyms there." She looked at her mother.

The other little girl, clearly a twin, looked up with the

same pleading expression. Cuteness exploded across the room. "*Are* there gyms?"

Alina's expression turned thoughtful. "Can you really escape the frigate?"

Cassie gave her a confident smile. "We have a plan. Should work."

Alina's thoughtful look turned to one of decision. "I'd like to come with you."

Remy blinked. "Why?"

Cassie turned instantly suspicious. "Not a chance." She scrutinized Alina's features. "Unless…" She strode to Alina and got in her face.

Alina jerked back.

Cassie gently wiped the makeup off Alina's left eye. The woman winced, but Cassie persisted. A faint tinge of black turning green from a recent bruise became visible.

Cassie answered her own question. "Never mind."

Remy sighed. "I respect your reasons for coming with us, but you can't stay here."

Alina hugged herself. "Why not?"

Cassie explained. "This is now the president's Number One target. He'll boil the seas trying to catch us."

Remy clarified, "We think he'll fail, but this is not going to be the safest place in the world. Think of your girls."

One little girl defended her mother. "We'd like to stay."

Cassie put her hand over her eyes. "How about this? We're not going back to Rivendell, so nobody's going to drop any more cruise missiles on it. We could take them there."

Alina gawked. "Cruise missiles?"

Remy looked doubtful.

Cassie whispered to Remy, though Alina could probably hear. "I know we can't invite every stray we run into to go to the fort, but this is sort of a special case."

Remy's silence was not consent.

Cassie came up with a better justification. "I've got it! Maybe we can use her as leverage with the president and get him to shut down Gamma. What do you think?"

Remy sighed. "I think that's both immoral and ridiculous, but you win. They're with us until we can get them to Rivendell."

Belyaev grimaced. "That complicates things."

Alina looked at them with suspicion. "What exactly are you planning to do to me and my family?"

Remy turned bubbly. "We're thinking of sending you to our home in Orinoco. Let me get you some pictures. It's beautiful, secure, and far from everything."

Alina responded with thick skepticism, "And it's a fortress that people shoot cruise missiles at."

Remy waved that away like cruise missiles were no more problematic than hard rain. "The missiles are in the past."

Cassie added, "It *is* a fortress, though. Lots of troops on guard." That was not precisely true. The EStormers had duties other than soldiering, but they were all combat-capable. Exceptionally combat capable, as they'd already proven.

Alina, demonstrating an Olympic level of acuity when it came to protecting her daughters, pressed another point. "If it's far from everything, what about schooling?

Cassie gave a belly laugh. "Oh, don't worry on that

score. We have the best educational system in the world. Trust us on that one."

17

WRAPPED UP

Cassie turned to listen as Belyaev coughed for attention. "Captain?"

The captain offered a gentle reminder. "Speaking of the frigate, perhaps it is time for you to reveal the plan to me. Perhaps I can help."

Remy spun to the door. "Good point. First step, head for Orinoco." She started for the bridge.

Alina asserted, "I'm coming too." She pushed a button by the windows. Water swirled and flowed to the sides of the pool.

Cassie peered at the flowing streams, trying to figure out what was happening. Her jaw dropped. "Is the bottom of the pool rising?"

Alina answered with smug pride. "The bottom of the pool is also a dance floor. He put it in for me." She looked at her daughters and spoke sternly. "When the floor's dry, forty minutes of ballet before you do your homework."

The girls blew out exasperated sighs in stereo. "Yes, Mom."

Alina followed the others out the door.

The captain got on the intercom. "This is it, people. We're about to turn toward Orinoco, violating the president's orders. Something will happen." He wet his lips. "Cassie and Remy assure me it will be all right. For now, take your flood control positions." He nodded at the helmsman. "Proceed."

The helmsman heeled the boat to port and pushed the engines to max, then frowned. "I don't think we have enough fuel for this, sir." He tapped the fuel gauge.

Cassie cursed. "I forgot to fix that." She strode to the control panel and delivered a straight punch to the fuel indicator. The dial shattered, and the needle spun a moment. Cassie ripped it out.

The helmsman and the captain stared at her.

She shrugged. "Forgot to tell you. While I was bringing the lights back up, I also installed your new power supply. The diesel engines are disconnected. You won't be needing fuel anymore."

The captain looked nonplussed.

Alina chuckled. "I guess you really *do* have this figured out."

Awe infused the helmsman's voice as he made his next announcement. "We're going almost ten percent faster than max."

The captain shook his head. "Your new power supply, I take it?"

Remy issued a warning. "We'll have to watch the electric motors carefully. They might overheat. Or worse."

Cassie disagreed. "It's just a little uprating. Should be fine." She muttered, "I should wire in a supercharger button in case we need extreme speed at some point. Now, *that* would burn out the motor if left on too long."

The captain offered the next warning. "This is all very well, but the frigate's still faster than us. We can't outrun it."

Remy bubbled. "Of course not, which is why we should start Phase Two any time now."

The captain frowned. "When?"

A stern voice came in on the radio. "Captain Belyaev. Return to course!"

Alina whisked to the control panel and had a brief argument with the captain. He rolled his eyes and showed her how to use the comm. She picked up the mike.

Alina had her own version of a command voice. "Captain, stand down. One of my girls has come down with a severe case of Buruli Cysticercosis. There's a hospital in the Orinoco capital—" she looked at Cassie with a questioning look, urgently mouthing the word, *"Capital?"*

Cassie whispered, "Ciudad Bolivar."

Alina repeated the name for the frigate commander. "They have a hospital that specializes in this rare disease."

Remy's eyes brimmed with laughter. "What exactly is Buruli Cysticercosis?"

Alina glared at her and muffled the mike. "Just a couple of medical words. Sounds good though, right?"

Cassie murmured to Remy, "She already fits right in, doesn't she?"

The frigate captain was no more satisfied than Remy. "Then take the chopper. The ship must continue to the Port of Sucre."

The captain retrieved the mike. "I'm afraid the helo's down. We're working on it."

The frigate commander growled. "I'll send *my* chopper."

Alina grinned, then spoke with sorrow. "There's no place to land, Captain, with the broken helicopter on the helipad."

They could almost hear the faraway commander stomping back and forth. "I'm coming to you." He broke off.

Remy clapped. "A beautiful performance."

Cassie concurred. "That went much better than I expected."

Moments later, the helmsman announced, "Got him on radar. He's closing." He shook his head. "Full power."

Remy stood next to him. "Will he reach us before we enter Orinoco waters?"

The captain studied the plot. "Hard to say."

Cassie shrugged. "Give me the comm. I'll tell Jorge we might want him to get involved prematurely."

The commander of the Russian frigate *Admiral Gorschkov* did *not* stomp back and forth on the bridge. He wanted to, however.

The navigator offered his analysis. "We should reach the *Glory* before they reach Orinoco waters. It'll be close, though."

The commander grunted. "When all is said and done, I really don't care. What's the government of Orinoco going to do, send out a fishing boat to intercept us?"

A call came through in the clear. "Commander of the

Admiral Gorschkov. This is Jorge Cabello, President of Orinoco."

The navigator goggled at the speaker. The commander rolled his eyes. "Just what I needed." He grabbed the mike. "This is the commander."

"Ah, very good. Your boat seems to be charging into our national waters. Please turn around and go someplace else."

The commander did *not* scream into the mike. "We are escorting an important Russian ship."

Jorge sounded unimpressed. "It's just a yacht, Commander."

The commander's voice held barely suppressed violence. "It's not just any yacht. That yacht belongs to—" He cut off abruptly. No one could know the *Glory* belonged to the president of Russia. Every goddamn bounty hunter and navy vessel in the world would descend on them, seeking treasure and prestige. A Greek frigate had been sniffing around his tail for weeks now.

The Orinoco president explained his position. "The yacht has clearance to come to the capital, but I am not going to authorize a military vessel in our waters."

The commander had reached the limits of his patience. "If you try to stop me, I'll rain missiles down on you. Stay out of my way."

Jorge sighed. "I feared this." His voice turned sorrowful. "Don't say I didn't warn you."

A few minutes later, the commander received another warning, this one from his radarman. "That dirigible is heading our way again, sir."

The commander blinked. "I thought it had left."

The radarman shook his head. "I thought so too. It just appeared in the middle of the scope. I think it dropped down and hovered just over the waves. Now it's back."

The commander grabbed a pair of binoculars and aimed them down the airship's bearing, then swore. "Battle stations." Was he about to be attacked by a dirigible dragging an immense Welcome banner?

The dirigible veered to a new course. The commander could see its probable path when the radarman announced, "She's going to pass in front of us."

The commander tensed. "How close?"

"Pretty close. Not close enough to drop a bomb, but close enough to shoot a Harpoon missile." He snickered. "Think they have a Harpoon on board?"

It seemed doubtful. "Just track it for the moment."

"Aye aye, sir."

The minutes ticked by. The commander's vigil was joined by all the sailors without other pressing duties and half the others.

As the dirigible crossed the T, it released the Welcome sign. The banner fluttered into the ocean in front of the *Admiral Gorschkov*. "Bear to starboard," the commander ordered. "Go around that thing."

"That thing" sluggishly came alive and drifted in the direction the commander had ordered the ship to veer. Coincidence or enemy action?

He considered his options. He was not going to turn to

avoid a deadly confrontation with a Welcome banner. He could not depress the main gun far enough to shoot it, and launching a missile seemed like overkill. He could probably swing one of the thirty-millimeter rotary barrel autocannons into position to hammer it.

He gave the order.

A thousand tiny water jets marked the places where the rounds struck the banner. The banner seemed unaffected. It didn't even supply enough resistance to set off the explosive charges in the shells.

The commander was about to order right full rudder when the banner rippled and sank out of sight. He exhaled in relief. "Full speed ahead."

"Aye aye, sir."

A few feet beneath the waves, the four tiny submarine drones, one at each corner of the banner, received instructions from Tina aboard the *Renegade*. The drones swung in unison to drag the Welcome sign beneath the Russian frigate. Inevitably, the banner got caught in the prop wash. The propellers sucked the banner into the blades with such force that the drones were ripped from their moorings. They drifted away after a job well done.

A normal banner would have shredded and swirled away with the rest of the detritus thrown out behind such a ship. This banner, however, had been manufactured using Kevlar. It did not rip.

As strips of Kevlar wrapped tighter around the propellers, the ship's velocity decreased. Meanwhile, the spangles that had spelled out the message started to disintegrate. Oddly, those had been filled with binary epoxy, the components of which remained liquid until they came into contact with one another. When they merged, they hardened on whatever surface they contacted, even when submerged in seawater.

The propellers on a naval craft are precision sculptures embodying the mathematical perfection of fluid dynamics. Only such perfection could produce the thrust necessary for the high speeds of military vessels. Major espionage efforts had gone to stealing propeller designs and propeller manufacturing equipment in the past and would do so in the future to enable a less technically competent nation to achieve a more technically competent nation's propulsive power.

A propeller covered with epoxy barnacles no longer conformed to the mathematical shape of pure power.

As a consequence, even after the commander sent divers down to clear the Kevlar ribbons, the propellers remained severely impaired. The fishing boat the captain had chortled about earlier could have outrun the *Admiral Gorschkov* in its current condition.

The commander invented a number of new blasphemies when the divers told him about it.

18

INVISIBILITY

The Russian satellite surveillance analyst rolled over in his sleep. His phone gave off a harsh ring. Unthinkingly he shut it off.

It rang again and seemed more insistent, though that had to be a trick of his mind. The same ring couldn't become more demanding, could it?

He struggled up. "Yes?"

"Get down here now. All hands on deck. We have a priority search."

The analyst shook himself awake. "What are we looking for?"

His boss whispered into the phone with an intensity that matched the ringing of the phone earlier. "It's the president's yacht. It's been hijacked."

Huh. Just like all the other yachts since the last war. The analyst considered going back to sleep.

His boss knew what he was thinking. "Now!"

The analyst finished his scrutiny of yet another ocean picture empty of ship wakes of the right shape to belong to a megayacht like the *Glory*.

The wake was one aspect of a major ship that could be seen and tracked from space. Once you had identified a likely wake, you could zoom in to inspect the ship, but the satellites could not scan the whole ocean at that level of resolution. You had to start with the wakes.

The analyst complained, "It's not here. Are you sure this is the right area? Do we really have no clue where they're heading?"

His boss wrung his hands. "The frigate commander said the *Glory's* captain claimed he was going to Ciudad Bolivar in Orinoco, but everyone's skeptical. The *Glory's* captain had clearly been compromised by the hijackers."

The analyst bit his lip. "How far could the *Glory* go with the fuel it had?"

The boss lit up. "That's a great question." He hurried off and hurried back. "They were heading to Venezuela for fuel. They can't go far."

The analyst studied the map. "They can probably make the Orinoco capital, but that's about it. All the refueling places they can reach outside Venezuela are on the Orinoco River." He got excited. "Get me images of that river ASAP!"

It took only minutes to find what he sought. "There's a megayacht, possibly the *Glory*, approaching the capital right now." He looked at his boss. "Next time a satellite comes into position, we can zoom and confirm."

The boss shook his head. "No time for fooling around with confirmation. We need to deliver actionable intelligence now." He gulped. "Or heads will roll. Maybe even yours."

The analyst gulped. "Okay, then. Tell them, I guess. The *Glory's* pulling into the Orinoco capital."

The Spetsnaz lieutenant whose career had been destroyed when he lost the *Glory* to a pair of girl pirates grinned. He watched the river come into view from the window of the Halo helicopter transport they'd borrowed from the Venezuelans.

The lieutenant's superior, a captain who had just arrived on the *Admiral Gorschkov* a couple of days before, looked at the lieutenant's hungry grin and smiled. "Fear not. We will take the ship back."

The lieutenant growled, "They caught me off-guard last time. This time, I'm prepared." He muttered, "This time, we'll put those bitches down."

The captain pointed at an enormous yacht tied up at a dock. "That one."

The pilot grunted. "You're sure? We're blatantly violating international law. That better be it."

The lieutenant huffed in exasperation. "Do you see anything else half that size around here? That has to be it." He peered at the vessel as its outline became clearer. "Wait! That's not the *Glory*!"

The captain stared at him. "You're positive?"

The lieutenant's face became a mask of pain. "I'm absolutely certain!"

The captain considered that. "Yet our orders are clear."

He started formulating wild speculations that weren't true but might exonerate him at a trial. "Perhaps they sent us here because the hijackers left the *Glory* and are here now. Perhaps our mission is to get them, not the yacht." He muttered, "It must be something like that."

The pilot interrupted his musings with an urgent question. "So, do we go in or not? Where do you want me to set down?"

The lieutenant knew they were making a mistake, but he understood they had no choice but to make it. He tried to help. "At least we have overwhelming force on our side. We can overpower everyone on the yacht, search for the two women, and get out before anyone gets too upset."

The captain nodded and told the pilot, "Drop us on the dock right next to it."

The chopper screamed a few feet over the water and popped up when it reached the dock. The commandos dropped lines and fast-roped down. Three descended too eagerly and wound up in the water.

The captain heaved a sigh of relief. "Everybody's down, no casualties. Looks like nobody's home on the yacht. Should be easy from here." He led his men toward the helpless ship at a trot.

A barrage of machine gun fire met them, blowing two of the Spetsnaz commandos back into the water. The rest dropped and fired indiscriminately, hoping to hit something or someone or at least make the enemy duck.

Someone bellowed, "Cease fire!" and the invisible shooters on the yacht did.

The captain echoed the order. "Cease fire." He turned a

grim smile on the lieutenant. "Shouldn't waste ammunition when we can't see the enemy. Looks like we'll need it later."

A man wearing a colonel's uniform stepped out, waving empty hands. "You people picked the wrong yacht to try to hijack."

The police cars that screamed into the dock area emphasized his point. The lieutenant also saw two American Stryker armored personnel carriers rolling up. "Sir, I fear we underestimated the enemy."

The captain followed his gaze and pursed his lips. "We are Spetsnaz. We will persevere." He brightened. "Perhaps we can confuse them as much as we are confused."

He rose and shouted, "This ship, the *Glory*, belongs to the president…" He swallowed the rest of the sentence. He'd forgotten again. "This ship belongs to the Russian Federation. Hand us control at once."

Another man came out, this one in a custom-tailored business suit. "You are very confused. This is *my* yacht. It belongs to Freeton McClain Minerals." He straightened his tie defiantly.

The Orinoco colonel took control of the conversation back. "For the moment, I will presume you've made an honest mistake. The *Glory did* request landing privileges here."

Another group of heavily armed men came out, tightly packed around another man in a business suit.

The colonel gasped. "Mr. President, you should not expose yourself like this."

The president chuckled. "Oh, quit worrying. These fellows know they're outgunned." He tapped the colonel's shoulder with his fist. "We faced greater danger when we were street thugs." He glanced around. "And their target is not here." He turned to the Spetsnaz captain. "You can call me Jorge, by the way."

The lieutenant goggled at the leader of Orinoco. He now understood why there was an army of guards here and why the police had responded so quickly. With Strykers.

He and his captain had gotten some very bad intel. The captain tried to recover. "Where is the *Glory?*"

Jorge shrugged. "I honestly have no idea. Remy Tambook called me and asked for permission to enter our waters, and after I granted it, she disappeared. I doubt her ship is even within Orinoco's territorial boundaries anymore."

The colonel tried to match his boss's nonchalant manner. "You should put your weapons down and let us arrest you. Presumably, your government will negotiate for your release. Then you'll be out of here."

A black woman skittered across the deck. "But not until I've gotten some video for our TikTok fans. We generate huge numbers of page views when someone shoots at us." She gave the Spetsnaz officers a beautiful smile. "I'm Odalis, by the way."

The captain stared at her in disbelief.

She pointed her cell phone at him. "Please try to look a little more sinister for the camera. Going live now."

On a military base near Moscow, the analyst who had supplied the intel for the assault studiously watched his screen as his boss stumbled up to him in a panic. "They just hit the docks in Ciudad Bolivar. That yacht wasn't the *Glory*."

The analyst didn't move or cease his intense scrutiny of the current photo. "Huh. Not as surprised as I could be, I guess."

The boss trembled. "What are we going to do?"

The analyst answered with determination, "We're going to keep looking." He tore his eyes from the display and looked up. "We're into long-shot territory now, right?"

Hope filled the boss's face. "Anything."

"Fine." The analyst popped a series of photos onto the screen. "This is a timed sequence of wide ocean shots starting shortly before the *Glory* left the *Admiral Gorschkov*'s radar range."

He pointed at a white wake. "That's the *Glory*." He pointed at another. "Still the *Glory*, heading south." He pointed at a red circle on another photo. "That's where the *Glory* should have been. It couldn't have gotten farther than that."

He zoomed in, and the resolution got worse. Finally, he had a very pixelated image. He marked another area with a red highlight. "I think there's a wake there. Very small, very fuzzy."

The boss snorted. "Everything's fuzzy."

"No kidding." He stepped through a couple more photos, each of which had a red dot. "In each of these, there's a strange bubbling trail that might be a wake in a place where the *Glory* should be."

The boss pursed his lips. "Awfully thin guess."

The analyst nodded. "You have anything better?"

The boss slumped. "What do you want me to do?"

The analyst handed him a sheet of paper. "I want a very high-res series of shots in this area. If those foam crescents belong to the *Glory*, we'll see her."

"You know those kinds of images are not free."

The analyst shrugged. "Desperate times, desperate measures."

The boss went off to order the pictures.

When the photos finally came in, the boss watched over the analyst's shoulder in tense anticipation.

The analyst sighed. "Well, we found that streak I thought could be a wake, but whatever it is, it's not from a ship. There's nothing there but solid blue."

Cassie saw Alina peering at the dirigible hovering directly over the yacht. The gymnast asked, "So, the top of the *Renegade* is solid blue?" The airship floated so low that Alina yielded to the temptation to stand on tiptoe and try to reach it. The distance was much greater than it appeared.

Cassie thought about reaching up to touch it as well. She figured she was fighting a trick of perception with an object so big and so close. "It's mostly blue. Our paint job was imperfect." She shrugged. "But the scattered streaks of white just look like foam on the crests of waves. It's all good."

Alina headed for the fantail. "And you did something to our propellers so we don't have a wake anymore."

Cassie winced. "Not exactly. There's a patent on Ship Wake Signature Suppression from the nineties. Turns out you can greatly reduce the number of microbubbles that form the wake if you hit the prop wash with a one megahertz ultrasonic acoustic blast."

She pointed at a long, thin metal object hanging from the rear of the ship, bouncing in the turbulence. It looked like a huge version of a home theater sound bar. "It takes a lot of energy, but with the wiffle ball, we have energy to spare."

The tension left Alina's muscles, and she sagged in relief. "So, we're invisible as long as we have the *Renegade* overhead."

Cassie nodded. "In a couple of days, we'll be far enough from the popular sea lanes and the usual satellite surveillance areas that we'll be able to send the *Renegade* on her way. We'll be just a dot lost in the vastness of the ocean." She twitched her nose. "But that will be irrelevant to you. You're going to Rivendell."

Alina shook her head. "How will I get there from a dot lost in the ocean?"

Cassie smirked. "By submarine, of course."

Alina's eyes went wide. "Submarine?"

Evgeni stood in the corner of the conference room again, hands folded before him, watching the president at the far end of the table.

The dictator's expression of implacable disdain had not changed, but anger touched his voice. "I want every resource we have tracking down my yacht. And tracking down the people who stole my yacht." As an afterthought, he added, "And finding my mistress and daughters."

He looked at the man in charge of surveillance satellites. "Why haven't you found the ship? They can't be hiding it under the ocean."

The intelligence officer grimaced. "It seems to have disappeared. We think they must have taken it to Orinoco and somehow camouflaged it on the beach."

Evgeni knew that was ridiculous. Half the men in the room knew it was ridiculous, but it demonstrated clever thinking on the officer's part—a fine bit of outside-the-box deception. Evgeni thought that if the president made this man disappear, Gamma might retrieve him and give him a second chance.

The president turned to the nearest admiral. "Send the frigate to Orinoco and cover every inch of that coast. The rivers, too."

Evgeni shook his head. The rivers as well? Did the president think a frigate could float through jungles without getting beached?

The admiral sat stiffly erect. "Yes, sir."

Apparently, the president had caught Evgeni's headshake. He thought Evgeni was a minion, so he glared at the Gamma director. "I want every covert operative working on this matter as well." He scanned the faces of the secret agency leaders in the room. "All of them."

By the time Evgeni had walked to his office he had calmed down somewhat. He found Grisha within, pensively clipping his nails.

Grisha raised an eyebrow. "Wow. Haven't seen you this angry since we lost Andrey."

Evgeni remembered that Grisha, a master assassin, was also a master at reading expressions.

Grisha drew the obvious conclusion. "What does our boss's boss's boss want now?" He said the word "boss" the way other people would say "lackey."

Evgeni sighed. "He's ordered all hands on deck to find his yacht and the people who took her."

Grisha chuckled. "Including us?"

Evgeni rolled his eyes. "It's okay to indulge a president as long as he's only wasting the lives of thousands of young men, but his interference with the projects and the people who make Russia strong has to stop."

Grisha pointed out another avenue of approach. "We're pretty sure we know who stole the yacht. I presume it would be strategically unwise to tell him?"

That penetrated Evgeni's dour mood. "You make jokes at the oddest moments. He wants to take the perpetrators alive so he can personally introduce them to the acid bath by his office on the floor above us."

Grisha sounded uncertain about how to interpret that. "So, that's a no?"

Evgeni rolled his eyes. "More fundamentally, our nominal local boss seems more afraid of the president than he is of us."

Grisha snorted. "Idiot."

"He's insisting we commit all our resources as well."

Grisha laughed. "And a fool. Of course, that was why we chose him." He pulled out a long knife with a double-edged blade of a type Evgeni did not recognize and ran his finger carefully along the edge. "Is it time to replace that fool with another? It's been several years."

From time to time Evgeni and Grisha found it necessary to remove their managers when said managers became confused and drew the erroneous conclusion that Gamma worked for them. "We could help him fall out a window. That seems to be a popular form of accidental death in the upper tiers of Russian society these days."

Evgeni pursued his thoughts out loud. "I think it's time to make a fundamental improvement in our state of affairs. The vacuum effect strikes again."

Grisha looked up from his blade. "'The vacuum effect?'"

Evgeni nodded. "As a dictator strives for total power, he has to demand ever more perfect loyalty from his subordinates. As he squeezes them tighter, it becomes ever riskier for them to tell him something contrary to his current fantasy beliefs. He eventually squeezes all truth out of his surroundings, leaving only a vacuum."

Evgeni sighed. "It's much the same effect we achieve with the Ruby Ragers when we embed them within customized dead internets, and it's a major reason why dictators wear out."

Grisha sat more alertly, knowing Evgeni was developing a plan far more comprehensive and effective than anything he would have developed. "Where's this leading you?"

Evgeni did not answer. Rather, he went to the bookshelves and pulled down a dusty tome called *The History of the Russian Empire, 1721-1917*.

Eventually, Evgeni snapped the book shut. "I think we need to go the next step this time, Grisha."

Grisha gave him a gleaming smile when he realized he was going to get a more interesting assignment.

Evgeni waxed philosophical. "Thomas Jefferson said it best. 'The tree of empire must be refreshed from time to time with the blood of tyrants.'"

Grisha peered at him. "I think your version is somewhat different from the original."

Evgeni waved that away. "Close enough." He spoke like a teacher giving a lecture. "It's common for Russian dictators to die after losing a war. Why not stick with tradition?"

19

BLOOD IN A DESERT

West of the University of Cincinnati, on an undistinguished street of single-family and duplex brick dwellings, very close to the invisible line separating Lower Price Hill from East Price Hill, Dale watched children play in the street. Their mothers watched them like hawks. He muttered to Cassie, "You grew up around here? I hate to say this, but didn't you stick out a bit?" Almost all the faces in the neighborhood were black.

Cassie stood next to him, smiling and occasionally kicking a basketball back to players who had lost control. "I learned a lot of good life lessons here." She picked up the latest escapee basketball and threw it at the distant hoop but missed. "I didn't learn much in school, however. Then I had to leave."

Dale dragged her back to the present. "So, now you're going to repay them for those life lessons. We're doing an incredible public service." He did not mention they were also getting paid for it. They were undertaking a small experiment in the new corporate direction Dale wanted Dread Nought to take.

Jake spoke from his perch on the top of one of the nearby buildings. Even Dale had no idea which one. "Here comes Contingent One. From the north."

Dale casually looked up the street. The newcomers were wearing their signature Cincinnati Reds caps—a popular piece of apparel among members of the Bloods. The bright red color around the C was an insult to the Crips, even if no Crips lived around here to appreciate it.

Cassie's leather jacket wrinkled as she clenched the collapsed baton within it.

Dale sympathized with her desire to pull out a weapon. He murmured, "Trust Jake and our other people." His eyes flicked to a black Dread Nought agent trimming a hedge close by.

Cassie ground out, "I understand." She looked at the rooftops and spoke for Jake's benefit. "Forgive me for not wanting to depend entirely on others for my safety."

Jake chuckled. "No worries. Contingent Two coming from the south."

Dale looked around. A gang who wore no identifying coloration approached. He tried to remember its name and failed. Pretty low-key as gangs went.

The mothers gathered their offspring and withdrew into their houses.

Cassie eyed the local gang as well. "I get that we're doing an incredible public service, yet I'm having trouble getting excited. All this trouble just for a grocery store?"

The mission had been born in a brainstorming session with one of Buddy Warwick's reinsurance VPs. He had talked to a friend, who'd talked to a friend, who'd collected some friends and enemies and called Augustus.

Since Dale had been in on the project from the beginning, he had not been surprised when Augustus called him with a new kind of gig. The Dread Nought CEO sounded elated. "I just got a call from a consortium of grocery store chains. They want us to help expand their market."

Dale acted astounded. "Grocery stores want us? For what?"

Augustus chuckled. "Come in and let them explain it to you." He turned serious. "Bring Remy or Cassie, whichever you can get your hands on." He turned angry. "I agreed to this crazy deal using the Memwriter 'only for good deeds' in the expectation that we'd get some good value in trade." He groaned. "You have no idea how complicated this re-org has made my life, creating this Boy Scout subdivision in Extreme Risk."

Indeed, Dale had no clue. "What's difficult about it? It looks fine from here."

Augustus sounded exasperated. "Of course it looks fine from your viewpoint. It all revolves around you, doesn't it? I'm the one who had to matrix-manage your Puritans, mixing and matching them with the rest of the team for specific projects, only to have your people question my ethics."

Dale chuckled. "You do walk the slippery slope of morality, Augustus. Who knows? Having us question you occasionally might make you a better person."

Augustus grunted. "So says the original Boy Scout." He

cleared his throat. "Anyway, I want this grocery store deal to be a joint operation. Let's see how much value their intel sources can bring to the party."

Dale acted surprised again. "What intel do the grocery stores need?"

"Org charts for the drug gangs."

Dale listened politely to the man in charge of the grocery consortium, nudging Cassie periodically to keep her eyes from glazing over.

Augustus Luther glared at her for her inattention, and Cassie muttered, "Sorry. Big storm in the Atlantic. The helicopter ride was a bitch."

The man in charge of the grocery consortium stood in front of the conference table, talking about his slides. "So you see, it's a simple math problem. In these areas…" he highlighted one of the jagged outlines of a chunk of Chicago, "the theft rate chews up about three percent of the revenues. Typical grocery store profits are only about two percent of revenues." He continued with an attempt at dry wit. "We tried making it up in volume, but we just lost money faster."

One of his minions chimed in. "These so-called food deserts are a serious problem. We're leaving a fortune on the table because we can't build grocery stores in these areas."

Dale pressed his hands to his temples. "Why don't people just drive to a grocery store farther away?"

Cassie explained. "Lots of people in these places don't

have cars, and the public transport sucks." She glared at the grocery boss. "Right?"

The slide presenter nodded. "It's almost as big a problem for them as it is for us. People in these areas have staggering rates of diabetes and other health problems."

Cassie kept most of her anger out of her voice. "You might even say it's a bigger problem for them than for you."

The presenter gawked, not understanding any difficulty as great as lost profits, but he wasn't interested in quibbling. "Good point."

Augustus smoothed the waters. "It's a win-win no matter how you cut it if we can bring the grocery stores back."

The minion brought them back to the main point. "So, the question is, how can you help us? We've been thinking that a radically more aggressive approach to basic rule enforcement might make the difference."

The presenter pointed his finger at his colleague. "What he said. We understand you folks have experience with direct interventions." He leaned forward. "Can you help?"

Augustus pointed at Dale. "What do you think?"

Dale leaned forward to make his pitch. "I think there's a chance we can make this work. Understand, Dread Nought is too expensive to supply you with ongoing enforcement within your budget. We've had internal discussion about ideas to leverage the existing force structure in these communities." He explained the current idea.

The consortium leader looked both doubtful and hopeful. "It's worth a try."

The minion suggested the next step. "We'd like to try it with the deserts in Chicago. Lots of potential there."

Cassie frowned. "Those aren't just food deserts, though. Those are death traps. Shouldn't we try this someplace a little more...I don't know, nonlethal? Amenable to upgrade?" She tapped on her phone.

Augustus frowned at her and whispered loud enough for everyone to hear, "It's our client's request."

Dale was torn. He had been indoctrinated in the corporate mantra, "The client might not always be right, but the client is always the client." He chose a middle course between siding with Augustus and siding with his partner. "Cassie, you have a suggestion?"

Cassie was lost in an analysis of whatever was on her phone.

After waiting until he could feel his pulse throbbing in his head, Dale coughed. "Cassie?"

Cassie looked up and smiled. "I think I do. How about Cincinnati?"

The presenter looked at her with intrigue. "Cincinnati?"

Cassie slid to the edge of her chair. "Absolutely. First of all, it's a big opportunity, just like Chicago. Forty percent of the people in Cincinnati live in food deserts."

The minion nodded vigorously. "Sounds good."

Cassie continued. "I've been looking at the Price Hill area. I presume the reason it's a food desert is that the crime rate is about fifty percent higher than normal for the city."

The presenter gave her a wry smile. "That would do it."

Cassie raised one hand dramatically. "*But*. It's all property crime, not violent crime." She shrugged. "From the perspective of a grocery store, it might be almost as bad, but from an overall perspective, it's lower risk."

The minion looked thoughtful. "Might help with the insurance premiums since we won't have as much exposure to employee lawsuits from being mugged near the store."

Augustus gave her a piercing stare, then nodded in approval.

Dale sighed in relief.

Cassie added one last item. "In addition, I have personal contacts there, so we already have a leg up on the intel."

Cassie watched the leader of the Bloods swaggered up. Cassie's fingers itched to grasp her katana, which was impossible because Dale had made her leave her sword at the motel.

Dale glanced at her. "Remember, you have backup."

The Blood leader eyed her, then turned to Dale. "Yo. You say you have money for me?"

Dale looked bored. "I said I have a job. You get to make a bid for the work."

The leader of the local gang, a bunch of kids who had given their group a name Cassie had already forgotten, stepped into the conversation. "So, what's the job?"

Cassie suppressed a grin as she listened to Dale try to explain without numbers. "My employer wants to build a grocery store here, but thieves steal more than he can afford. We need lookouts to encourage people to pay for what they take."

The local leader watched the Blood leader carefully as he clarified the offer. "What's in it for us?"

Boy Scout that he was, Dale led with his best offer. "You'd earn half a percent of the store revenues."

The local fellow countered, "One percent."

The Blood boss snorted. "Talk all you want. Go ahead, build the store. It's one hundred percent mine."

Cassie glared at him. "You guys don't know when you're looking at a good deal, do you? You're like the Ebola virus, killing your host before you can spread."

The Blood stepped into her private space. He didn't know *how* he'd been insulted, but he knew he had. "Another word from you, bitch, and I own you as well." He glanced at Dale. "No matter what the white wimp says."

Dale squeezed the bridge of his nose. "Cassie, you made your point." He turned to the Blood leader. "I tried to be polite, but I'm over it. You're done here. Leave the neighborhood by morning or die."

The local leader stared at him. The Blood leader laughed in his face. "Guess you're mine too." He pulled out a gun.

A rifle cracked, and the Blood leader's head exploded.

The local gang's members backed away, pulling out knives and waving baseball bats.

Half a dozen Bloods pulled out firearms.

The Dread Nought agent by the hedge no longer held trimmers. He raised an Uzi and started firing three-round bursts.

Between Jake on the rooftops and the agent on the grass, the armed Bloods dropped before they could figure out who to shoot.

The Bloods who had either come unarmed or had

moved too slowly to gear up ran back the way they had come.

The locals stared around, wide-eyed. Their leader muttered unhappily, "They'll be back."

Cassie grinned at him. "No, they won't. We have really good intel." Courtesy of the NSA, they had every cell phone call by every person in the city recorded and stored in the Utah Data Center. Cassie and Andrey had drawn up full org charts for every gang in the city and developed résumés for every member of every gang. "Each of the survivors is about to receive a FedEx package. It will contain a grenade—disarmed, of course—and a note telling them to apologize to you and ask for the opportunity to join your team."

Dale nodded. "When they join your team, they join our team. Is that good with you?"

The leader looked at the Dread Nought agent, who was still hefting his submachine gun. He nodded slowly.

Dale finished the negotiation. "Like I said, half a percent of revenue." He gave the young man a stern look. "Do a good job and reap the rewards. Do poorly and," he nodded at the corpses on the ground, "we get a new partner."

They swiftly agreed on the terms.

After Cassie gave the gang leader a homie handshake, the gang left. Before the police arrived, Cassie commented to Dale, "The Bloods really *are* like Ebola."

Dale raised an eyebrow. "Too violent? They seem to do okay."

Cassie shook her head. "Not in Cincinnati, they don't. They've tried to establish a presence here before." She gave him a smug smile. "The cops always shut them down hard."

She snickered. "This time, the cops don't have to do anything but clean up."

Dale looked at her thoughtfully. "I see." His eyes brightened. "I told you we'd do something really good here. We should celebrate. Come with me to dinner?"

Cassie jerked to a halt. Dinner with Dale? Why not? "I know a place across the river that's really expensive. You're buying."

Dale laughed and thrust an elbow out.

Cassie wrapped a hand around his upper arm. "It'll have to be a quick dinner. I have to get back to the ship. The Russian crewmen and the EStormers are still sorting themselves out."

Dale nodded. "Where is the ship, anyway?"

Cassie shot him a sidelong glance. "Wouldn't you like to know?"

20

FOR THE CHILDREN

Grisha stood by the jungle road with Max and a couple of the survivors from the Rivendell assault. Everyone looked grim.

Big diesel engines rumbled down the snaking road from the north. Max gave orders, and the Ragers dragged several concrete barriers into the highway. Grisha stepped out into the middle of the road to face the oncoming convoy and raised his hands.

Max hissed, "We could take over the enemy trucks and roll through the gates undetected."

Grisha smiled at him. "We *could*, but this time, Max, we need their help voluntarily. Our homeland is facing a terrible crisis, the kind of danger that comes from within. We must purge Russia of weakness at the top to make her strong again before we can expand the imperium as the Ruby foretold."

Max nodded, then waved the troops into the edges of the jungle. "If anything goes wrong—"

Grisha finished, "I'll give the signal, and we'll do it your way."

Max disappeared moments before the first truck came into view.

Grisha waved his hands, and the truck slammed to a halt. A shout arose, and Orinoco troops jumped out of the half-dozen vehicles in the convoy.

Grisha yelled, "Could you give me a ride, please?"

Grisha sat up front in the first truck, squished between the driver and the captain in charge of the convoy. Grisha wiggled his hands, which caused the chains between his handcuffs to clink. "Lot of troops if you're just delivering basic supplies. I'd guess you're bringing weapons of some sort." He raised his eyebrow. "More Stinger missiles, perhaps?"

The captain glared at him and poked his combat knife deeper into Grisha's side. "Classified."

Grisha nodded. "Of course." He twisted to avoid having the knife dig deeper. He felt perfectly confident that if needed, he could take out this captain and hijack the truck, but he'd get hurt in the process, and it would defeat his purpose. That was the last resort.

The radio crackled, and a voice he recognized spoke. Cassie sounded astonished. "Captain, you're telling me a man who calls himself Grisha Chernyshevsky voluntarily surrendered to you?"

The captain answered. "Yes, ma'am. I've got him right here."

Cassie sighed. "Put him on."

Grisha leaned toward the mike. "Cassie. So good to hear your voice again."

"I should have the captain shoot you where you sit."

Grisha shook his head. "Tsk. I'm here to be useful to you. We have a mutual enemy."

Grisha enjoyed the resulting silence. Alliances in the world of covert ops changed every day, sometimes every minute. Cassie and Remy had forged teams with agents from AID and Dread Nought before. Why not Gamma too?

Cassie blew out a sound of disgust. "Very well. I'll tell them to let you in."

Grisha had a parting request, "Bring Alina too, please. She'll want in on this."

Grisha hopped down from the truck. "Thank you for the ride."

The driver frowned at him and put the truck in first gear.

As Grisha passed the Rivendell sign on the sward, he saw a pale man with thinning hair laboring to replace a pane in the front wall of the damaged main living quarters. Grisha stopped in his tracks. The meeting with Cassie and hopefully Alina was his priority, but he had to take a minute to investigate this mystery. He had to know.

So he strolled over to the pale man. "Michael. How have you been?"

Michael turned from his caulking efforts. "Sir." He

stared into the distance for a moment. "How fascinating to see you here. I never would have expected it."

Grisha smiled. "The world contains more twists and turns than anyone can predict."

Michael looked into his eyes, but his gaze lacked the reverence he had once shown. "So I have learned. I suspect I understand that truth far better than you. Nothing is as simple as it seems, no matter how much our yearning for illusory pattern recognition demands simplicity."

Uh-oh. That did not sound like the man he'd known before. Somehow, Michael had shrugged off the quasi-religious thrall Grisha saw in all the Ruby Ragers.

How did this very different person feel about him? Grisha took a step back.

Michael watched him shift to defend himself and covered a smile with his hand. "Don't fear me unless you intend me harm." Hope entered his eyes, quickly replaced by mirth. "I surely know the answer to this question, but I have to ask. Are you here for the Awakening?"

Grisha gawked at him. "The Awakening" was an EStorme catchphrase that referred to the time when everyone would see the Estormers' beliefs for what they were—the truth.

Had the EStorme cult psyop systems been so much stronger than the Ruby indoctrination that they had hijacked Michael's mind? That didn't seem possible. If the EStorme engineering was that good, they would be fielding sturmers and meat bombs of their own in larger numbers.

And where had the reference to illusory pattern recognition come from? Grisha tried to clear his head by shaking it. "Not the Great Awakening. That's just an EStorme fairytale."

Michael chuckled. "I agree. I'm referring to the *real* Awakening."

Grisha felt alarm. "What happened to you?"

Michael put his caulking gun on the window ledge. "As you know, when I joined the Ruby, I was susceptible to religious cult conversions. That was why your psyops engineers were able to transform me into a Rager."

Grisha had a sinking feeling. "It was the clarity of your thinking that brought you to us, not some cult vulnerability. We showed you how all the pieces of the world fit together." As he said it, he understood how Michael's comment on illusory patterns fit in. The Rager belief system was completely woven from such falsely connected dots.

Michael chuckled. "Oh, please. Don't embarrass yourself by pretending you believe that stuff." He looked into the distance. "Anyway, Cassie and Remy trained me with the critical thinking skills to see my vulnerability. Before them, I didn't have the tools to cope with the bandwagon effect, false induction, sampling bias... The whole panoply of assaults on the thinking mind."

He glanced at Grisha. "I'm still prone to religious conversion." He snorted. "I still call it an Awakening, after all. But really, it's just an enhancement in the coherence of my analysis of..." His voice faded.

Grisha brought him back to the conversation with a sharp question. "Analysis of what?"

Michael looked surprised. "Everything." He stepped forward and, in a friendly way, grabbed the assassin by the arm. "Even you." He stepped back after releasing the arm. "Who knows? Even you might someday be Awakened."

He turned back to the window he had been fixing. "I'm not holding my breath, however." He hummed as he went back to work.

A stern though melodious voice yelled across the yard, "Grisha! *Yoohoo!*" Fenya, the hooker from the Nuclear Sanctum, gave him a peremptory wave. "Over here."

Grisha followed her with considerable bemusement. "You're working for Cassie and Remy now?"

Fenya's hair shimmered as she shook her head. "Sort of. They're more or less customers." She pointed him to a chair in the living room, whose exterior wall had been blown out by Grisha's Ragers.

So, Cassie and Remy were customers of Morte Noir. Good to know. Very important news.

This trip had already paid off twice over, and he hadn't even gotten to the good part. He did find himself wondering how much Morte Noir had overcharged him for the information on where he could find Alina. It seemed likely that Morte Noir hadn't had to look for her at all. Alina had fallen into her lap.

That forced him to wonder why she'd shared the info with him. Wasn't Alina's location part of another customer's secrets, or had Morte Noir discussed it with Cassie and Remy and Alina, and they'd made a group decision to let him in? If so, how much of today's festivities were pre-scripted performances?

His chair faced a giant monitor on the intact inner wall. As he made to sit down, he put a hand on the back of the chair.

A red dot appeared on his wrist. Adrenaline coursed through his veins.

He turned to face the outdoors, and additional laser dots appeared on his chest. He turned back and rolled his shoulders as if he were trying to remove an itch and sank into the chair.

Fenya sat close enough so he could smell her perfume.

Grisha gave her the rabid wolf smile that denoted amusement. "I get it, but you don't have to engage in performance art for my entertainment."

Fenya laughed gaily, giving him yet another dose of entertainment. "Of course it's art. If I need you dead, I'll do it myself."

Grisha watched her thoughtfully, then smiled. "It would be my delight to see you try." They stared at one another, eyes full of love—the love of combat.

Time for business. Grisha looked around in puzzlement. "Where's Cassie? She talked to me at the gate."

Fenya relaxed in her chair. "We hooked her up remotely. She's on the yacht she just stole from you. Probably. She delegated you to me." She leaned forward with wicked glee. "She told me to do whatever I thought was appropriate with you."

Well, he didn't really need Cassie. "Alina?"

Fenya sat back again. "I told Alina about your request, but she declined."

Grisha grunted. "I suppose I wouldn't be thrilled if a Russian assassin sought me out either if I were she."

Fenya confessed to herself that she was enjoying this engagement. "Glad you can see Alina's point of view." She waved at Brett, who was standing in a corner and watching attentively. Brett had arrived in Rivendell the same day she had, though his journey had been even stranger from Fenya's point of view. The EStormers had dug an artificial lake in the middle of the barren triangle of land wiped out by the hypersonic missile. He'd dropped the airship on the edge so that on a low-res, wide-scan satellite image, it looked like part of the water.

Brett crossed the room to Fenya, bearing a tray with tea things and pastries.

As he offered a cup to Grisha, the two men eyed each other like bears establishing dominance.

Fenya shook her head. Testosterone. If she needed Grisha taken out, maybe she should let Brett have a go. It would be a good graduation exercise for his martial arts memwriting.

Fenya accepted a cup as Grisha continued his entreaty. "It's really Alina I came here to talk to."

Fenya scowled. "About what?"

"About the president's plan to kill her."

Fenya shook herself. She had expected the president to put a hit on his lover, as had Alina. However, they had expected Grisha to fill a considerably different role. "Aren't you in charge of the assassination team? I thought your visit would be a ruse to take her out." As she said it, she realized it could be a ruse to take *her* out.

Grisha laughed mockingly. "Let me remind you how

Gamma works. The president hardly knows we exist. Executions such as the one planned for Alina are carried out by the FSB." He shrugged. "They are loyal to the president." A note of pride entered his voice. "*We* are loyal to Russia."

Fenya pursed her lips. "Where does that difference in loyalty lead you?"

Grisha pointed a finger at her. "Exactly the right question." He leaned forward and spoke softly, as if someone in Moscow might hear his words despite the intervening ocean. "Gamma has decided we need to upgrade the caliber of person fulfilling the duties of the presidential office."

Fenya got a warm glow at the thought. She had considered undertaking that project on her own more than once, but her Mistress had a stern prohibition against pro bono public services. "So, you're going to assassinate our president." Funny that she still thought of Russia as her country despite everything.

Grisha shrugged. "We are going to clear a path for the early succession of a superior candidate."

Enlightenment came. "And you want Alina's help to clear that path."

Grisha sipped his tea. "The president spends all his time these days in his private part of the bunker below the Kremlin. Really, his paranoia has become tiresome."

Fenya could see that it would be annoying to an assassin to have a target who acted on the paranoid belief that he was in danger all the time.

Grisha finished, "Alina should be able to lure him out. She could make the difference between success and failure."

Fenya sighed. That sounded legitimate. She threw her head back and talked to the ceiling. "Did you hear all that? I guess I believe him. Alina, you want to join us?"

Cassie sat on the deck of the yacht, basking in the sun. She cradled her tablet in her lap and sipped a cup of tea as she watched and listened to the meeting with Grisha. This was really the *only* way to attend meetings, she decided. With no one even knowing she was there unless she was needed.

Alina glided into the living room in Rivendell with her gymnast's grace on full display. She wore black leggings and an exercise bra. Her eyes held fury, and her scarlet hair seemed to hold flecks of fire as it moved in the breeze that entered through the front wall. She burst out, "Why should I help you? Here in Rivendell, I and my daughters are safe for the first time."

She threw him a sarcastic follow-up. "You yourself have demonstrated how safe Rivendell is. I've seen the video of your soldiers burning like candles."

Fenya laughed. "Enough. We are all Russians here. No need for confrontation. We can lie and pretend for each other and still hear the truth, as only Russians can do."

Cassie had to chuckle at that one. She concluded Fenya had said it just for her.

Grisha answered Alina patiently. "You know even Rivendell is not completely safe. Consider the missile." He paused to let her reflect on that.

Alina started to say something, but Fenya shook her head.

Grisha continued. "And neither you nor your children can leave here as long as our president is alive." He leaned forward to emphasize the point. "Think of your children if not yourself."

Alina seemed paralyzed. She spoke in a meek whisper. "Why do you need me?"

Grisha explained his plan. "It's the only surefire way of carrying out the strike."

Alina slumped. "So I'll be alone with him and with his goons." She pointed at Grisha. "And I'll be wholly dependent on you to save me."

Grisha grimaced. "My people are superbly trained, and they'll move in at lightning speed. Your risk will be as minimal as we can humanly make it."

Alina pursed her lips.

It looked like the deal might go sour. Cassie realized she wanted it to succeed, so she punched the button to bring her image up on the display in the living room. "Actually, Alina, I can fix this."

Alina's mouth worked, but nothing coherent came out.

Grisha smiled. "Cassie! I was wondering if you'd put in an appearance."

Fenya sighed. "It was fun while it lasted."

Grisha returned to the point. "You have a solution to make Alina safer?"

Cassie nodded. "I can fit her out with an army."

Grisha shook his head. "The president will not show if she brings a combat team. Not even for her."

Cassie chuckled. "Oh, he'll show. He won't know about the army."

Grisha and Alina looked at her like she was crazy.

Fenya looked at her with dawning understanding and approval.

She explained, "Alina will have a one-woman army." She smiled warmly at the gymnast. "Fear not. The president will never know what hit him."

21

LASER FOCUS

Late afternoon sent long shadows streaking across San Diego Harbor. Morte Noir brushed the single star on the sleeve stripe of her uniform that denoted her rank as a rear admiral (lower half).

Rudy Ross shoved his hand through his hair. "I'm both excited and scared. I've never been a secret agent before."

Morte Noir grabbed his arm and stopped him. She leaned in and whispered fiercely, "You never will be again if you say one more word like that here. You're a project director for Kratos. Understand?"

Rudy gulped. "I get it, Mistress."

Morte Noir went nose to nose with him. "Who am I?"

Rudy's eyes flew wide. "Admiral Sinclair."

The Dark Mistress straightened his tie, not that it needed it, and patted his chest. "You look every bit the high-power executive. Next time, we'll make you a VP, Dr. Peabody."

Rudy closed his eyes for a moment to get into character. "It's a promotion I've been planning for, Admiral."

They turned and marched to the gangplank of the *Portland*. The petty officer of the watch saluted. "Admiral Sinclair. We expected you earlier."

Andrey had broken into the Navy's comm systems and set up the appointment for earlier, knowing that if he specified a time too late in the day, the *Portland's* captain would want to negotiate another time. Morte Noir wanted to arrive as late as possible, so she carried the ruse forward. "Our planning meeting ran late, which threw off our entire schedule."

They boarded the ship, and the admiral brushed off the officer of the deck's attempt to assign them a guide or introduce them to the captain.

Dr. Peabody spoke testily. "We're already late, and I need to see the LaWS while we still have some daylight. I'm going to be inspecting it well into the night as it is."

The officer looked at him with imperfectly masked disbelief. "You plan to inspect it? I thought you were a project manager."

The admiral chuckled. "He's a man of many talents."

Dr. Peabody raised an eyebrow. "I used to be an engineer. Still am." He paused. "I need to examine the spectral beam's combined fiber lasers for signs of wear. All six of them. We've had reports of problems from other users."

Morte Noir added, "We've also been in contact with one of your engineers, an ensign I expect to meet us later."

The officer admonished, "Just remember, we leave port at daybreak."

The admiral assured him, "We won't interfere with your schedule."

As they climbed the stairs, Morte Noir sarcastically

muttered, "Signs of wear on the lasers? The solid-state lasers?"

Rudy chuckled. "Hey, it worked, didn't it?"

They reached their destination. Rudy first ran a hand around the optical sensor of the LaWS. The SEQ-3 Laser Weapon System was a one-of-a-kind prototype anti-drone weapon that had worked well enough that the Navy had decided to deploy it on the *Portland* after they completed their testing.

Rudy spoke reverently. "This is the telescope used for target tracking. They say having this on board is like having a Hubble Telescope at sea."

Morte Noir grunted in acknowledgment. She had to be patient with geeks.

Next, Rudy ran his hand down the main laser tube. "Okay, baby. We're going to move you to a place where you can do a much bigger job, and we'll be giving you a huge upgrade to do it."

Morte Noir thought he might kiss the laser, but he refrained. She sighed. "I still don't see why you needed *this* one of all the laser weapons under development today."

Rudy bent over to examine the swivel mount. "Because this one uses commercial welding lasers to generate the beam. I figured it would be easier to scale up if we started with a system that was already integrated with off-the-shelf gear."

He stood back up. "Which reminds me, I also ordered the lasers." He winced. "A hundred of them."

Morte Noir goggled at him and choked out, "How much?"

"Forty mil." Rudy smiled sheepishly. "I got a good deal for buying in bulk."

Morte Noir glowered at him, but the fading twilight reduced the impact.

Rudy soothed her. "Andrey said it was no problem."

Morte Noir relaxed. Of course, Rivendell could afford this at least as easily as she could. Someday, she'd have to talk with Remy or Cassie about cost-sharing for their joint fortress.

Someday, she also still had to talk with them about *making* it a joint fortress. She didn't like thinking of herself as a mere renter.

In the glimmer of the lights of the harbor, Rudy pointed toward the stern of the ship. "Shall we go get the girl?"

The *Portland* was an amphibious transport dock, a ship that carried troops, tanks, and landing craft. Like many of the modern ships in the fleet, the vessel sported no deck on the sides. From the top deck to the waterline, the ship was a seamless wall of metal, only a slight cant making it less than a vertical precipice.

One of the features Morte Noir most prized was the floodable well deck in the back beneath the helipad. This formed the ship's equivalent of a beach, into which you could motor with your landing craft and step onto a dry platform.

Morte Noir had expected to have to pull rank on someone to open the outer door to the well deck, but for whatever reason, they had left it open this evening.

As she and Rudy watched, the dim outline of a small black dome popped out of the water. Rudy smiled.

The neoprene hood rose, followed by the rest of the person. Esin waved at them. She opened her mouth to say hi but remembered in time that they were covert. She climbed onto the dock, dragging an enormous bag, and whispered, "I made it."

She rifled through the bag and pulled out an ensign's uniform. As she stripped, Morte Noir asked the question that had worried her. "Any trouble with detection? Any reason to think the sonar pinged you?"

Esin, now nude, shook her head. "I swam along the bottom as you told me to and came up directly beneath the ship." She grabbed her hair and wrung it out.

Rudy studiously stared out the back of the ship the entire time.

A few moments later, Esin looked the part of a sailor. "Where's our laser?" She struggled to lift the bag she'd brought.

Rudy reached out. "Let me carry that."

Esin looked reluctant, but Morte Noir nodded. "Always let the big men carry the heavy stuff. It's easier than arguing with them."

Esin giggled.

They returned to the LaWS, and Esin pulled out a set of floodlights and arranged them to light the mount that held the laser.

Rudy scrounged through the bag. "Try this."

Esin put her back into it, but in the end, she failed to loosen the bolts.

Morte Noir coughed. "I think we need a big man's help

again."

Rudy smiled. "See? I knew you brought me along for a reason."

Morte Noir was the next person to root through Esin's bag of goodies. "Here's the balloon." The "balloon" was a tough rubbery skin they could pull over a large object, then seal and inflate it. She pulled it from the bag and shook it out.

Once they had the LaWS disconnected from the ship, sitting precariously on the mount and vulnerable to passing waves, they wrapped the balloon over and under it. Esin started to fill it with air.

Morte Noir cautioned, "Not too much."

Esin nodded. "We want it to sink slowly, not float."

Rudy rubbed his hands together. "Okay, we've got Part One as ready as we can get it for now. On to the sea-wiz." The sea-wiz, otherwise known as the MK15 Phalanx CIWS or Phalanx Close-In Weapon System, was the gatling gun used to try to shoot down incoming missiles when all else failed.

Morte Noir blinked. "What do we need to do with the sea-wiz?"

Esin explained. "The LaWS uses the CIWS for target acquisition."

Morte Noir pointed at the LaWS. "I thought it had its own targeting system."

Rudy shook his head. "It has target tracking it uses to point the laser and fire, but to find the target, it needs a wide-sweep target acquisition radar."

Esin was heading for the ladder. "We should hurry."

The CIWS was larger than the LaWS. The white cylinder's domed top gleamed in the harbor lights. Morte Noir could barely see the forbidding black barrel of the gun as a shadow against the backdrop. "We're never going to get that into a balloon. It's too large."

Rudy pointed at Esin. "That's one of the reasons we have her."

Esin's proud smile supplied more light than the harbor illumination. "I'm tiny. I can fit inside the radar dome."

She scrambled up the metal handholds on the side of the radar cover and scrutinized the screws holding the top in place. "Pass me the hex wrenches, please."

They organized a system. Esin would request a tool, Morte Noir would find it, and Rudy would pass it up.

Esin lifted the cover very carefully and slid it a little way. She scooted over the lip and down into the cylinder. Her voice came out muffled. "It's a little tight in here. And dark."

Morte Noir called her on her cell phone. When Esin answered, she explained, "Use the light on your phone." She looked at Rudy. "She hasn't fully assimilated Western tech yet."

Rudy laughed, then winced. "I've been memwriting her with advanced integrated circuit design, and she doesn't know she has a flashlight."

Morte Noir explained, "She grew up in a very isolated community." She skipped the part where Esin had almost been stoned to death by her village. "Everything she knows about tech, she's learned very recently."

Esin interrupted, "I'm looking at the base of the radar,

and I don't know what we need and don't need." She sounded frustrated. "I don't think Rudy can help me."

Morte Noir explained how to deal with it. "We'll set you up on Zoom. You'll point your camera at different things, and I'll show them to Rudy on my cell."

"That should work."

Rudy gave Esin a running description of what she was seeing, and Esin responded with a—usually correct—assessment of whether they needed it.

Morte Noir stood by, controlling a desire to tap her foot. This was taking too long.

On the bright side, it was clear that Esin had soaked up a tremendous amount of engineering knowledge. Morte Noir wondered what it would be like to learn so much so quickly. She'd really like to try the Memwriter. Should she push harder for them to make an exception for her in the deal with Remy and Laurie?

Esin reached a conclusion. "This is where we have to separate the key part of the radar from the rest of it."

Rudy nodded. "Exactly."

"I can't just disconnect it. Cassie was right." She exclaimed, "I get to use the thermite!"

Esin chimney-climbed up the radar housing to the top, on which the dome still perched precariously. "We'll have to move this to get the radar out." She started moving it to the side very slowly.

Rudy called, "Wait." He walked around the cylinder to get into position to catch it.

Too late. The dome teetered, fell off, and hit the deck with a loud clang. The dome acted like a bell and sent the sound of the disaster reverberating across the ship.

Morte Noir yelled at her frozen teammates, "*Hurry!*"

While Esin and Rudy hauled the radar out and wrapped it in a balloon, Morte Noir assumed her most commanding military posture and headed for the steps.

The officer of the deck met her, backed by two men. He saluted. "Ma'am. What's happened?"

Morte Noir spoke with stiff arrogance. "A minor mishap. Nothing to worry about."

One of the men gasped and pointed. "They're stealing the radar!"

The OOD looked past the admiral and frowned. "Ma'am. You'll need to stay here while I get the captain."

Morte Noir sighed. "I understand." She moved close enough that the officer's body blocked his men from seeing her strike him in the throat with a taser.

As he fell, she held him up. "Help me," she ordered the two sailors.

When one reached out to take the OOD, Morte Noir tased him as well. The last man backed out of taser range.

Morte Noir dropped the officer, hopped lightly over the body, and kicked the survivor in the head. He fell next to his companions.

She hurried back. Rudy and Esin had finished packaging the radar. Esin looked concerned. "I don't think we have time to take this back to the well dock."

Morte Noir chuckled. "I never expected that to work. Esin, get back into your scuba gear."

Rudy looked puzzled. "If the well dock's not the plan,

what is?"

Morte Noir pointed over the edge of the deck at the smooth, canted hull. "We'll roll the radar over the edge."

Rudy goggled at her, then ran to get the balloon. A series of muffled clangs accompanied his labors as he heaved it one step at a time to the edge of the deck. Fortunately, he did not have far to go.

Esin came back suited up and helped push the balloon the last step. It rolled down the side of the ship, bumping and bouncing.

Morte Noir pointed at Esin, then at the ship's side. "You're next. Grab the balloon and head out."

Esin slipped over the side without hesitation. She bounced and bumped less than the balloon. Morte Noir thought she heard Esin say, "Whee," but her voice was too muffled by the regulator to be sure.

The Mistress turned to Rudy. "Back to the LaWS."

The LaWS balloon was ready to roll, but Rudy was not. He stood on the edge of the deck and swayed unhappily. "I knew we'd escape using scuba gear, but I didn't expect to jump off a cliff first."

Morte Noir explained with failing patience, "It's not a cliff. It's just a steep slope. You've been to Disneyland, right?"

Rudy peered at her. "Yes?"

"Since they closed Splash Mountain, think of this as the next-generation ride." She grunted as she gave the balloon a last heave. It slid, rolled, and bounced down.

Rudy observed. "Can't we just go back to the well dock and—"

Morte Noir grabbed him around the waist and pulled him over.

Down they went. The Mistress confessed to herself, *Okay, more a cliff than a slope.*

The occasional clang of the oxygen tanks on the hull ended as they hit the water and plunged into darkness.

Morte Noir unhooked her lamp and looked around. She could see Esin's lamp farther away from the dock as she presumably dragged the almost-floating radar balloon behind her.

Rudy's light landed on their balloon. She helped him rope it, and they dragged the LaWS until they caught up with Esin.

They continued to make agonizingly slow progress along the harbor bottom, moving north past the Navy docks, then north past the USS *Midway* Museum, then northwest to the Sheraton Hotel and Marina.

On the harbor bottom near the marina, another light shone, marking the location of their luxury submarine. It was sitting quietly, letting the sounds of the yachts at the Sheraton's dock mask whatever noise it made. They headed for it.

Once they'd attached the balloons to the sub, they climbed one by one into and through the airlock.

Dave helped them up. "Welcome back, everyone. Successful trip?"

Rudy had recovered his aplomb and gave Dave a thumbs-up.

Esin gave him a big grin. "That was fun!"

22

LETHAL WAYS TO LEAVE YOUR LOVER

The president of the reborn Russian empire watched from his helicopter as they approached his seaside home, which was referred to in legal documents as the Residence at Cape Idokopas.

His lover Alina generally referred to it as his Italianate fairyland, half in awe and half in disgust. He thought of it as his modest one hundred ninety-one thousand square foot palace.

The serene blue waters of the Black Sea rolled up within hiking distance of the palace. Getting down the steep sandstone slope to the beach presented a challenge, but the president enjoyed it. He got to show off his bare chest during a bracing dip in the water every morning.

Today, however, he had a more important event than a swim. His darling lover had returned.

He had experienced a rare moment of introspection when she called him from the palace. He had been surprised by her return. Upon reflection, however, he felt surprise that he had been surprised. He was, after all, the most powerful man in Russia and probably the world. Of course she would return. How could she not?

When his chopper landed on the helipad, he jumped out and hastened down the path through the trees. He forced himself to slow down. If someone saw him like this, they would conclude he was eager to reunite with Alina, and that wouldn't do.

He couldn't help himself. He sped up again.

Alina looked at herself in the full-length mirror a last time. She wore the translucent white nightgown the president loved, which fell in straight lines to the floor and presented every curve of her athletic body as a luscious outline. She wriggled. The gown shimmered, and the parts of her the president most enjoyed appeared and vanished. Good enough. "Time to go, Max."

Max Balakin bowed. "This will be a glorious day for the Ruby."

Grisha had filled Alina in on the conspiracy group of which Max was a leader. She suppressed a sigh, thought about how her own circumstances could now change if she played her part successfully, and answered with all her heart, "Yes, Max. Glory for the Ruby."

She led him down to the indoor swimming pool adjacent to the discotheque. She normally took the twins there to perform their rhythm exercises.

As she spread herself carefully on the couch at the far end of the pool, hidden from most of the room by multiple white marble columns, she looked up at Max. "Your men succeeded?"

Max nodded. "The Ruby granted us proper FSO credentials." The FSO was the Russian equivalent of the Secret Service, and their agents protected the palace when the president was away. "Quietly killing the real agents was easy after that."

Alina nodded. "Where are the bodies? It would be bad if the president saw them before he meets me here."

Max pointed into the distance. "We placed them in the ice palace. That way, I think."

Alina closed her eyes. "Very suitable." To get into her role, she languidly lifted her arm and waved Max away. "Go join your troops."

Max hesitated. "Are you sure?"

Alina chuckled. "I have never been so ready for a performance in all my years of gymnastics. It's as if I had been preparing for this day all my life."

The president stopped outside the swimming hall to catch his breath, then marched through the doors at a dignified pace. "Alina?"

Alina's voice held a low edge of lust. "Here, beloved."

The president forced himself not to run to the far end of the pool. His breath caught as he gazed at her, lazing on the couch. He thought about telling her how beautiful she was but chose to command her instead. "Come here."

She rose, rolling her hips, and approached him in a series

of spins, holding her arms high and pointing her toes, pirouetting. When she reached him, she draped her arms over his shoulders and brought her whole body into contact with his.

He instinctively put his arms around her waist and grasped her butt. "Where were you?"

She looked at him with wide eyes. "I was held on the ship." She rolled her hips to tease him. "I negotiated my way out."

Alina had worried that she would find it difficult to go through with the final act of this performance, but her fears were unfounded. The bastard didn't even ask about their children. All he cared about was using her body.

She nodded at the skinny man with greasy hair who led the bodyguards that accompanied him. "Another minion from the Wagner Group?" She shook her head and repeated a question she'd asked several times before. "Do you trust your own FSO so little?"

The president gave no sign of having heard the question.

Alina had stopped trying to read his expressions years ago for a very simple reason. He no longer produced any.

For decades, the president had treated life as a giant poker game. He had schooled himself to keep his face flat and frozen. No curl of a lip, no rise of an eyebrow, not even the blink of an eye gave a hint of his thoughts. Over the years, he had gradually forgotten how to smile and how to make his eyes look more alive than dead.

His muscles had atrophied, so he could not have

expressed an emotion if he desired to. He had less life than a zombie.

Yes, Alina could play this out to the end.

The sound of machine gun fire penetrated the walls.

The minions trained their weapons on the doors. "Mr. President, stand back."

The president backed away from the doors, away from the guards, and away from Alina.

Time for the next act in the play. She began her newest gymnastic routine. Alina stepped up to a guard, spun gracefully, and kicked his head with her left foot.

She landed so lightly that she seemed to float down, then bounced up with even greater amplitude. As the unconscious minion fell, she spun in the opposite direction and struck his jaw with her right foot with such force that the sound of his bones and teeth shattering echoed off the water, the marble columns, and the tiled floor.

"Thank you, Remy," she whispered. The men could not have the least clue what she meant. Remy had taught her how to weaponize her gymnastic skills, and she now understood. The dance of the assassin had interesting similarities to the choreography of *Swan Lake*.

She was a gymnast, however, not a ballerina. She flowed into the rhythm.

Jump, half-turn.

Backflip, kill.

Split-leap, strike.

Handspring onto the table, finish with a vault of death —not for a kill, but for the sheer beauty.

She stuck the landing to face her lover.

Alina had always been a fast learner, but with Remy's

silver-and-gold head thingie, even Alina had been surprised by how swiftly she had perfected her new abilities.

She floated nearer the president. He showed neither surprise nor horror nor even a determination to survive. Whatever soul he still had no longer shared a connection with the world or his body.

She felt sorry for him. So she struck him in the temple. He fell silently to the deck.

Alina turned to the door as it exploded open. "All clear," she shouted lest someone start shooting on general principles.

Max led a handful of sturmers into the room. His eyes widened when he looked at the president. "Is he dead?"

"He's been dead for years, but he might still be breathing." She held her bare foot over his mouth and felt him exhale. "Definitely breathing. So the plan's still on."

Max frowned. "About the plan."

Alina raised an eyebrow. "Something wrong?"

Max spread his arms. "As large as this palace is, it's only two stories tall. If we throw him from a window, he'll probably survive."

Alina grimaced. "That *is* a problem." She scoured her mental map of the estate for an answer. "I know. We'll take him to the beach." She pointed at a couple of Max's men. "Max, could your people bring him for us?"

The men offered no complaints as they carried the president down the forest path. Indeed, they were jaunty, anticipating the demise of the leader who had failed to expand the empire the way the Ruby had foretold. They knew in their hearts that the next president would do better.

Eventually, they reached the cliff path that led to the beach. They stopped there and looked doubtfully at Alina. "Do we have to carry him down?"

Max had deduced the plan. He bowed to Alina. "With your permission?"

Alina nodded graciously. "Please carry on."

Max pointed at a sharp precipice near the top of the path. "Just toss him over."

The men smiled. With great enthusiasm, they threw the president off the cliff.

Everyone craned their necks to watch him fall. A dull thud accompanied his arrival on the beach.

Alina grunted. "Can't tell from here if he's dead."

The men shuffled their feet uneasily.

She stepped to the barely distinguishable path that led down the side of the mountain. "Coming?"

The men stumbled cautiously in the ruts Alina showed them as she descended with the careless speed and èlan with which only an Olympian would traverse such an unforgiving, tricky slope.

Alina reached her paramour and leaned over to check for a pulse.

The president groaned. "Alina."

Alina unleashed a string of unbecoming curses. She looked up as Max arrived. "We'll have to do it again."

One of the sturmers gulped. "You want us to carry him back up?"

Alina brushed her hair back and grabbed his feet. "I will do it if you're afraid."

Having called their masculinity into question, they responded swiftly. Eschewing further complaints, the sturmers carried the president back up the cliff.

The second toss succeeded.

Bryce had snuck into the Doc's office while the admin was distracted. He wasn't here for an assassination, but he wanted to study the possibilities so if he did decide to make the hit, he'd have some tactical ideas.

The Doc came through the door, head down, apparently unaware of his surroundings, studying a tablet. "Bryce, I'm glad you're here."

Bryce sighed. He'd need new tactical ideas. He held out an elegant box. "Congratulations."

The Doc accepted the box and raised an eyebrow. "Congratulations for what?" He lifted the lid. "Cohiba Red Dot cigars." He pulled one out to study it. "Of course, I don't smoke cigars."

Bryce chuckled. "Neither do I. But it's traditional." He gestured for the Doc to put the one he held in his mouth and withdrew a lighter to ignite the tip. He put a second cigar in his mouth and repeated the ritual. Sharing cigars and befriending possible targets were not his specialties. Still, he knew something about them.

The Doc sucked on the Cohiba. "Okay, I guess." He took his chair behind the desk. "What's the occasion?"

"You were right about the Kinzhal missile. Even though

Cassie and Remy knew we shot it, they started a three-way war anyway. Gamma, Rivendell, and the Kremlin went at it. Very satisfying."

The Doc watched the smoke waft through the room. "Who lost?"

Bryce blew a ring. "The president fell off a cliff. It'll hit the news in a couple days, pun intended." He leaned forward. "How did you know the missile would start that battle?"

The Doc laughed. "Though Cassie and Remy knew we'd fired it, they also knew the Russian government had let us get our hands on it in the first place."

He shrugged. "So although I didn't know the outcome with certainty, I did know an outcome like this was statistically likely." He pointed a stern finger at Bryce. "Remember, I built EStorme. I'm not just a medical researcher who knows the physiological effects of rage or a psychologist who understands the flaws and defects in human thinking. I'm also an anthropologist and sociologist who has studied group dynamics and conflict excitation over the course of all human history."

Bryce shot him a look of admiration. For the first time in his life, he felt cold fear in the pit of his stomach. What could stop a man with so much perception? What were the consequences if the man with that perception also engineered systems of torture like the one at Camp No?

Bryce forced himself to radiate happiness at having a director of unparalleled foresight. "So, what's next, Boss?"

Grisha sipped the cognac Evgeni had slipped him. "So, Alina performed brilliantly. I asked her if she'd like to join Gamma. She clearly has the skills." From Max's description, she had incredible skills. Where had they come from? Was there something in the water at Rivendell?

His eyes slid to the speakerphone on which the Doc listened, but Evgeni intruded. "I take it she refused the offer."

Grisha sighed. "She only helped us to protect her children. If we run into someone else who threatens the twins, we should call on her."

The Doc grunted. "The president had slid into delusions comparable to those of Ruby Rage. Unfortunately, he did so without my guidance on what delusions to embrace."

He sighed. "I'm sure the next dictator will be better. Regression to the mean." He switched subjects. "But that is not why you called me. The coming and going of public tyrants is amusing but of little import. What help do you need? What news do you bring?"

Grisha cleared his throat. "Actually, I had an encounter while tracking down Alina at Rivendell that I thought would interest you."

The Doc was, as usual, frighteningly quick on the uptake. "Did you find Michael McKinney?"

Grisha swallowed hard. "I did."

The Doc lunged on. Instead of his usual clinical coldness, however, he grew warm with wrath. "Did he seem different to you?"

Grisha nodded. "He did."

"Tell me every detail."

Grisha told him about the conversation, the references to illusory patterns, false induction, critical thinking, and an Awakening.

The Doc's anger faded by the time Grisha finished. He turned pensive. "I suppose, for a Ruby Rager or an EStormer, it would seem like an Awakening when he escaped our programming."

Grisha shuddered. He always hated it when the Doc talked about programming people. Manipulating minds and running head fakes was all well and good, but "programming" seemed a little too mechanical. He'd always assumed it was just a figure of speech. He now wondered if it was more true than he'd allowed himself to believe.

The Doc sighed. "The Ruby Rage programming includes a buildup of resistance to counter-programming. Apparently, the enemy's technology is strong enough to break through even those barriers."

Grisha interrupted his meanderings. "What tech? And for that matter, what enemy?"

The Doc proceeded as if he hadn't heard. "This is a severe setback for our plans. Unless the threat is eliminated immediately, it could destroy all our work."

Grisha exchanged looks of astonishment with Evgeni, who objected, "One Rager escaped our psyops training. How is that a bigger problem?"

The Doc was silent for a long time. "I must now tell you of matters about which you heretofore had no need to know."

Grisha sat on the edge of his seat. He'd always known the Doc had his own agenda. Perhaps now he would glean some information on Gamma's psyops scientist.

The Doc went into lecture mode. "Let me tell you about the Memwriter."

The Doc told them about the research Laurie and Gerald Tambook had done and the machine that could give you days of practice and memorization in hours. He explained some of the hypothetical consequences, such as the ability to rewire a personality with false memories.

Grisha listened in horrified astonishment. He wondered if what he felt now was what a conspiracy cultist would expect people to feel upon being Awakened. "How do you know all that?"

The Doc grunted. "I have an opponent of sorts. Maybe a challenge partner. He and I went to school together and specialized in the same areas of chemical addiction, psychology, and sociology."

Evgeni figured it out. "The developer of EStorme."

Grisha blinked. Of course. Ruby Rage and EStorme had their beginnings in the corpus of knowledge shared by the Doc and his enemy-partner.

He also realized something about his personal frustrations, starting with the raid on the Nuclear Sanctum that had initiated his current journey. "We never really had a chance of catching Cassie and Remy, did we? They're superhuman."

The Doc chuckled. "Not quite that. They can learn and train to an expert level in multiple fields of endeavor, but they are still human. Neither is going to invent the solution that integrates general relativity with quantum mechanics or jump tall buildings in a single bound."

Evgeni sat entranced, as if he were seeing his first glimpse of paradise. "The things we could do with this Memwriter! We must acquire it."

The Doc's voice turned harsh. "Too late for that. If they unleash this technology, they can unravel both EStorme and Ruby Rage. We'll lose our sturmers, our kamikazes, and our current successes in transcontinental domination."

Evgeni got stubborn. "If we could get it, we would win everything."

The Doc relented. "Yes, yes. If you could capture Remy, that would be perfect." His voice turned commanding, as if he were in charge, not Evgeni. "But if you can't take her, we have to kill her."

23

EDGE OF SANITY

Every day, the Doc had the NSA take a photo of Rivendell to let him take the pulse of events in his enemy's heartland. So far, Cassie and Remy had kept their promise not to go back. Since that had been the goal of the exercise, the plan had technically succeeded. It had put them back on the run and vulnerable.

That part of the plan, however, had failed. Instead of staying vulnerable, the bitches had hijacked an even better hideaway.

He considered shooting another missile at the fortress on general principles, but more overt violence would attract unwanted attention. Besides, he should figure out why the first one had missed before trying again.

Today he brought up the daily photo, expecting to see nothing except the grass growing.

Instead, he saw a nearly completed dome under construction on top of the keep. Zooming in on the sward in front of it revealed the dismembered parts of several machines that tickled his memory.

He looked up the classified files on a recent altercation at the Navy's San Diego base, a contretemps that had diligently been kept out of the news. He looked at the files, then the photo, and back.

He started swearing.

Morte Noir sashayed across the sward to talk to Rudy. She wore a sun hat that covered more than her bikini did and carried a backpack that also covered more than the swimsuit. "Hey, Rudy, looking good." She waved at the EStormers working on the wiring and electronic assemblies for testing and positioning. Esin knelt next to the remains of the original LaWS, puzzling over one of the pieces.

Rudy rubbed his hands together. "We have enough of it up and running to test it. Care to join me?" Assuming she would answer in the affirmative, he walked across the grass to a control station with a drone lying nearby.

Morte Noir waved at Esin. "Have you seen the test?"

Esin looked up from the subject of her frustration. "He hasn't tried it yet. I think he was waiting for you."

Morte Noir smiled. "Cool." She nodded at Rudy. "Let's play."

Rudy entered the demo presentation mode of a natural entrepreneur. "Esin, Mistress. May I present the Rivendell Death Ray?"

He pressed a button, and a cylinder filled with a dozen tiny barrels peeked out above the main living quarters and pointed at them.

Morte Noir raised an eyebrow. "I thought you were putting the lasers on the keep?"

Rudy chortled. "We'll use the dome on the Keep too, but that's primarily for show. Let them shoot at that while I blast them from another rooftop."

Esin brought her hands together in delight. "Very clever."

Rudy pretended to tip his hat. "I thought so." He led Esin over to a display with a joystick the size and shape of a fighter plane's control stick. "I want you to point the lasers."

He handed Morte Noir a plastic box with twin joysticks. "If you want to, you can drive the drone."

The Mistress also gave him a bright smile. "Happy to." She pressed a button, and a drone rose. She maneuvered it over the outer wall and sent it into the sky.

Rudy clapped. "Now begin. Mistress, drive the drone into the fortress. Esin, burn her down."

Morte Noir sent the drone zigzagging across the field, zooming past the walls toward the main building.

Esin pursed her lips in concentration. She moved her joystick back and forth in ever smaller increments. At last she squeezed the trigger.

The drone did not burn or tumble out of control. It vaporized. One moment, Morte Noir was watching a drone. The next, she was watching a puff of smoke.

Esin chuckled. "Gotcha."

Morte Noir smiled wryly. "I somehow expected something more dramatic."

Rudy explained, "The original LaWS' power output was

thirty kilowatts. It would have punched a hole in the drone, which would have fallen to the ground."

Morte Noir chuckled. "I presume this is better."

Rudy continued, "Esin just hit that drone with one hundred and fifty kilowatts. That's enough to knock out a cruise missile."

The Mistress asked the logical question. "What about a hypersonic missile?"

Rudy's expression was grave yet determined. "Needs at least a megawatt laser." He pointed at the roof and the Keep. "When we're done, we'll have one point five megawatts of laser batteries. Ten times what you just saw. Should be plenty."

Morte Noir proceeded to the question all entrepreneurs and engineers hated. "How long until it's ready?"

Rudy scrunched his face. "About a week."

Morte Noir had learned to estimate project schedules by not only listening to the engineers' words but also watching their body language. She chuckled. "Two weeks, then."

Rudy frowned and shrugged.

The Mistress turned serious. "Look, as long as the lasers aren't in place, I'm a danger to everyone here, including myself. If any of several of my enemies discovers me here, you'll get another missile in the mail." She held up her tiny pack and swayed her hips. "Which is why I'm going on vacation 'til you've locked it in."

She turned to Esin. "You coming, or do you want to stay with Rudy?"

Esin looked at the two of them. She clearly wanted to

go with Morte Noir, but she didn't want to disappoint Rudy.

Rudy snorted. "Go. Have fun."

Esin turned to the main building. "Let me pack."

Morte Noir shook her bag. "No need. I have a variety of swimsuits and a couple of toothbrushes. Anything else, we can scrounge." She pointed at a nearby Hummer. "Let's go."

Esin ran to the vehicle.

Morte Noir gave Rudy a sober look. "Get this thing working before somebody shoots at us again."

Rudy saluted. "You bet, Mistress."

Months ago, before Jean Houston had boarded the plane for her flight back to Wisconsin from Rivendell, she had swallowed her disappointment and put on a cheerful façade. Her new best friend Tina, whom she'd met here in Orinoco, had hugged her tight. "I'm so sorry, but as the Emerald warned us when we arrived, they only need a few people right now. I'm sure you'll be Chosen when her needs expand."

Jean had hugged her back, but privately, her thoughts took a jealous turn. She understood that only a few of the most devoted EStormers, ones with specific skills, could stay.

She couldn't help asking one question, however. Why Tina and not her? Okay, Tina had beaten her in the marksmanship trials, but only barely. That couldn't be the distinguishing characteristic. Everyone who had gone through the memwritten sniper training had achieved extraordinary scores compared to the rest of the world.

Digging deeper, she realized what really bugged her was the change in Tina's commitment to the cause. When they'd arrived, Tina had been as full of zeal as Jean.

Over time, Jean's fervor had grown. Remy's upbeat incisiveness and razor-sharp thinking offered everything anyone could hope for in a leader when fighting desperately to save the world from overwhelming clandestine forces.

However, while Jean's excitement had grown stronger, Tina's dedication had waned.

Tina had withdrawn within herself, becoming distant from everyone and everything, including EStorme and Jean. She'd recovered in the last couple of days before Cassie had announced who would stay, but her late conversion smacked of artifice. Until that moment, artificiality had been the last thing of which Jean would have accused Tina.

It didn't seem fair for the Emerald to retain Tina, and it tore at Jean's heart. It got so bad that Jean's commitment to the whole EStorme enterprise had faltered. She'd blamed the Emerald, but in one of the occasional fits of analytical introspection she had suffered since her Rivendell trip, she convinced herself that there was another issue.

The Emerald's gem drops seemed to have deteriorated in quality. In the old days, the messages on the imageboard had formed a cohesive whole. The newer posts lacked that integrated trueness. Her mind kept looking at them and whispering, "False induction. X does not prove Y." Other times, she would look at a possible coincidence, decide it was part of the conspiracy, and realize, "Availability error. Once you see a conspiracy in one place, you start seeing conspiracy everywhere because the possibility of conspiracy is at the forefront of your mind."

The problem had grown so bad that her boyfriend, who had accompanied her to Rivendell, had noticed. Jean wasn't sure if he had left her or if she had left him, but they were no longer together.

When she diffidently asked the board if anyone else had noticed a problem, it had exploded in denunciations. Then everyone had gone on to ooh and aah over the next gem drop. All Jean could hear beating in her mind were the words "bandwagon effect."

Was the problem a change in EStorme? How could Remy have allowed that to happen?

Or was part of the problem within her? Had she lost her way?

How would she know?

She was sure of one thing. Her life was crumbling.

One cold Wisconsin morning, as she worked her way through the sixty cows in her family's dairy barn, sanitizing each cow's teats and hooking them up to the pumps, she struggled with her questions until she concluded only one person might help her. Did the one person she knew who had lost her faith and come back restored have the answer?

Tina looked sadly at the caller ID on her cell phone. Jean. They had met at Rivendell, and Jean had had so many talents that Tina had been sure she would be Called to stay at the fort. Only near the end of the testing and education process, when Tina finally understood the nature of the Call, did she realize that Jean's dreams were not meant to be.

Tina forced a smile onto her face and chipperness into her voice as Jean's face appeared on her display. "Jean! Great to hear from you."

Jean's hair straggled down the sides of her face. She looked like she'd been hit by a truck. "Tina. Sorry to bother you, but I had to call someone who might help me." Before Tina could answer, Jean forced chipperness into *her* voice and asked, "So, how is it going at Rivendell?"

Tina thought about the crazy events she'd participated in since Jean's departure and selected one she could share with an EStormer. "As we expected, the forces of the Dark have come after us with all the weapons at their disposal." She described the Ruby Rage attack on the fortress and the role she had played in protecting the Vault.

Jean listened in speechless wonder. "So, the battle is coming out into the open. Sounds like I could have been useful."

Tina sighed. "I'm sure you could have, but Remy only had a certain number of slots at the time." Lest Jean get her hopes up, she added, "I don't think we'll be expanding our team in the near future, either."

Jean looked away in despair, and Tina counseled, "Patience. Await your role in the Plan."

She then took them back to the original topic. "You said you needed help. What can I do?"

Jean answered quietly. "I've been having trouble with

the EStorme imageboards. Does it seem like they've lost their crispness?" She described her concerns. "Remy probably hasn't been able to give the boards the same amount of attention she used to with the battle against the Dark heating up. Is that the problem?"

Tina frowned. "I'm afraid I haven't been watching the boards as much."

Jean replied wistfully, "Of course not. You don't watch the news when you're in the thick of it."

Tina didn't know what to say.

An alternate interpretation of Jean's situation struck her. Perhaps she *did* know how to help. "Jean, I need you to think carefully about what you told me. You say the Emerald's recent drops cherry-picked a number of incidents to show they were linked in a grand web of deception."

Jean muttered in frustration, "It seemed that way to me."

Tina leaned forward. "Does that sound like something Remy would do?"

Anger pierced Jean's depression. "Absolutely not. Not our Remy."

Tina let a small smile unfold. "Jean, why do you believe Remy is the Emerald?"

Tina watched Jean's stunned expression for the least clue about her thoughts. Jean answered, "Because she told us she was."

"Is that the only reason?"

Jean's breathing got ragged. "Of course not. Remy *has* to be the Emerald. She's exceptional. If EStorme has an Emerald at all, it has to be Remy."

Tina held her tongue and prayed for her friend.

Someone answered her prayers, and Jean made the leap.

Her voice quavered; she was near hysteria. "Oh, no. There *is* no Emerald, is there?"

Tina held her hand up in a calming motion. "Hang in there. While you were here, Remy and Cassie taught us all how to think. It's time to use what you learned. *Think*, girl."

Jean grimaced, then shook her head. "It's too much. It can't be true. If there's no Emerald, how did the boards come into existence? How could they have attracted so many people?" She answered her own question. "Appeal to consensus. Jump to conclusions. Illusory patterns."

The time for Tina's own leap of faith had come. "Jean, Remy didn't tell us everything the Memwriter can do when she introduced us to it. It can give us memories that are suppressed until the right trigger is pulled."

Jean raised an eyebrow. "That doesn't seem possible. You're sitting there watching the images the entire time. You know what you've learned."

Tina looked away, embarrassed. "You can hear voices in your sleep, and the Memwriter can reinforce them but store them where your conscious mind doesn't know about them until sparked to awareness."

Jean scraped her lower teeth across her upper lip. "Did they do that to me?"

Tina rooted through her phone to find the last recording Remy had given her. "Let me play this for you. It will take you a little while to digest the message. Don't worry. I'll be with you on the call the entire time. When you're ready, we can talk." She started the playback.

The first words Jean heard were Remy's. "Welcome to the Disclosure."

For a moment, those were the only words she heard. Then her brain started to itch and more words followed, slowly at first but picking up speed until they were racing through her head. Peculiarly, no matter how fast they filled her, she still understood.

In this mind flood, Remy told her about AID and Gamma and the psyops engineers who'd created EStorme and Ruby Rage. Jean saw their connections to real events, from terrorist attacks to wars to the overthrow of governments. She learned about Remy's parents, their kidnappings, and the covert agencies' plans to subvert the Memwriter.

She took a steadying breath. "Ohmigod." She managed to focus her eyes on Tina. "The words whispering in my brain. Is this happening to everybody?"

Tina shook her head sadly. "Alas, no. Most people take their new-found critical thinking skills and apply them to reinforce their pre-existing beliefs."

Jean smiled. "Confirmation bias is, as we learned, genetically wired into us. Hard to break."

Tina continued. "About twenty percent experience the Awakening while they're here. Those are the ones who stay at Rivendell. Maybe five percent have your experience, in which your new critical thinking reflexes fight a slow but relentless battle in your subconscious to overcome those cruder instincts."

Jean looked away, despairing again.

Tina saw that and asked sharply, "What's wrong?"

Jean choked on her words. "We were wrong the whole time, weren't we?"

Tina gave her the smile of an old, wise woman. "Ah. Were we? Look deeper."

Jean tried but failed. "I don't know how to look deeper."

Tina chuckled. "You are right. We *were* wrong. But we were right the whole time, too. Do you see that?"

Jean frowned, still puzzled.

"Immense secret forces, on a global scale, in combat to dominate civilization. It's true. We just didn't understand that the real players work one level deeper than the people we thought were pulling the strings. And the hate for public figures we justified because they were Satanic pedophiles? Just a lie, but it contained a murky outline of the truth."

Jean closed her eyes and smiled. "Of course. The secret networks were always there, just submerged beneath a silver surface that reflected our thoughts."

She frowned. "There's still one disappointment in all this. Remy isn't the Emerald after all."

Tina toyed with the idea of letting Jean know that half the time, the person she knew as Remy was really Cassie, but she let it slide. Parts of the truth could wait for another day. Besides, regardless of the identity-switching, one truth remained—a far more important truth for a reformed EStormer to hear.

Tina's eyes glistened. "Yeah, Remy is not the Emerald. I thought about that long and hard too, and I eventually had to ask, isn't she? Did she not bring us the Disclosure? Has she not started the Awakening? Isn't it all according to the Plan?"

Jean gawked at her mentor. "Wow. In the deepest sense, Remy *is* the Emerald."

Tina nodded. "You must first realize that the Emerald does not exist before you can understand who the Emerald truly is." She laughed gaily. "Just don't tell Remy that."

Jean joined in the laughter. "Never. Promise."

24

LEVERAGE

Calvert Woodley Fine Wines and Spirits looked like an oversized Seven-Eleven without the gas pumps. Dale shook his head. "Is this really the best place in DC to buy champagne?"

Remy laughed. "That's what they say."

They entered the store. Racks of wine created aisles that marched back to refrigerated cases filled with fine cheeses.

Remy wrinkled her nose. "I don't know anything about champagne."

Dale reluctantly admitted, "Neither do I." He squared his shoulders with determination. "I'm sure we can figure it out."

Remy looked at him doubtfully. "Perhaps we should ask for help."

Dale was about to object—he was a man, dammit! He didn't need instructions—when Remy's phone rang.

Remy put it on speaker. "Andrey. What's up?"

Anxiety had hijacked Andrey's voice. "The world has become much more dangerous, especially for us."

Remy tried to calm him. "Tell me about it. What's the new threat?"

Andrey exhaled heavily. "I've been trying to identify the new director for AID. He's been hiding so effectively, I couldn't even get a line on him using the UDC."

Dale joined Remy in nudging him forward. "We've heard your earlier reports. Did you finally nail him?"

"Not exactly. I just put two and two and two together and got seventeen."

Remy tag-teamed him. "Lay it out."

Andrey mused, "You know, there's one other person I haven't been able to get a line on either."

Remy nodded. "The Doc." Remy didn't care half as much about the new director as she cared about the Doc, who had left her father more dead than alive.

Andrey. "Exactly. Here's the thing. Since Dallas Ferris's death, the amount of traffic in and out of Fort Meade using one-time-pad encryption has skyrocketed."

Remy perked up. "So someone associated with the Doc joined the AID HQ."

Dale gasped in realization. "Worse. It's the Doc. Right, Andrey?" He put his hand on his forehead. "The Doc is now the director!"

Andrey spoke cautiously. "I think so, but I can't prove it."

Remy stared at the phone. "No, but it fits. What kind of monster other than the Doc would destroy someone's complex with a hypercruise missile just to make sure they can't go home again, even if it cost a thousand people their lives?"

Dale could think of several other monsters who would, but he didn't have the heart to interrupt.

Remy continued with more conviction than was probably warranted. "It's the Doc. I'm sure. Thanks, Andrey."

Andrey continued grimly. "Wait. I haven't gotten to the worst part." He paused for effect. "I told you before that these one-time-pad users show up over and over in both America and Russia, so it's not just a couple of guys. It's a full-grown covert organization. A cabal, if you will."

Dale coaxed him along. "So, it's bigger than you thought?"

Andrey hedged. "Maybe. As I was trying to explain, not only have I looked across space for these interconnected users of unbreakable pads, but I've also looked across time. I still can't believe what I found."

Dale felt like reaching through the phone and shaking Andrey until he spilled, but Remy spoke first. "Give it to us straight."

Andrey gathered himself. "This cabal is older than the internet. It's older than the earliest data the NSA has moved into the UDC from its earliest databases."

Dale heard the panic in the words. "Drop the other shoe, Andrey."

"Though they've been around for generations, their activity picked up after the founding of AOL when the first experiments in mass digital communications started. Their operations expanded with the growth of Facebook and Twitter, but another event coincided with an even greater explosion of activity." He cleared his throat. "A very personal event."

Remy looked puzzled. Eventually, she figured it out.

She looked like she'd been struck by lightning. "My parents' kidnapping."

Andrey sighed. "They've been in a frenzy since the invention of the Memwriter."

He continued after a pause. "It's as if they were in a state of hibernation for decades, waiting. Waiting for the invention of social media, and above all, waiting for you."

Augustus Luther sat at his desk, staring at the numbers on his laptop. They were disturbingly good.

Dread Nought's stock had gone up steadily for weeks. Since he was a major stockholder, that should have been cause for celebration. Augustus's problem was, he didn't know *why*. Nothing in the business fundamentals had changed. Revenues were strong and profits were good, but not radically so.

He now suspected someone was trying to do a buyout. That was not a big deal. More than one government had tried to take control of the company. Key assassinations had always taken care of the problem.

Joyce was investigating the new purchasers of shares. In the past, attackers had come in through shell companies, but Joyce had pierced their veils to find the single central enemy. This time, however, the attack was so complicated that he wasn't even sure he faced an attack.

A couple of the buyers were re-insurers, which made

sense. In retrospect, he wondered why that industry hadn't gotten in on the high-end security business earlier.

One of the buyers was a VC firm. Strange, but not particularly threatening. Another was the country of Orinoco.

Could they be attacking him? Why? The previous state-level attacks on Dread Nought had been performed by organizations with something huge to gain. Orinoco did not fit the profile. Also, they owned less than a controlling percentage of the new investments.

He remained concerned, however. Some of the investors were the kinds of shell companies used for a classic hostile takeover. Even Joyce could not penetrate a number of them.

Worst of all, if he *was* under attack, what could he do? Who would he counterattack? Bottom line: who should he kill?

His phone rang. It was Pierce Fletcher, one of his allies on the board of directors. "Pierce. What's up?"

Pierce whispered in a raspy voice, "We're under attack."

Augustus heaved a sigh of relief, and his uncertainty was replaced by eagerness to strike back. "Who?"

"Apparently, it's a consortium. I found out just now when they tried to recruit me." He barked a laugh. "Crazy collection of buyers you would not believe. "

Augustus did believe. "Who's leading it?"

Pierce grunted. "I'm not sure. Whoever it is knows the business inside and out, though. Could it be an insider? It would have to be a top-level executive."

Augustus considered. "I can't guess who."

His door opened without a knock. Two security guards

came in, flanking Dale Strickland. Dale carried a bottle of champagne and spoke loudly for the benefit of the person on the phone. "Pierce, is that you? Everything's under control. You can hang up now."

Dale had not planned to run this op for a few more days, but when Fletcher had reacted with unmitigated hostility to the proposal one of Dale's directors had made, he'd realized he had to move now.

He set two champagne flutes on the desk and popped the cork. "A toast to new horizons."

Augustus picked up a flute, brought it halfway to his lips, and stared at it. He was clearly wondering if it was poisoned.

Dale snorted. "Oh, please. This is a business transaction in a high-level corporate headquarters. We're not in a jungle." He looked at the picture of Augustus on a lion-hunting safari on the wall. "Well, we're not that deep in a jungle." He grabbed Augustus' champagne glass and switched it with his. "I'll take the poisoned chalice. Drink up." He took a sip.

Augustus reluctantly played along. "To what do we owe this celebration?"

Dale launched into a short marketing pitch. "Dread Nought is about to pursue a new and exciting strategic direction."

Augustus raised an eyebrow. "Do tell."

Dale's smile would have been familiar to any hammerhead shark. "In a moment. That is not what we're celebrating. Not yet."

Augustus tried to match Dale's smile and failed. "So, what *are* we celebrating?"

"Your magnificent golden parachute. Your retirement."

All humor left Augustus' face. "Guards, please escort Mr. Strickland out of the building."

Dale leaned back and spoke quietly. "It's okay. You can leave us."

The guards nodded and departed.

Dale chuckled. "Hearts and minds, Augustus. When infiltrating an enemy stronghold, it pays to make friends with everyone." He turned serious. "Anyway, I wanted to thank you."

Augustus glared at him in disbelief.

Dale smiled again. "Seriously. You built an extraordinary corporation from a company that barely broke even selling deadbolts and renting warehouse guards. It's amazing." He gestured around. "It just needs a little redirection. With great power comes great responsibility and all that."

Augustus sneered. "Boy Scout." He pulled out his phone.

Dale waved his finger. "No, no. Before you do anything rash, let me make sure you are fully informed." He pulled out his phone. "Joyce, have the caterers arrived? Excellent. And you've gathered everyone from the Extreme Risk division in the conference room? Yes, Joyce, I understand that half of them are out on missions, but the rest are here? Excellent."

Dale hung up and pointed at the door. "Let me brief you

along with the others." He patted Augustus on the shoulder. "And cheer up! It's going to be great."

Domed trays of food covered several tables at one end of the conference room.

When Dale walked to the head of the table with Augustus, the room quieted. Dale murmured to Augustus, "Let me do the talking. Seriously."

Remy had struck up a conversation with the Slip, who had earned her nickname while preventing a terrorist detonation of a South African nuclear warhead. Judging by the look on the Slip's face, Remy was astounding her with some tale of derring-do. Dale realized that Cassie and Remy would find many fellow adventurers here.

He spotted Curtis at the far end of the table. A blend of satisfaction and fury touched the hacker's face when he saw Remy. Curtis ran his finger over the place on his own cheek where he had scarred the cheerleader.

Okay, they weren't *all* fellow travelers.

When Remy saw Dale, she broke off to join him.

Joyce, who was standing near the head of the table, kicked it off. "Augustus? What's up?"

Augustus gave her a grumpy frown, so she redirected. "Dale?"

Dale began his new pitch. The old pitch had been aimed at investors. This pitch was aimed at the key players. He hoped it would work.

He forced his doubts from his mind and focused on enthusiasm. "We have exciting news. We are about to embark on a new path." He took a deep breath. "We're going to go after the cartels, the mafia, the tyrants, the thieves, the con men, and the saboteurs, collecting damages and retrieving stolen wealth."

He laughed. "That's a lot of wealth, folks. Expect to see really surprising bonuses once we get this ball rolling."

The Wasp made a droll comment. "So, we'll target our customers."

That got a murmur of laughter. Dale spread his hands wide. "Some of them. There are plenty of others." He gave the Credit Suisse accounts example.

Carrie Baer, a petite woman known as the Bear, spotted the difficulty. "Are we gonna spend half our time protecting ourselves from these people once they know we're their enemies?"

The Slip shook her head. "We're gonna spend half our time killing them." She looked at Dale and Augustus. "Right?"

Augustus glared at Dale. Dale glared back.

Curtis asked the question they all wanted to hear answered. "Just who is the boss, anyway?"

Dale cleared his throat. "With a new era and new challenges, our CEO has agreed it is time to step down." He blushed. "The new CEO is, uh..."

Remy stepped up next to him and clapped. "Everyone, meet your new CEO, Dale Strickland."

Half-hearted applause came back.

Carrie raised her hand. "Not to be a spoilsport, Dale, but do you really have the background to run a multi-billion-dollar enterprise?"

Dale gave her a warm smile. "Thank you, Carrie. I

should have talked to you beforehand to make sure you asked that question."

That got some chuckles.

Dale projected his voice. "The answer is no, I do not have that expertise. Not yet. And that is why I've thought long and hard about who to pick as the COO. Someone with the knowledge, the wisdom, and the respect to run operations in a way we can all trust." He watched the audience ponder this difficult question and ask themselves who would qualify.

He continued. "So, assuming she can forgive me for making this surprise announcement, let me present the new Chief Operating Officer. Joyce, congratulations."

Joyce gawked at him and pointed at herself. "Me?"

Joyce's promotion provoked raucous clapping. She had saved the lives or missions of every person in that room at some point.

After the cheering died down, someone in the back shouted, "Holy crap. We're working for a Boy Scout."

Remy glared in the direction of the voice. "Is that a problem?"

The Wasp drawled, "Hell, no. I have a confession to make, folks. I always preferred the jobs where we hit the bad guys. Who agrees with me?"

Murmurs of assent turned into more clapping and cheering. Remy started a cheer. "Boy Scout! Boy Scout!"

Dale continued to blush as people came around and congratulated him.

Curtis stood in the back of the congratulations line with a couple of hitters Dale had worried about from time to time. He whispered to Joyce, "Are we recording this meeting?"

Joyce pulled out her cell and tapped a few keys. "Now we are."

"Good."

Dale eventually shook hands with Curtis. "I hope we can improve our working relationship. You're exceptionally talented, Curtis, and I want you to succeed in the new plan."

Curtis gave him an unconvincing smirk. "No problem, Dale."

When the party broke down into a generalized celebration, Dale led the new COO to his office. Augustus decided to follow. Dale welcomed him. "You can help if you're not too furious. I'll happily offer you a consulting contract if you're up for it."

Augustus was too furious to help his betrayers, but he could pretend to be helpful long enough to scoop up some dirt that would let him decide how to respond.

Already stepping into her new role, Joyce voiced a concern. "Isn't this all premature, Dale? I had Augustus describe the list of investors for me and looked up the size of their holdings. It's not enough."

Augustus crossed his arms. "I'd like to hear the answer to that myself."

Dale chuckled. "Leverage, of course. Specifically in the form of junk bonds."

Augustus saw where that was going. "Issued against the value of the company, I presume?"

Dale nodded.

Augustus grunted. "That should work." Junk bonds, otherwise known as "speculative high-yield bonds," were risky issues bearing high interest rates.

Joyce squinted. "So, the Boy Scout is going to sell bad debt to perform a turnaround that will make so much money he can pay off the bad debt? One that will allow him to put all the bad guys away as a side effect?"

Dale clapped her on the shoulder. "Beautiful, isn't it? Junk bonds save the world."

Augustus rolled his eyes. "Okay, irony makes the world go round. I get it, but *seriously*?"

He stepped closer. "I can still stop you. I can trash your junk. I can hammer you in the courts for years."

Dale gave him a cold stare, the likes of which he'd never seen from the Boy Scout.

Dale spoke softly. "You come out of this smelling like a rose, Augustus. You have an exceptional life ahead of you. Why would you trade that for an unmarked grave in a third-world country?"

Augustus' heart crept into his throat. Fear. Admiration. In the end, he looked upon his successor with thoughtful yet approving eyes.

Perhaps the Boy Scout *did* have the stones to run Dread Nought.

25

SUIT UP

Bryce entered the director's office with his hands spread to show he held no weapons. He knew the display was unnecessary, but it seemed like the safe course to follow.

The Doc grunted. "I'm afraid I'll have to postpone our meeting. I have a job for you, but something came up."

Bryce was not easily blown off. "What's happening? Even if I can't help, I'm happy to listen." He needed to gather every scrap of data he could to help him understand this scientific torturer who seemed destined to rule the world.

The director eyed him suspiciously, then shrugged. "I have disturbing evidence that members of the EStorme cult are breaking free at artificially augmented rates."

Bryce blinked. "We're losing EStormers?"

The Doc explained, "A cult like EStorme usually loses followers at a quantifiable low rate. We have data on this from numerous conspiracy cults, and the outcomes are easily predicted and reliable."

He pursed his lips. "But the rate of loss for EStorme has

recently increased by a statistically significant percentage, and there is a correlation." He muffled a growl of frustration.

Bryce leaned forward, actually interested in what was happening. He'd always felt that the rise of EStorme and Ruby Rage had attracted a disproportionate amount of attention when the age-old profession of assassination clearly produced better and more reliable results. "And the correlation is?"

The director pointed at an image of Rivendell on the monitor behind him. "The growth in departure rates began after EStormers started going down to Cassie and Remy's fortress to interview for jobs."

Bryce sat back, puzzled. "I would have expected that people exposed to Remy as the Emerald would become more devout, not less." He chuckled. "Let's face it. If there really was an Emerald, Remy would be perfect."

The Doc glared at him before producing a shallow smile. "True." He went back to studying a series of numbers that left Bryce out of the conversation. "Nonetheless, that is the correlation."

He muttered, "I'll have the NSA run an analysis of who went to Rivendell, who came back, and who stayed. I'll have to line them up with the participants on the imageboard who are trying to change the form of discussion and asking disturbing questions. The Awakening seems to be a popular topic that I am having trouble controlling."

Bryce offered his thoughts. "I still can't believe Remy or Cassie is responsible. Let's consider the worst case. Suppose they used the Memwriter to alter the personalities of the people who went down there. Even then, you'd see an increase in devotion of the cultists, not a decrease."

The Doc rubbed his face. "They *are* using the Memwriter. The people who stayed at Rivendell learned exceptional combat skills in ridiculously short periods of time. Also, some of those who returned came back with new skills that enabled them to move up in their careers or move into new professions. My evidence is anecdotal until I acquire more data, however."

He clenched a fist. "And I'm suspicious they are all working under an oath of secrecy that I'm having trouble penetrating."

Bryce went back to his point. "They might give their elite cultists new skills, but I repeat; it is not credible that they would use the Memwriter to rewrite personalities. Their personalities preclude such an undertaking." He looked at the director shrewdly. "Who else might sabotage EStorme? Is there anyone?"

The Doc stared at him, thunderstruck. "*Him.*" He cursed.

Bryce gently asked, "Him who?"

The Doc's cell phone emitted a peculiar chime, and his mood brightened. "I need to take this." He turned away and listened. "That is excellent news if true, but are you sure you have the right package?" He listened for a moment, then replied, "Very good. I'll accept your assessment as preliminary evidence. I'll deal with it immediately."

He turned back to Bryce. "The mission I planned for you is canceled. I have something much more important."

Bryce did not have to feign eagerness. "Where am I going?"

Cassie settled into a lounge chair on the deck of the *Glory*. She placed her cell phone on the table next to the intriguing thriller she had just started reading. She had lately discovered she enjoyed thrillers. They were low-key and slow-paced compared to her life.

Finally, she relaxed in the sunshine.

This was the life she had imagined since they'd snatched the Quantum Key from the Kremlin—the life of unrepentant luxurious wealth. Somehow, between the heists and the battles and the kidnappings, her vision had gotten pushed into a distant and blurred future.

Her respite wouldn't last long, though. Too many enemies hungered for satisfaction.

Yet here she was, living for today. She still wore oversized sunglasses, but not to fool the facial recognition algorithms. Today, they kept the sun out of her eyes. How odd.

A member of the ship's waitstaff stepped up, careful not to block the sun. "Ma'am, Morte Noir's submarine has arrived."

"Most excellent." They would have to bring the yacht into port someday, but for the moment, they were doing just fine with Morte Noir delivering fresh food from time to time.

Life was good.

Barefoot steps announced the arrival of someone who prowled rather than stomped. Cassie opened her eyes. "Morte Noir. Welcome."

Morte Noir wore a cherry-red bikini smaller than her own. Cassie felt a moment of smugness since she thought her bikini, a glittering mesh of metallic purple and emerald, was more striking.

Morte Noir nodded in approval. "Looking good, girl." She apparently agreed with Cassie's conclusion that the red bikini was too drab. She untied the knots, let the pieces drop on the deck next to a lounge chair, and laid on it to work on her perfect tan.

Fenya and Esin came over, looked at the other two women, and followed Morte Noir's lead.

Morte Noir smirked at Cassie and observed, "You might be overdressed."

Esin suppressed a giggle.

Cassie wished Remy would show up. Remy would wear a swimsuit of some sort. Well, Cassie was pretty sure she would. At least, Cassie hoped she would.

Another member of the waitstaff appeared with a bottle of wine and glasses. Cassie thought the gold rims of the glasses were a tad over the top, but she could live with it.

Morte Noir explained, "I took the liberty of raiding the yacht's wine cellar. Small, but excellent."

Cassie snorted. "Ludicrous." She'd investigated the cellar and thought about the fortune she could make selling the ancient vintages. Then she'd reminded herself that she had enough money and left the wine.

After popping the cork, the young server gave each of the ladies a full glass. Morte Noir raised hers. "A toast to life in the eye of the storm!"

Fenya offered an addition in a cheerful tone. "For tomorrow, we die."

Cassie corrected, "For tomorrow, we party." She waved her glass. "We die the day after."

Morte Noir nudged her protégé and Esin spoke shyly. "To wonderful friends. And friendships."

Everyone took a sip, even Esin.

Alina showed up next. Cassie breathed a sigh of relief. Alina wore a modest one-piece suitable for racing.

Cassie grinned. "You came along too? Where are the twins?"

Alina shook her hair back. "The Mistress persuaded me that my daughters could use a break from training." She almost laughed, a hopeful sign that she was finally loosening up after living a life of pure anxiety for many long years.

She gave Cassie a crooked smile. "And she persuaded me that I could use a break from my daughters."

Cassie pointed at the lounge chair to her left. "Come join me on the side away from the nudists."

Fenya snorted. "Americans. So prissy." She glared at Alina. "Show us."

Alina rolled her eyes, then pulled off her swimsuit and slid onto the lounger next to Cassie. She muttered, "It's just like a girl's locker room." She put her hand over her eyes to shield them from the glare. "Only brighter."

Cassie closed her eyes and thanked the heavens that she was tanned enough not to show her blushes. "You Russians might not be prissy, but if you don't put on some suntan lotion, you'll turn the color of Morte Noir's bikini."

Cassie contemplated a sort of silver lining. Dale and Andrey weren't here to look at all the drop-dead gorgeous women and drop dead.

Her cell phone rang.

"Dale! How'd the meeting go? Just as expected, then.

Excellent. Remy? She's not here. I thought she was still with you."

Cassie sat up in the lounger. "No, Dale. She hasn't shown." Her heart turned over. "That's good. You go check that."

She abruptly rose to her feet and looked at the characters in the sunbathing circle. Ohmigod. How could darkness spill across a place filled with this much sunshine?

She closed her eyes and breathed. When she opened them, though no one had moved and nothing had changed, her vision had transformed, and she was filled with an unnatural calm.

A moment earlier, she had seen a festival of erotic beauty. Now she beheld a battlefield occupied by blooded warriors, killers all. She spoke harshly. "Ok, bitches. Suit up."

She choked. "They've got Remy."

THE STORY CONTINUES

Cassie and Remy's story continues with book five, *Infinity Option*.

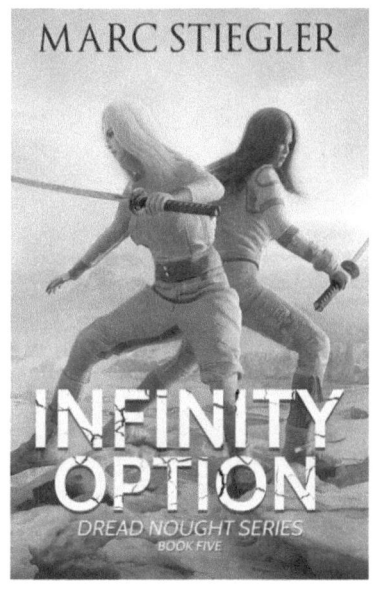

Claim your copy today!

AUTHOR NOTES

If you think it is unrealistic for a dictator to have an Olympic gymnast as a mistress, I have news. The current dictator of Russia has just such a mistress. He also owns an immense palace on the Baltic Sea that includes every feature mentioned here and a yacht with a pool that turns into a dance floor.

At the time of writing, I invented the idea that the yacht would be trailed by a warship for protection. Silly me. Of course such a yacht has such an escort. This is the second time I have had to thank the Russians for retrofitting reality to match my prose.

When I worked with Fort Meade long ago, baby-puke green was a critical component of the color palette. Hopefully, they've redecorated since then. Moreover, I've never been to the deepest level, so I do not know if the baby-puke feng shui extends to there.

The Vortex satellite, the Echelon surveillance network, and Five Eyes were all operational at the time of the

Snowden classified documents leak. Those systems surely still operate today, though the names have probably changed. Name changes are popular within that community since that allows intelligence services to clean up their act by shutting down a program without needing to change its activities.

Narco-submarines come in a wide variety of flavors. At the top end, they carry almost eight tons of drugs and cost two million dollars. A sub like that can generate one hundred million dollars in revenue on its first trip, so the return on investment is satisfactory. The US Coast Guard reckons they catch about eleven percent of them.

Unverified reports suggest there *is* a narco-submarine graveyard in the Canary Islands. The steps outlined in the story for the evolution of this global resource are so obvious that they hardly qualify as extrapolations.

So, while you can't buy a sub in Gran Canaria this afternoon, give the entrepreneurs a little time. Remember, you read it here first.

The Wagner Group, now famous for its operations in Ukraine, is also very active in Africa. Their forces in the Central African Republic are stronger than the state army, the rebels, or the Islamists. Saying they own the country is not far from the truth. Whether they own it for Russia or for themselves is less clear. In late breaking news, the leader of the Wagner Group was recently assassinated. Only time will tell the impact. They are so useful to Russia one suspects they will continue operations, though the name might change to protect the guilty.

Reinsurance is a real thing. One of the world's richest

AUTHOR NOTES

billionaires started with reinsurance as his core multi-billion-dollar business, though he now has many other multi-billion-dollar businesses as well. I doubt he knows as much about AID and Gamma as Buddy does, however.

The transponder system used by major ocean-going ships was designed in a gentler time for a more civilized world. Jiggering the transponders is now routine, especially for yachts, oil tankers, and wheat transports dodging embargoes and impounds. You just can't trust Western civilization to leave the Russian oligarchs alone with their ill-gotten gains.

The amphibious transport dock vessel *Portland* did carry the LaWS at the time of this writing. I have periodically wondered how much fun it would be to slide down the canted side of one of those modern streamlined ships and plunge straight into the water. As is often the case, the only problem might be the landing.

The thirty thousand accounts at Credit Suisse are real, with a caveat. Many of them are ancient history, and others have been closed. Does that mean the problem is solved and Dale's and Remy's Dread Nought business plan is obsolete? You're kidding, right?

Well-crafted conspiracy systems would indeed generate rage cycles as a part of managing the anger-opioid addiction levels in their subjects. You can't keep your victims at peak rage all the time. The excess of hormones would cause neural cell death.

Fortunately, the conspiracy systems of today are not generally well-crafted. In a typical conspiracy community, a continuous free-for-all prevails as diverse speakers spin rage-inducing fantasies in a chaotic war for clicks, likes, and dominance.

Marc Stiegler
February 7, 2023

EXCERPT FROM INFINITY OPTION

The following is an unedited excerpt from The Dread Nought series book 5, Infinity Option.

Prolog: 1945

Colonel Meyer watched his breath turn to mist as it drifted across the immense ice cavern. When he inhaled, he tasted the bitter cold of despair.

He frowned and forced his back ramrod straight once more. Despair could not be permitted in his vocabulary, much less in his thoughts.

He touched the skull-and-crossbones insignia on his black uniform and remembered who he was--not a member of the Nazi SS as so blatantly proclaimed by his uniform, but a member of the oldest and noblest secret society in history.

He tried to focus on the Great Plan as the Eldest had admonished him to do so often during this project. While the twin experiments with Nazism and Leninism would clearly fail in the near future, it was a minor setback within the context of the ancient journey of the Elder Guides.

Indeed, the Guides had learned so much from the Hitler and Stalin projects, the Eldest had grown confident that the Guides could end the chaotic flow of uncontrolled history in just a couple more generations.

The leader of the Guides, however, was also elderly. He had lived and breathed the Great Plan all his life, and had accepted his place therein.

The Colonel was young and eager. He had dared to hope that the Plan would come to fruition within his own lifetime, and that he personally could play a key role in its blossoming.

Instead he now commanded development of the backup plan. So he opened the log book to the first blank page and surveyed the room to identify matters that deserved a notation.

He looked to the front of the enormous underground retreat people were already calling the Fulcrum. The masons had finished implementing the exterior of the sanctuary, a solid brickwork that extended across the floor, up the walls, and across the arch of the ceiling.

A team of slaves scurried to put up the next layer, a confection of wool and of the recently-invented "fiberglass" insulation. He would have preferred pure fiberglass, but the material was scarce, and not even the Guide's agents in the Reich Research Council could get more.

A layer of plaster would cover this insulating layer, and another layer of insulation would cover the plaster. Finally an innermost layer of brick would form the interior wall.

He thought steel reinforced concrete might have been

better than brick, but it had been easier to acquire slaves skilled in brick laying, so once again he made do. Some future member of the Guides, whoever replaced him in some distant future, was more than welcome to upgrade.

The outermost wall of brick extended halfway to the far end of the cavern. He walked to the center where the masons now labored, and peered to the far end, where naked ice still formed the walls, where the work on the power plant proceeded.

They had drilled a hole up to the surface for an exhaust port for the diesel generators that now powered the lights. In the beginning Meyer had urged that they also use diesel for the permanent plant, but he now saw a significant flaw in his early thinking. The duct to the surface was so cold, the exhaust turned frigid on its way up, ceased to rise, and trapped the polluted air beneath. He could see the men working on the main reactor coughing as the fumes threatened to overpower them.

The diesel exhaust would not actually kill them, of course. A far more horrific fate awaited. Colonel Meyer shuddered as he considered their future.

While the Allies had destroyed the Norwegian plant producing heavy water, and had destroyed the stocks along with it, in fact one large shipment had escaped demolition. The senior Guides had gone to heroic lengths to hide the shipment from both Axis and Allied powers. They kept it for their own needs, though they had not yet known what those needs might be.

Preparing for threats hidden beyond the veil of tomorrow was as natural for the Guides as breathing.

When it became clear that the current effort to tame

civilization with Communism or Fascism was doomed, the Guides had hatched the plan to build this sanctuary. In that moment the value of the heavy water became clear.

So at the far end of the cavern a team of slaves, a mix of Jews and homosexuals, labored to build a nuclear reactor using a design somewhat improved over the sketch taken from Heisenberg.

Start with a child's ceiling mobile. Replace all the birds and flowers with cubes of uranium. Make it tall, with layer after layer of branches all replete with more and more cubes. Now slowly--very slowly!--lower the dangling array into the heavy water.

As the heavy water slows the neutrons they become easier to capture by the uranium in the other cubes, causing fission. Lower enough cubes into enough water and get a sustained reaction. Seal the container and run normal-water heat exchanger coils around the container to drive a steam turbine. The ice outside the cavern made a very efficient cooling system for the cycle.

At that moment a cheer went up among the men working on the reactor. The leader, whose name Meyer had already forgotten, ran over to him beaming. "The water has started to bubble."

Meyer nodded sharply. "Excellent work. Seal the tube, and tell your men to take a break before continuing." He forced a smile. "The sooner you finish, the sooner you can go home, as we discussed when I brought you here."

The man nodded back and returned to his team.

Meyer unclenched his hands behind his back. He hated allowing these particular slaves to get so close to him, but it was critical for them to not know they were already dead. Each had already soaked up enough radiation to kill a battalion.

The main entrance from the outer world opened up, and what looked like a teacher with a classroom of kindergarten children on a field trip entered.

The progeny from the Nazi experiments in genetic engineering had arrived. The Nazis had thought they were running the project with the Lebensborn association to create a generation of pure-blood Aryans. But in fact the Guides had molded the experiments that molded the children. Each of these youths represented a vision for the creation, not of an Aryan man, but of a superior man.

Meyer had had to leave a few of the less-advanced superior children in the outer world so that the Allies would think they had ended the experiments, but the Colonel had managed to save most of them. Bright-eyed, healthy, and frightfully intelligent, they represented a better future indeed. Their arrival was an event most worthy of logging in the book.

Before he greeted them, however, he made a mental note about another small problem he needed to write up.

Corpses. He would have to figure out how to store or get rid of the corpses of all the slaves who would die here over the next hundred years.

Chapter One
Frenzy

Remy stepped out of the Uber and thanked the driver before looking up at the Spirit of Washington Heliport.

The heliport lay not too high off the ground. It didn't need to be high to have wide clearances though it resided in the heart of DC. The architects had built the port on a dock sticking out into the Potomac. Hence, the heliport only needed to be high enough to ensure that helicopter propellers cleared the tops of the yachts parked all around it.

The noise of an approaching helo drowned out her thoughts. Her ride whirled overhead and bounced onto the concrete. Remy stepped aboard.

A person she'd never seen before sat in the back, smiling unpleasantly at her. He carried himself like a young man though he appeared middle-aged, with thinning hair and an aquiline nose that suggested his ancestors had belonged to the German aristocracy.

His eyes filled with satisfaction. "Remy. I'm so glad we finally meet."

Remy peered at him. "Who--" She stopped abruptly as she spotted the other man half-hidden behind her own seat.

"It's about time," Bryce crowed as he threw a bag over her head.

Remy struggled, but she knew she'd lost even before she felt a needle slide into her neck and inject a cool stream of helplessness.

EXCERPT FROM INFINITY OPTION

Remy sat unable to see or to move, wondering why she was still conscious. She guessed Bryce had injected her with something more like curare than ether. Why would he do that? Was this his way of helping her to keep situational awareness so she could escape when the time was right? Or had he done it to taunt her?

Or had the other man wanted to torture her with her powerlessness? Which led her to wonder, was this other man the Doc?

Bryce spoke, confused. "Aren't we going to Ft. Meade?"

The bald man chuckled. "That's not where I have my laboratory." He turned grim. "I used to have a nice lab in Cuba, before you allowed it to be destroyed. Now I'll have to take her to my primary lab."

Bryce could not prevent a hint of horror from entering his voice. "Are you going to do to Remy what you did to the people at Camp No?"

Aha. Remy now had confirmation that this was indeed the Doc. She would have jerked but the drug prevented it.

The Doc chided Bryce. "I already told you, once I had Remy, I could abandon those lines of inquiry. I won't have to torture anybody any more." He paused reflectively. "Not physically, anyway."

Even the drug could not prevent a cold chill running down Remy's spine.

Bryce sounded relieved. "Right. Now that you've got Remy, you can force her to tell you how to build a Memwriter." His voice once more contained a hint of worry. "Uh, won't you have to torture her first to get the Memwriter, before you can switch to Memwriter-based research?"

More chuckling foreshadowed the Doc's next words. "If I'm right about how the machine works, I don't need any more help from Remy. I just need her body."

For a moment Remy wondered if he would kill her now.

Bryce echoed her thoughts in disbelief. "So you're just going to kill her, after all this?"

The Doc sounded annoyed. "Waste not, want not."

Bryce relaxed. "So what's the plan?"

"I was planning to operate on her when I got her to the lab. But..."

The Doc did not continue for a long moment. Remy's anxiety grew.

Finally the Doc spoke with abrupt decision. "The procedure should be straightforward. I've waited too long already. And who knows if someone will interrupt us? Best to proceed."

Remy heard the zipper of a bag opening.

Bryce asked in amazement. "You brought a medical bag? And a scalpel?"

The Doc went back to chuckling. "Always be prepared, Bryce."

Remy heard him rifle the bag again. He finished, and placed something hard against her head. "Now I just have to find it. Where did your father put the chip, Remy? Tell me now, and we can finish more quickly."

The instrument moved around her head, down her face, across her neck.

Bryce cleared his throat. "What's that?"

The device swept down one arm.

The Doc explained. "It's a broadband electromagnetic

radiation sensor. I'm probably looking for a Bluetooth transceiver, but it might be wifi."

The Doc shifted to inspect the other arm.

The sensor warbled.

The Doc spoke with a child's delight. "There it is!"

Remy struggled to move in her desperate despair. No use.

Bryce still sounded perplexed. "There's what?"

The Doc explained. "Based on a couple of semi-coherent comments Gerald Tambook made as his mind was dissolving, before his speech turned to pure gibberish, I came to suspect that the key component of the Mindwriter was embedded in a chip in Remy's arm." He tapped the machine. "Looks like I was right."

Pain seared Remy's flesh as the Doc cut deep. Remy wanted to scream, but she could not, and she would not had she been able.

The Doc poked and prodded inside her arm, setting off spasm after spasm of agony. He stopped. She felt something being slid out of her body.

Smug satisfaction laced the torturer's announcement of triumph. "I have you at last."

Bryce sounded incredulous. "That's the Memwriter?"

The Doc answered, "That's the part that contains all the secrets. The rest is easily duplicated."

Remy felt nimble fingers pull the edges of the surgical cut together. Strips of tape clasped the sides of the wound.

Remy felt the sensor come into contact with her arm once more. The machine warbled again, a different though similar sound.

The scientist paused the machine. "Oh, my, what have

we here?" His fiddling with the machine while still contact with her arm shot random jolts of pain across Remy's senses. "A miniaturized Apple Airtag, too. Naughty girl."

He chuckled. "Can't have that." He ripped away the bandages he had just placed and drove the scalpel into her arm once more.

An infinity of agony later he withdrew the blade. "Bryce. I have a job for you." He explained his plan.

Bryce reacted with disbelief. "You want me to do what?"

The Doc cleared his throat. "Now."

After a bit more nudging, Remy thought she could hear Bryce gulp. He growled. "Happy?"

The Doc's voice turned jaunty. "That should make her conspirators much easier to deal with."

The background thrum of the propellers changed pitch. The helo descended. Remy strained to make out any sounds that might give her a clue about their location. Nothing.

Bryce spoke slowly. "You're sending me back to headquarters? I'm not coming with you?"

The Doc spoke with an edge of anger. "Still worried about Ms. Tambook here? Where are your loyalties?"

Bryce remained silent.

The Doc returned to patient lecture mode. "I already told you not to worry. Indeed, I have good news. The next time you see her, she'll be much nicer."

He paused thoughtfully. "Pliant and obedient, even."

EXCERPT FROM INFINITY OPTION

Mere minutes had passed since Cassie had told her fellow sunbathers on the megayacht *Glory* about Remy's capture. No sunbathers remained.

Morte Noir, Fenya, and Esin had seemingly pulled combat fatigues, assault rifles, and combat knives from thin air. She presumed the head steward had helped conduct the miracle, but he had remained offstage.

Alina had not gone full military, but she had managed to get into more sober clothes, jeans and a T-shirt.

Cassie stood there holding her cheerleader baton, wearing a bikini, feeling under-equipped. It couldn't be helped.

Morte Noir allowed amusement on her face. "All dressed up but no way to know where to go. And no way to go if we did know where to go."

Cassie smacked her forehead. "The helicopter. It's still in Florida waiting for Remy." She looked over the side of the yacht. "We could take the submarine, but--"

Esin finished the sentence. "Too slow."

Alina shrugged. "I would like to go back to Rivendell on the submarine, if you don't mind."

Cassie stared at her a moment. "You don't want to help?"

Alina struggled with multiple emotions before answering. "Of course I want to help." She looked away. "But I need to protect my children most of all. They're all alone without me."

Morte Noir's harsh laugh mellowed as she accepted the answer. "Of course. Family first."

Cassie suppressed her initial observation that Alina's children were only alone if you discounted the dozens of

EStormers with mad sniper skills who would die to protect them.

Instead, Cassie forced herself to lie. "I...understand."

Fenya was the first to make a practical observation. "Even with Cassie piloting the copter, we wouldn't have room for Alina anyway. Just four seats."

Morte Noir leaped to the next problem. She turned, and a steward appeared before her. "Tell the captain to call the helicopter back immediately."

Cassie, calming down, grabbed her phone and started making calls. "Even if the helo were here, we wouldn't know where to take it. Time for a video conference."

She needed a couple of minutes to bring everyone together. Andrey, Laurie, and Tina from Rivendell. Grandma in her Arizona missile silo. Dale and Joyce from the Dread Nought HQ. Cassie was so sure Bryce had taken Remy, she thought about getting him on the phone just to demand he tell everyone where he'd taken her, but she refrained.

Morte Noir, in addition to listening to the conference, talked softly on her own phone.

Dale spoke with agonized anxiety. "Have you found her?"

Andrey beat Cassie to the answer. "No."

Jewel's head poked into the shot from Dread Nought and whispered to Joyce.

Joyce smiled savagely. "We've tracked her to the Spirit of Washington Heliport on the Potomac. She boarded a helo. We lost her there."

Andrey jerked in his chair. "Let me run that backwards and forwards."

While he worked, Cassie asked him gently, "What about her tracker?"

Andrey shook his head as he typed. "I'm trying, believe me. Can't get a connection."

Grandma muttered while the geeks worked. "I can't believe I'm stuck in this damned bunker."

Laurie gave her mother a sharp look. "You can't be serious. Stay where you are."

Andrey exclaimed in triumph. "Gotcha! Footage of the helo at its last stop before getting Remy, about to take off." He popped some fuzzy video on the screen. Two men clambered aboard, one that looked bald, and a tall one who looked jaunty. No faces were visible.

Cassie hissed as she recognized the tall one just from the arrogance of his posture and stride. "Bryce."

Andrey asked, "Anyone recognize the other one?"

Morte Noir cleared her throat. "Hard to tell from here, but I suspect that's the new Director of AID."

Cassie groaned. "The Doc."

This assertion led to another round of hisses from those who knew about the Doc's work turning Remy's dad into a vegetable, and his gruesome experiments at Camp No: Andrey, Laurie, Dale, and Grandma.

Laurie pointed out how bad this news was. "That's the man who started this mess and killed and tortured so many people just to steal the Memwriter."

Cassie gawked at her. "Ohmigod. If he knows where to look, he's got it now, even if Remy refuses to help him." The secret, proprietary part of the Memwriter that AID had sought so long resided in a chip in Remy's arm.

Laurie nodded grimly. "Forget about EStorme and Ruby Rage."

Morte Noire's voice went low. "He's inches away from the real tool for global domination."

Esin thumped her foot against the deck. "What can we do?"

Fenya put a hand on her shoulder. "We can wait for the geeks to find her." She tapped her assault rifle. "Then we can kill him."

The megayacht *Glory* steamed with all the speed her wiffle ball could muster towards the USA, to hasten the moment when the ship's helo would reach them. Cassie paced, unable to bring herself to move from the sun deck and the multinational video conference until they had more information on Remy.

The beginning of the next phase started with a photo finish. Joyce broke the tense silence. "Nassau Airport in Yulee Florida. I've hacked into the FAA's flight plans for the helo."

Andrey stepped on her words. "Confirmed. I'm following the radar tracks." He popped a picture onto the Zoom display. "It's barely better than a dirt track. The strip is paved with concrete, sort of."

Joyce joined in dryly. "It has as many cracks as smooth patches."

Dale added, "I'll have a Dread Nought team on site in forty minutes."

Morte Noir was working her phone. "That's just north

of Jacksonville, right?" Without waiting for an answer, she spoke urgently into the cell. "I need eyes on the Nassau Airport ASAP." She listened, then hung up. She said in a smug voice, "I'll have a contractor there in half an hour."

Cassie could see how this kind of competition could produce some very interesting results. "Will your people be able to snatch Remy back?"

Dale spoke with pride. "My men can deal with any opposition handily."

Morte Noir frowned. "My man can handle it himself, as long as it's ok to kill everyone." She raised an eyebrow at Cassie.

Grandma broke in before Cassie could consider. "Do it! If you leave enough bodies perhaps those bastards will learn something."

Laurie, who had never seemed particularly bloodthirsty to Cassie before now, chimed in. "It's called a teachable moment, Mom."

Grandma cackled. "Very good, girl. Teach away."

Cassie rolled her eyes. "Hold on a moment. Could we instead--"

Andrey interrupted. "No good. The helo's landing early. They'll be gone before anyone can arrive."

Joyce squelched a scream. "That can't be! The flight plan says they won't land until Morte Noir's man arrives!"

Andrey answered grimly. "The radar doesn't lie."

Morte Noir tapped her cell. "Faster. Bonus applies."

Cassie heard the thundering prop wash of the Glory's own helo as it approached the ship. "About damn time," she muttered.

Andrey made an announcement. "I'm getting another

radar track coming into the airfield hot." He whistled. "I mean really hot. It's a jet of some kind."

Cassie looked at the image of the landing strip again. "Can that airport even handle a jet?"

Joyce answered, "Not a chance."

Laurie asked the naive question. "Could it be a coincidence?

Cassie, Morte Noir, Fenya, and Grandma answered in chorus. "No."

Joyce studied her other monitors. "Whatever that jet is, it hasn't filed a flight plan."

The helo bounced onto the ship's deck, and the rushing whir of the rotors subsided.

Cassie turned toward the helipad. Grandma's voice overrode all the others. "Where do you think you're going, Cassie?"

Morte Noir chimed in with a dry chuckle. "You might want a destination before you take off."

Fenya gave her a wicked grin. "And considering how prissy you are, you might want to put on some clothes before departure. Or is that a battle bikini?"

Cassie stopped in her tracks and moaned. "I hate waiting." The steward appeared with jeans and a leather jacket, and she started to change.

The next interminable minutes passed in stressed silence. Morte Noir's phone chimed once again. Everyone jerked to attention as they strained to listen in. Morte Noir proceeded calmly to her asset. "Go."

She listened a moment and pursed her lips. "Did you get anything at all?" She nodded. "Excellent work. Thank you."

Cassie demanded, "What happened?"

Morte Noir transferred several images to the conference video. "He arrived too late to do anything, but he got two shots of vehicles departing. The first was a sports car."

Everyone looked at the blur of a silver Lamborghini racing past the photographer.

Cassie delivered the disgusted answer before anyone else deduced it. "Bryce."

Next a photo of an odd looking airplane pointed toward the tree line took center stage. Joyce spoke for most of the group when she said, "What is that?"

Cassie asked a more precise question. "Are those empty rectangles engines?"

Andrey looked at the picture with awe. "I think that's a, well, ahem. Let me confirm before I say something crazy. Hang on." He stepped off camera. "Rudy, have you ever seen one of these?"

Rudy Ross appeared on the screen. "Hi, everybody. What did you want me to look at?"

Andrey pointed at the photo.

Rudy stared with his mouth open for a moment. "Wow. It's just like the Jetoptera prototypes, except I think this one's full size." He grew excited. "My God, someone did it!"

Cassie tapped her foot on the ground. Since she was still buckling her pants, barefoot, no one heard the impatience in the tap. "What did they do?"

Rudy went rapturous. "It's a fluidic propulsion system." He highlighted the empty rectangles wrapped in the box-shaped tail of the plane. "No propellers or exterior turbines. There's a compressor in the body of the plane that squirts high-speed exhaust into the cavity and entrains a large volume of air."

Andrey added, "This, like the small scale Jetoptera prototypes, can tilt the exhaust for vertical takeoff and landing."

Joyce muttered, "So that's how they landed a frickin' jet at the dinky airport."

Esin stared at it with delight. "How fast can it go?"

Rudy shook his head. "Best guess is point eight Mach."

Laurie added a bit of trivia. "So, faster than a Boeing Dreamliner."

Morte Noir gave them an angelic smile. "I need one."

Grandma growled. "Get in line, Missy. I need one first."

Claim your copy of Infinity Option today!

OTHER BOOKS BY MARC STIEGLER

The Braintrust
The Braintrust - A Harmony of Enemies (1)
(Prometheus Award Nominee)
The Braintrust: A Crescendo Of Fire (2)
The Braintrust: Rhapsody For the Tempest (3)
The Braintrust: Ode to Defiance (4)
The Braintrust: Requiem (5)

Dread Nought Series
Triple Cross (1)
Double Tap (2)
Power Plan (3)
Zero Sum (4)
Infinity Option (5)

Valentina
(Hugo Award Finalist)

OTHER BOOKS BY MARC STIEGLER

David's Sling
(Prometheus Award Finalist)

EarthWeb

The Gentle Seduction (anthology)

CONNECT

Follow Marc on Social Media

Facebook

https://www.facebook.com/MarcStieglerAuthor/

www.ingramcontent.com/pod-product-compliance
Lightning Source LLC
LaVergne TN
LVHW041746060526
838201LV00046B/915